THE SACRIFICIAL CIRCUMCISION OF THE BRONX

THE SACRIFICIAL CIRCUMCISION OF THE BRONX

A NOVEL BY
ARTHUR NERSESIAN

BOOK TWO OF
The Five Books of Moses

AKASHIC BOOKS
NEW YORK

This is a work of fiction. All names, characters, places, and incidents are the product of the author's imagination. Any resemblance to real events or persons, living or dead, is entirely coincidental.

Published by Akashic Books
©2008 Arthur Nersesian

ISBN-13: 978-1-933354-60-6
Library of Congress Control Number: 2008925941

First printing

Akashic Books
PO Box 1456
New York, NY 10009
info@akashicbooks.com
www.akashicbooks.com

AUTHOR'S NOTE

The character of Paul Moses is a fiction, loosely built around a handful of facts as described in Robert A. Caro's biography, *The Power Broker: Robert Moses and Fall of New York* (Vintage, 1974). The "Mkultra," though fictionalized in this novel, was an actual series of science projects developed and financed by the CIA dealing largely with mind control; files related to it were destroyed by CIA Director Richard Helms in 1973.

Then the Lord said to Cain, "Where is Abel your brother?"
He said, "I do not know; am I my brother's keeper?"
—Genesis, 4:9

1

Paul had a tall skinny younger brother and a short shy sister. His mother, Bella, was an overbearing bull of a woman who despite everything always meant well. His father, meek and weak, was an utterly henpecked man. Robert, his brother, jumped when Mama spoke; since Paul was the eldest, the mantle therefore fell upon him to stand up to the Czarina Bella Cohen.

The first girl he ever loved was a stunning Jamaican named Maria who was about ten years older than him and always had a cigarette burning. Bella had seen how hardworking and honest Maria was at Madison House, the do-good organization, and hired her as a domestic. Young Paul couldn't take his eyes off of Maria's unbelievable curves. He was raised in turn-of-the-century affluence, with money from both sides of his family rushing in and swirling around him. His childhood was spent mostly up in New Haven, Connecticut, where the servants called him *Mr. Paul* and his younger brother *Mr. Robert*. He'd tell them to just call him Paul, but his brother was always Mr. Robert.

When Paul hit his teens, the flood of cash rushed the entire family through some subterranean pipeline, flushing them out into a plush new brownstone on 46th Street just off of Fifth Avenue. As he and his younger brother reached college age, their mother wanted them to go to Yale, their hometown university. Mr. Robert was glad to comply, but Paul found the old school stodgy and was looking for a more liberal education. Woodrow Wilson, the progressive, opinionated president of Princeton, had just announced that he was running for governor of New Jersey. This excited Paul to such a degree that the young man selected Princeton as his first choice.

When he got his letter of acceptance six weeks later, he tore open the envelope right at the dinner table and made the announcement. Though his father Emanuel seemed happy, Bella silently nodded her big head in dismay. By making a major decision for himself, Paul hoped to teach his younger brother that he didn't have to be such a little mama's boy. His father opened an expensive bottle of cabernet and made a toast. His mother just sat there. To further irritate her, Paul guzzled down several glasses of the wine as though it were water.

While the others at the table talked, Paul's head began spinning from the wine and he had a strange daydream that he lay suspended, just floating in darkness. When he closed his eyes he felt as though he were submerged, bouncing along the sides of some kind of giant underwater conduit.

"Paul, what do you think?" asked his dad.

"I'm sorry, I wasn't listening."

Paul's father suggested that he consider a career in banking or finance. Lightheaded, Paul pretended to listen as the alcohol just floated him along.

2

While attending Princeton, Paul Moses had lofty ambitions of being either a scholar or statesman. During his freshman year, he hung out with young gentlemen who dressed in herringbone tweed and fussed over sybarite subtleties, such as unusual pipe tobacco and exotic teas. In his sophmore year, however, Paul decided that it was all just a competition of vanity that gave rise to legions of nancy boys and self-involved powder puffs. Soon, he dismissed the whole Ivy League as nothing more than an extension of European royalty, American aristocracy at its most pretentious.

During school breaks, nonetheless, he displayed his newly acquired sensibilities to his brother and sister, reciting French Symbolist poetry and discussing the latest advances in European art. Although Paul's father was proud to hear his son's growing sophistication, Bella rolled her eyes. Paul further enjoyed irking his mother by taking an active interest in the Zionist movement. Gradually, as he read more and more about how fellow Jews were being mistreated around the world, he became firm in the opinion that only when their people had the security of their own homeland would the persecution end.

"None of this would happen if they simply blended into the countries they're living in," Bella would say.

"But *we* are Jews," Paul would shoot back. "Do other groups have to deny who they are?"

The Jewish settlements in Palestine occupying unpopulated lots in the desert gave hope toward a permanent homeland for all Jews. Paul's other liberal sentiments were

rooted more firmly in the plight of the working man, particularly as championed by Eugene Victor Debs and the
Socialist Party of America. It was primarily for this reason
that he joined the Democratic Reform Club, a leftist organization at the college. In a fit of zeal he soon accepted
the nomination and ultimately the office of its presidency.
Although the position didn't offer many privileges, he did
meet more girls.

What captivated him most about Millicent Sanchez-
Rothschild was her strong, defiant face and cascades of
shiny thick, black hair. He was delightfully surprised when
he heard her explaining to another student why Oliver
Wendell Holmes was the greatest juror who ever sat on
the high court.

Millicent had just arrived from the University of Pennsylvania to hear a lecture that his club had organized.
Williams Jennings Bryant, the Democratic presidential
candidate of 1900, was giving a talk on how the Supreme
Court was stonewalling labor reform.

After spending the majority of the evening talking with
Millie, Paul asked her on a date.

"If you want to make the trip down to Philly, I'm all
yours," she replied.

He took the first train the following week. In Philadelphia, they spent the afternoon just chatting. Or rather, she
talked and he listened. She was from a wealthy Sephardic
Jewish family who had settled in Mexico City. Despite the
fact that her parents were rich conservatives, she was very
progressive in her views. Rights of the working man, so-
cialism, the suffrage movement—they were in agreement
about nearly everything.

Though Millie had many suitors, Paul continued seeing
her throughout the semester, taking the train down from
Princeton on weekends and holidays.

Over the next few months, she shared various aspects
of Mexico—its history, its conquest by Cortéz, the destruc-

tion of the native culture by the Catholic Church. "The Mayans produced vast libraries that Bishop Diego de Landa ordered his priests to collect and burn in huge bonfires," she explained, "though a few books survived as the Maya codices, preserving some record of their heritage."

Millie's family, which made its fortune in mining, had benefited greatly under the repeated presidential terms of Porfirio Díaz. Yet she was part of a consortium of young Latin compatriots studying in the United States who despised "El Presidente."

Aside from her own desire for social justice, her beloved cousin, Pedro Martinez—her rebel mentor—was a prominent member of an anti-Díaz group. Following a national convention of various liberal clubs in 1901 and 1902, the Díaz regime arrested a group of their leaders—including her cousin—and suppressed their publications. When Pedro was finally released, he migrated to the United States along with other radicals and they unified as the Mexican Liberal Party. In 1906 they published a manifesto entitled *El Programa del Partido Liberal* calling for, among other things, guarantees of civil liberties, universal public education, land reform, and a one-term limit for all future Mexican presidents.

"How many times has Porfirio been elected?" Paul asked on one of his visits.

"Six, but last year he promised to retire at the end of this term, so we're all waiting anxiously."

Suddenly, Paul felt a strange jolt through his body and his knees buckled.

"You okay?" Millicent asked, taking his arm.

"I just feel a little light-headed," he said, and when he closed his eyes and let her lead him, he felt once again as if he was submerged in warm liquid.

"Paul, what's the matter?" Millie demanded, brushing his arm nervously.

"I'm sorry. I think I have a touch of the flu."

3

During spring break, Millicent joined Paul on a trip home to meet his family in New York. They arrived late in the afternoon and Millie found herself seated with Paul's parents and siblings for a wonderful dinner. His sister Edna brought up a recent strike that had been in the news. Millie commented how the American government was behaving like a Pinkerton private security force for various robber barons. Paul's mother Bella politely responded that things might be changing, as indicated by the fact that Teddy Roosevelt had been the first president to stand up to big business, ordering them to negotiate with labor unions during a major strike several years earlier.

"But he didn't go far enough."

"What was it like growing up in Mexico?" Edna asked, trying to steer her away from controversy.

"*Very* traditional," Millie replied tiredly.

Bella stared out the window tolerating Paul's precious coquette. As coffee and dessert were served, Edna asked a casual question about the suffrage movement and whether Millie thought a constitutional amendment giving women the right to vote could actually get passed. It compelled Paul's date to launch into one of her signature arguments for women's rights.

"Tell me, dear," Bella finally said, "what exactly is it your parents do?"

"My father is the head of a mining company down in Mexico."

"And do you think he exploits any workers there?"

"My own guilt doesn't excuse anyone else's," Millie replied.

"Young lady, I don't know who taught you the fine art of hypocrisy, but—"

"It's my life mission to give restitution. What's your excuse?"

"You can't talk to my mother like that!" Mr. Robert interjected, rising to his feet.

Paul had to bite his lip to keep himself from laughing. After an awkward silence, his father Emanuel made a comment about the weather.

When Millie left early the next day for the train back to Philly, Paul's mother called him into her study and explained that she didn't want him seeing "Señorita Obnoxchez" ever again.

"I love her," he said simply.

"How can any man love such a sanctimonious and vain person?"

"I can ask the same of Dad," he snorted back.

"Paul, I made an effort to be nice to her and only got scorn in return."

As Paul stormed out of the room, he bumped right into the maid, Maria, nearly knocking her down.

"Pardon me," he said, but the words sounded strange, like they were muffled behind some invisible wall. Hard as he tried to reach out, he couldn't.

"Paul, are you okay?" Her face seemed to ripple as she spoke.

"I'll be fine," he muttered, and left.

4

Though his younger sister Edna liked Millicent, neither his mother nor brother had anything nice to say about her. On a visit home toward the end of the year, Mr. Robert inquired whether Paul was still seeing "that opinionated young lady."

"Sure I am, and I plan to see her as much as I can."

"You're certain you're not just using her to anger Mom?"

"Mom is such a stick in the mud. Everything angers her."

"I know she can be pretty bullheaded, but she is our mother."

"We're her children, not her whipping boys."

Mr. Robert nodded silently.

That fall, to his mother's great joy, Mr. Robert began attending Yale. Soon the two brothers fell out of touch.

One day the next spring, Paul, as president of the Democratic Reform Club, was invited to a tea hosted by the dean of Student Affairs. There he was introduced to the tall, dapper Woodrow Wilson, who was now serving as governor of New Jersey. He had come earlier that day to meet the constituents of Princeton, where he had formerly presided. Paul and a few lucky others had the opportunity to chat with the bespectacled politician for nearly twenty uninterrupted minutes.

"Regarding workers," Paul asked, "what exactly would you do to alleviate their hardships if you occupied the Oval Office?"

"Well, I'm not running for president, but if I was, I'd

probably draw up a bill of rights for the working man."

When Paul called to tell his sister that he had met his hero Wilson—who incidentally supported the idea of a Jewish nation—she interrupted to say that Robert, who had been captain of the Yale swimming team, was in the middle of a huge imbroglio with the head of the university's sports funding.

"What happened?"

"He tried to get more money for the swimming team and ended up resigning."

"Good for him," Paul said, happy to hear that his brother was finally standing up for himself. He wanted to congratulate Robert for confronting the administration, but still felt uncomfortable about how they had left things regarding Millie and Mom.

On the morning of the summer solstice, Millie called him in tears. She'd just heard that President Díaz had formally declared that he was running for a seventh term—he had lied!

"Well, I'm sure he'll be defeated," Paul said, not knowing how else to respond.

"No, he won't," she retorted. "People are afraid to run against him." Millie told him that a prominent member of a respected Mexican family, Francisco Madero, had announced that he was going to oppose Díaz in the election, but Díaz had Madero thrown in jail, effectively destroying the hopes for a democratic nation that so many had spent years patiently waiting for.

Over the next month, her like-minded compatriots at different universities joined together and formed an emergency organization, Latin American Students and Teachers Still Concerned about Mexico—LAST SCaM.

Now, every time Paul visited Millie in Philadelphia, she talked obsessively about how Díaz was taking some new and diabolical action to destroy Mexican civil liberties: abolishing freedom of the press, then undoing all the land reforms that had been put in place before him. American slaves and Russian serfs had been set free, yet Mexican peasants were still captive.

Paul spent much of the summer helping Millie, who along with her committee launched a letter-writing campaign to raise money for the cause of those oppressed in Mexico. When she heard that Francisco Madero had escaped his captors, she called Paul and declared, "You know what this means? Porfirio's days are numbered!"

"Well, there's still the small matter of getting him out of office."

"Díaz has everything but the people. And the people *are* everything!" she countered. Even Paul found this a little hokey, but he didn't want to discourage her optimism.

One morning in early September, a week after he had started a new semester at Princeton, Paul got called to the pay phone in the noisy hallway. Pressing the earpiece against his temple, he heard Millie shouting, "It's about to commence! People are racing down to Mexico. The revolution's starting!"

"That's great!"

"I'm heading down there too. I'm going with four other women and six men from the committee."

"Sweetheart, you don't want to get killed. Why don't you think this over some more?"

"They can't kill all of us. Mexico is about to go into the fight of its life!" she shouted. "These blackguards are trying to steal the country from my people. There's no way I'm just going to sit here quietly while this is happening. I'm leaving tonight!"

He told her that she couldn't go without seeing him one last time.

"We're all boarding a train at 9:35 this evening," she said. "If you want to come, you better head over here now."

The commuter train from Princeton to Philly left six

minutes past every hour and took roughly ninety minutes. He barely made the next train.

He arrived in Philadelphia at 8 p.m., dashed several blocks to the University of Pennsylvania, and headed across the sprawling campus. Men were not allowed up inside the women's dorm, so, trying to catch his breath, he called from the reception desk downstairs. When Millie came down, she led him into a dark alcove; once alone, she threw her arms around him and gave him a passionate kiss.

"Please don't do this," he pleaded.

"I don't expect you to understand," she whispered. "But this is my own . . . escape." It was as though she were drunk with the possibility of a new life awaiting her.

"Whatever does that mean?"

"It means when I'm visiting you at Princeton or even when I'm here at the campus, everyone looks at me as this proud, smart, annoying girl, but that's only because I've done such a great job hiding my true self behind this pale face."

"But what does that have to do with you now?"

"I was raised in Mexico City. I didn't know a word of English until I was six. Heck, my mother's father fought against the gringos when this country stole the northern half of our land more than fifty years ago."

"Look, fifty years ago my family were Jews living in Prussia," Paul replied.

"All I'm saying is that I'm stuck outside my country, trapped in a petticoat and a social strata. Your mother was right when she said I was living on my father's blood money. And this is my chance to make amends."

She's going to get herself killed, Paul thought, and kissed her hard on the lips.

"Unacceptable! Unacceptable!" one of the university matrons shouted over to them, clapping her hands loudly.

"I still have to pack my bags," Millie said. She kissed him again and dashed back upstairs.

Paul paced tensely in the reception area. Some from Millie's committee had already come down with their steamer trunks and suitcases. A taxi sedan had arrived and was waiting out front. Once they all squeezed in with their luggage, there was no room left, so Paul stood on the running board, hanging on the side. Despite the wind as they drove, he kept shouting to Millie through the window, "Please reconsider! This is a dangerous idea!!"

They finally arrived at the huge marble-columned station where redcaps with large wooden hand trucks grabbed their trunks and heavy leather bags. They met up with others who had come from various points nearby. After exchanging greetings they all headed to the gated ticket windows. Paul waited until he was alone with Millie, then dropped to one knee and said, "Marry me!"

"What?!"

"Be my wife!"

The surprise in her eyes melted to a slightly amused sadness. "I'll do it if you come with me."

"That would defeat the whole point."

"Which is to keep me here."

"To keep you *safe*," he clarified. "Is there something wrong with that?"

"No, but I do love you, Paul," she said. "And one of the reasons I love you is because I know that if we were in Mexico City and you heard that America had been taken over by a tyrant, you'd come back up here to oppose him."

Not if I were a woman, he thought.

One of the fellows on the LAST SCaM committee, a skinny young man named Victor Gonzalez, handed her a train ticket and the group walked over to their track. The first leg of the trip was an express train which would take them as far as St. Louis. Paul walked alongside Millie and a redcap valet to the door of the train.

"I'll write you at every opportunity," she said.

Paul boarded the locomotive with her. The entire committee had bought sleeping berths in first class.

"Where can I write to you?" he asked nervously.

She proceeded to scribble down her family address in Mexico City, as well as the addresses of three friends living in the countryside. "I'll write you as soon as I get down there, but if you don't hear from me, one of these people should know where I am."

"A person's life is defined by the caution of their choices," he said in an effort to sound authoritative. "This could be the worst decision you will *ever* make."

"Despite what you might think, I'm not trying to be a hero and I have no desire to die, but I love my country and I have to do this."

He remained with her on the train until the conductor called out, "All aboard!"

She walked with him to the Dutch door at the end of the car and watched as he stepped down onto the sunken platform. The conductor lifted the wooden step and jumped on board. As the train started pulling out of the station, Millicent waved.

Paul stood alone on the platform until the locomotive slowly vanished into the night.

5

Paul took the next train back to Princeton and returned to his dorm room just past 3 that morning. Unable to sleep, he skipped his French and Spanish classes and remained listlessly in bed. As he eventually began his daily routines, he once again felt strangely captive. It was as if he were sealed in some kind of long, narrow tunnel, wanting to get through it quickly and out the other side. Without her, all alone, he felt as though he were drowning.

Roughly a week later, he got the first postcard from Millicent, sent from St. Louis. She explained that they were about to board a second train that would take them to Galveston, Texas. She had to be in Mexico by now, he thought. A second postcard came two days later from Texas saying they were about to cross the Rio Grande.

Two and a half weeks later, a letter arrived detailing how it was too dangerous to go to Mexico City, so they were instead heading west to Baja. Apparently, several revolutionary organizations had formed their own governments in the area and Millie's group felt it could have the greatest impact there.

October went by without a single postcard. The Mexican postal service wasn't very efficient, and Paul figured that the political turmoil must have further delayed the delivery of foreign correspondence. Hard as he tried to invest himself in schoolwork, Paul found himself suffering from repeated attacks of vertigo. He would usually just lay in bed trying not to imagine the worst: short, fat, oily soldiers with large, dirty sombreros taking turns violating Millie as she spat out blood and noble slogans.

The only ideas distracting him came from *The Physical Sciences*, the primary text for his Introduction to Physics class that he was taking to fulfill his science requirements. Reading the principles of physics from Galileo and Newton, he found himself mesmerized as if he was engrossed in a mystery novel.

Finally, on November 3, he received another post from Millicent. The letter had been given to a friend who was heading into Texas. It began: *My beloved Pablo, I'm assuming you didn't get any of my other letters as I haven't received any from you* . . . It went on to explain that her committee had broken up. Two men had joined Pancho Villa's contingent in the northeast; four others had joined Señor Zapata in Chiapas; but she and one other were still in Baja in a commune run by the Mexican revolutionary Ricardo Flores Magón. Despite these different factions, Madero was still generally regarded as the new hope for Mexico.

> *You'll be happy to hear that Señor Flores is a pacifist. He doesn't even have a military attachment. He's simply trying to lead by example. The other day a calvary of federal soldiers galloped through, almost daring us to provoke them. We've been wearing clothes we bought here, trying to blend in with the locals, but we spend our days heading down the peninsula trying to familiarize the peasants with the issues of the impending revolution* . . .

The letter had been sent from somewhere called Córdova. As November progressed, stories about the brewing troubles in Mexico began appearing in the *New York Times*.

Bella called to invite Paul up to New York for Thanksgiving, saying she missed her eldest boy and wanted to hear how he was doing. He ended the short conversation without uttering a single word about Millie, knowing that nothing would bring his mother greater pleasure than hearing of the girl's reckless voyage.

Opening the New York Times on November 20, Paul saw the headline: *TROUBLES IN MEXICO! CALL TO ARMS!* While still a fugitive from the law, Madero had announced from Texas that it was time for the people of Mexico to revolt against the tyrant who was holding their country hostage. Paul feared this would end with widespread bloodshed.

During the early train ride the next day for Thanksgiving, Paul felt on edge. When he finally arrived in New York City, he briskly walked the fifteen or so blocks from Penn Station to the family brownstone on 46th Street, near Fifth Avenue.

Upon greeting the maid Maria, he learned that his mother had been in a foul mood all day. Paul took a stiff belt of Scotch and listened as Bella bossed the help around. He couldn't stop wondering if the federales garrisoned in the small Mexican village of Córdova had noticed the young students arriving from abroad.

He retreated into the study and located some paper and a fountain pen. He started writing Millie a passionate letter about his constant fears and boundless love for her. Before he got very far, however, he was interrupted by joyous shrieks. Mr. Robert had just arrived home from Yale. His mother squealed in delight, and showered her son with kisses. Paul could hear Robert giggling boyishly in response. Though Bella had been told the story numerous times, she made Robert once again relay the heroic events in which, despite his having to resign, he raised an unprecedented amount of money for the Yale swimming team.

When Paul's sister Edna arrived, Bella's mood shifted. She started bellowing about how her favorite charity, the Madison House in Lower Manhattan, was misusing her funds.

"You should've donated the money to Lillian Wald instead," Edna said.

"Paul, come on down and say hi to your brother," Bella called out, ignoring her daughter's comment. Paul quit trying to write and joined them.

When their father showed up late, Bella berated him for

making them all wait while the dinner grew cold. Emanuel didn't sound contrite enough, so his wife went on about how he was a lazy ne'er-do-well, spending his days just laying about the house.

"You were the one who forced him to retire," Paul muttered softly to himself.

Robert sat with a frozen smile on his face, waiting for his mother's tantrum to pass.

Bella looked angrily around the room and, seeing Paul glaring at her, she said, "Please tell me you broke up with that mustached shiksa." Robert snickered.

"First of all, she's Jewish. Secondly, save your rancor for those who are afraid to defend themselves."

"Hey, Princeton boy," she replied, "don't forget who pays for you to learn how to recite French poetry!"

"Well, you can keep your damned tuition," he lashed back. "Cause I'm done with that . . . that finishing school for robber barrons!"

"I'll believe that when I see it!"

As Paul furiously headed for the front door, he heard Robert saying to his mother, "Let him just simmer down."

True to his word, when Paul got back to Princeton, he waited until Monday, then went to see the dean of Student Affairs and applied for a multisemester leave of absence that wouldn't affect his grades. Next he returned to his dorm room and packed his bags. He was about to call Bella, but instead dialed Robert. The phone rang until someone in the hallway of his brother's dormitory answered and said Robert wasn't around.

Paul kept calling over the next four hours until he finally got ahold of Robert. As soon as his brother said hello, Paul explained that he had just withdrawn from classes.

"Please say you're joshing."

"Absolutely not."

"Mother was just having some fun, but this is downright spiteful."

"I didn't do it out of spite."

"The semester's almost over, and then you only have one more year to go!"

"Robert, I have no choice. Millicent's down in Mexico and I'm sure she's in distress."

"Oh my," Robert said. "So what are you hoping to do, go down and rescue her?"

"I suppose." It sounded melodramatic even to Paul.

"But you're not seriously planning on fighting the government of Mexico, are you?"

"No, of course not, I just want to protect Millie."

"Paul, you're handsome, rich, and young. You don't have to get yourself shot in another country to save some wetback mistress. Hell, you can sleep with Maria—I know you fancy her."

"Damn you, Robert!"

"I'm sorry, Paul, but this is just crazy."

"Look, it's one of those things that if I don't do, I'll spend the rest of my life regretting."

"And how about if you get yourself killed? Do you have any idea how angry Mom would be if that happened?"

Paul smiled, but then realized that Robert was serious. Robert wasn't afraid of his older brother's death, only concerned about upsetting their mother. Paul replied that he simply had no choice.

"So you're really going through with it?"

"I am, and I hope you'll learn from this."

"What exactly am I supposed to learn, Paul?"

"That you shouldn't be afraid to fight for something you believe in."

Paul heard a sound that could've been a snort or a chuckle. He wasn't sure if Robert was indignant or amused.

"Good luck," Robert finally remarked.

Paul hung up the earpiece on the cradle of the candlestick phone. Trying to stand, he found that his left leg and right arm had fallen asleep—like he had pinched a nerve. After several minutes of nervously shaking his body, his circulation returned to normal.

He gave away many of his possessions and put the rest in storage, then packed a single rucksack of necessities. He headed straight to the train station and mapped out as direct a route as he could to the tiny Mexican village of Córdova. The trip was six days of continuous travel with four connecting trains. The food was awful, but Paul enjoyed watching as the passengers, climate, and landscapes slowly changed while they moved southwest. He also became friendly with most of the Negro Pullman workers on the trains. It was the first time he had traveled out west. The wide-open ranges and the soaring mountains stretched his imagination, but the endless rolling desert filled him with an inexplicable déjà vu.

As Paul's train eventually approached the Mexican border, he changed into a new suit to extinguish any suspicion that he was aligned with the revolutionaries. He didn't have a passport, but when the two federal soldiers marched slowly down the aisle, Paul handed over his Princeton University ID. One of them looked it over and handed it back to him.

The train stopped three more times, and each time a different pair of menacing soldiers walked down the aisles of his train, carefully checking the identity of foreigners and asking what business they had in Mexico.

"Just vacationing," he always replied with a tight smile.

When Paul eventually descended from his final train in Mexico, he felt a painful crick in his neck; it seemed as if an invisible force was pinning his head in place. He assumed it had something to do with the pinched nerve he had suffered earlier, so he simply trudged along in discomfort.

6

Following a full day of travel on a mule-drawn carriage, Paul finally arrived at the small village of Córdova in the state of Sonora. Millicent's last mailing address turned out to be a home full of peasants.

"Are any students from America staying here?" he asked one of the men in his passable Spanish.

Paul was directed to Victor Gonzalez, one of the original committee members, who said that Millie was running the canteen attached to a small brigade roughly fifty miles to the east. It was headed by Colonel Ceasar Octavio-Noriega, a short man with a bushy white mustache.

Paul was able to catch a ride there the next day. As rebel soldiers stopped the wagon upon his arrival, Millie came racing up with her arms spread wide.

"Paul!"

He kissed her hard on the mouth and squeezed her tightly.

That night, over soggy corn-flour burritos with rice and beans that tasted like they had been refried one too many times, she filled him in: Things had not been going well. When Madero escaped his captors and made his formal call to arms, he expected to find a trained army of sympathizers waiting to assist him when he crossed the Rio Grande. A small crowd was gathered there, but the ragtag group hardly constituted an army. Madero was forced to retreat back up to Texas. In Mexico, there were some minor skirmishes, but the expected uprising fizzled. Nonetheless, word spread and various insurgent leaders started joining together. Peasants began to grasp the significance of the fight and joined the insurrection. In the state of Chihuahua, Madero supporter Pascual Orozco took over the town of Guerrero. At the end of the November, Francisco "Pancho" Villa captured San Andrés. Back in Sonora, another revolutionary, José María Maytorena, organized a series of small bands which soon infested the north. From the southern state of Morelos, the great Emiliano Zapata sent a delegate to Madero to discuss cooperation in fighting the Díaz regime.

"I can't believe you came all the way down here," Millie said excitedly to Paul.

"Believe me, I didn't want to," he replied, putting his bag down.

With a wide smile and a beautiful tan, Millie looked like someone else. She led him around the camp proudly showing him off to her various friends and colleagues.

"Who is this?" Colonel Octavio-Noriega asked suspiciously.

"My fiancé," Millie replied.

"Good, then he'll stay in your tent."

That night, Paul and Millie made love for the very first time. Over the following weeks, as the band rode east and then south, Millicent introduced him to a variety of zealous young comrades, many of whom had come from abroad to help with this struggle. All seemed to believe that a worldwide revolution was imminent. Paul sat quietly at night around the campfires.

"Civilization comes to the point," one Italian volunteer named Carlo struggled to say one evening, "where iz no longer need for the leaders who divide and exploit the work man."

Listening to them, Paul found a renewed faith in the American system of government. To Millie's displeasure, he told her that he had decided to stay out of all combat in Mexico. His sole task would be protecting her.

"Can't you see how bad it is here?" she appealed. He

replied that he did, but that he just didn't think these people were ready; the poor seemed to accept their fate and the rich clearly felt entitled to theirs. His noninvolvement soon became an ongoing argument between the two of them.

It all changed by accident one day, when a young Russian anarchist who was an expert sapper arrived under orders from Pancho Villa. Vladimir Ustinov, who wasn't much older than Paul, had ample experience with bombs from his time in czarist Russia. He had been sent out to teach various militias, some of whom were filled with foreign fighters, how to build homemade bombs to be used against the local garrisons.

In the turbulent state of Chihuahua, almost none of the peasant fighters spoke anything besides Spanish. Other than Russian, Vladimir only knew French. It often took him three hours to give a twenty-minute lesson, but that day he was pressed for time. Getting a full demonstration with all the equipment, Paul, who had studied French at Princeton, spent an hour learning from the Russian before the man had to gallop off to his next mission.

"So should I teach your soldiers?" Paul asked the colonel after the Russian departed.

"Teach them what?"

"What Señor Ustinov taught me—how to use the explosives."

"You're our official sapper," the commander said to him in Spanish. "Just instruct them as you need."

"But I'm not a volunteer," Paul explained. "I'm just here to protect my fiancée."

"Congratulations, you've officially been conscripted," the commander replied.

"Look, I'll teach your men what Vladimir taught me, but I refuse to kill people in a war that I don't believe in."

The commander pulled an old pistol from his cracked leather holster and pointed it at Paul's forehead. The young

American stared angrily at the older man, refusing to believe that the bastard would pull the trigger.

"I'll teach and oversee your men, but I simply can't kill anyone. If you really are going to execute me, so be it."

The commander put the gun down and told him to wait outside the tent. Five minutes later, the man sent for Millicent, who he greatly respected. The two spoke alone for five minutes, then Paul was summoned.

"Okay, I've agreed to your terms. You can instruct Millie here."

"Millie?"

"Yes, she'll be your hands. Your first mission is tonight."

"I'm not going on any mission," he replied.

"Fine, then she'll do it alone. Instruct her as best as you can. She's going out in a few hours."

"What's the mission?"

"There's a supply train passing two hours from here. She's going out with a detachment of the European volunteers to blow up the track."

"Millie can't do it."

Before Paul could opine that most of the European volunteers were criminals who'd sooner rape her than follow her, she spoke up: "I've done missions before."

Paul finally relented and agreed to be the militia's official sapper instead of Millie.

Along with a dozen men, most of them Italian volunteers, they rode out on horseback. From a distance, Paul could see a large regiment of federal soldiers patrolling both sides of the tracks. He had his men tie up their horses at a safe distance, then waited until night. He brought three men with him, proceeding forward on foot. They were almost caught when a passing patrol found their tracks in the moonlight, but they cautiously advanced from tree to tree and rock to rock and reached the target undetected. Paul and Carlo hastily wedged three dynamite sticks under each of the tracks, while the others kept watch. Paul lit a slow-burning fuse and they ran like hell.

Over the next twenty-eight months, his little group, known as the Italian Brigade, carried out twelve more missions. Complicating matters was the fact that they began running out of supplies. One sweltering afternoon, however, Vladimir Ustinov returned with several large spools of wires and a plunger detonator. Due to the surge of federal troops there, he had been sent back into the region.

After giving Paul instructions on how to attach the fuses, he explained that with the plunger they could dramatically increase the amount of federales killed. Paul nodded, not revealing that he really didn't want to be responsible for any casualties.

That night, passing a bottle of tequila over the large bonfire, the two men chatted. Vladimir explained in French how the food and liquor were killing him here—constant diarrhea—but he greatly enjoyed the work.

"Since the bloody attack in St. Petersburg by the czar's army on unarmed citizens a few years ago, Russia is much like Mexico these days," Vladimir explained. "Right on the verge."

"Then why are you here instead of mother Russia?"

"Waiting for the right moment," Vladimir answered. "Everything has that moment when you can tip it over with a feather. One day soon America will have its own moment."

"I can understand your feeling that way about Russia, but in America we have an elected government."

"The United States has the same vast disparity between the rich and poor that every other country has, and its elections are rigged all the time. America just needs a single major event to topple the old apparatchik."

"I met Woodrow Wilson and he's a good man. If anyone can fix things, he will."

"He might make some small differences, but he can't change the many social inequities that divide your country."

Paul wasn't interested in arguing, but Vladimir and the other young radicals in his brigade could talk about little else. Over the ensuing weeks, every time they met, the Russian youth would ask him if he was ready to help start the new American revolution. And every time, Paul would answer that America's major problems would be settled by Woodrow Wilson.

Soon it became a running joke. If the weather was bad or the federales had repelled an attack, Vladimir would say to Paul in broken English, "Don't worry, your Wilson will fix."

"We kill Czar Alexander, we kill your McKinley, and we can kill Wilson when iz time," Carlo declared. Paul sighed and wondered how he'd gotten himself mixed up with all these nuts.

Paul was able to send a letter home from the small town they were using as a central hub. Six weeks later, Edna wrote him back and explained that when his mother had heard what he was doing, she threw such a fit that his father had to call a doctor to settle her down. Since then, his name had not so much as been mentioned. Robert was still in school and had a new girlfriend named Mary. Paul's favorite maid, Maria, had also met someone and was falling deeply in love.

7

Several months later, Paul received a tightly scripted postcard from his sister informing him that poor Maria had fallen on hard times. She had married that fellow, some Italian-Jewish guy from Rome. He had worked and saved and managed to buy an old house at a good price in a section of the Bronx called East Tremont. No sooner had she moved in with him than he got her pregnant. Then the guy just vanished into thin air. One of his friends claimed he had returned to Italy; allegedly he was connected with the Mafia.

Please give her five hundred dollars from me, and tell her to take it easy until she has the kid, Paul wrote back.

One day, while they were planning a complicated two-site detonation, Vladimir explained that Paul would need a watch in order to coordinate the second explosion. When Paul said that his wristwatch broke long ago, Vladimir gave him his own pocket watch, a beautiful gold piece with a miniature image of a handsome older gentleman glazed on the inside.

"Is this your father?" Paul asked, staring at the resemblance.

"It's the father of a Russian industrialist I executed, which is why I had to flee the country," Vladimir replied. "But he looks like my father, so I'm very much attached to it. And it keeps perfect time. You'll give it back to me the next time I see you."

Vladimir had to depart quickly to aid with another vital operation further south. Several days after Paul completed his mission, he heard that the young Russian had been caught by the federales and was summarily executed.

Even so, Paul discovered that over two hundred federal soldiers had been killed during his two-site detonation, he was horrified. While the others in the Italian Brigade celebrated, he went to his tent and began packing.

"What are you doing?" Millie asked, entering quietly.

"This has gone on long enough!" he yelled. "Over two hundred men are dead because of me, and I never even *joined* this cause!"

"You in it now!" called Carlo drunkenly from outside the tent.

"Paul, we're winning. It's just a matter of time now."

"You manipulated me into this. And it's over. To hell with you, I'm going home."

"Octavio's outside," she whispered. "If you leave now, he'll have you shot."

"You tricked me into this and now look! You've made me into a damn murderer."

"Paul, don't ever say that. You came down here on your own. You knew my loyalties from the start. I never lied to you. Listen to me," she appealed softly. "You've given me everything I want. In return we'll get married and we'll have a family and a nice place near the city. We'll be very happy together."

He nodded his head and left the tent.

Under the two charismatic generals, Zapata and Villa, the tide was clearly turning. Díaz had begun appealing publicly for peace, but Madero flatly rejected his efforts. To try to win back popular support, the tyrant attempted to reinstate land reforms. He even went so far as to dismiss most of his conservative cabinet, but it was to no avail.

Soon places that were Díaz strongholds like Veracruz, Chiapas, and the Yucatán began seeing heavy insurgency. By spring, the rebels had seized over twenty major cities.

Finally, when the revolutionaries encircled the city of

Juárez, Díaz resigned. Within days, Madero was sworn in as the new president. Victory celebrations blanketed Mexico. The revolution was over.

"It's time to go home," Paul said to Millie upon hearing the latest news.

She nodded in agreement. But the very next day, the new president, who was expressing reluctance to enact some of the key reforms of the revolution, was suddenly assassinated. Several revolutionary leaders boldly declared themselves the rightful heir to power. Colonel Octavio-Noriega held his brigade together, waiting to see what compromise might be reached, but by the week's end it was clear that a new struggle for power had begun.

"They just need us a bit longer," Millie informed Paul.

"This isn't fair," Paul said with clenched teeth. "I came here to protect you and now a big chunk of my life is gone!"

A week after the assassination, Colonel Octavio-Noriega led Paul into his tent late one night and explained that the American was an indispensable part of his command.

"Carlo knows everything I do about explosives," Paul replied tiredly.

"It would have a detrimental effect on morale if I were to just discharge you," Octavio-Noriega said. Then, in a low voice, he added, "However, if you and Millie were to take a mule and leave one night and vanish forever, there would be little I could do."

The next morning, Paul hugged Millie tightly to his chest and whispered into her ear, "We're leaving tonight."

"We'll be shot."

"He's letting us go."

"But the fighting isn't over."

Paul explained that he had been given an unofficial discharge.

"But that wasn't our agreement," she said, turning away from him.

"You said that when we could leave without getting killed, you'd go with me," he replied sternly. "You promised!"

She didn't say a word to him the rest of the day, refusing to even make eye contact.

Early that evening, after packing a handful of essentials, Paul went out for a final meal with his comrades.

When he returned to his tent, he found that Millie hadn't packed her trunk. She was lying facedown on her cot, weeping uncontrollably.

"What's the matter?"

"I love you dearly, Paul. Truly, I do. And I know the sacrifice you made coming down here and helping me in this struggle. And if it's worth anything, these people love you and need you. So, if you want, we can marry and live here. We can even have children and—"

"You agreed to come back north!"

"I'm really sorry. I just can't abandon my country," she said, embracing him.

"You betrayed me to get me to kill people for you!"

"Paul, I love you. I swear it!" She wept aloud as he stormed out.

Taking one of the regiment's old burros, he rode and walked nonstop through the night and all the next day. Arriving at the nearest train station, he bought a ticket west that would take him to another train north. Caked in dirt and sweat, utterly exhausted, he had an odd succession of thoughts. *Did you abandon your post? Did you abandon a people in crisis, a people in need of you? Did you abandon a situation that you were culpable in creating?* He sensed somehow that the thoughts were not entirely related to Millie and Mexico, and that they were coming from somewhere else altogether.

On the third night of his slow train ride across the dry landscape, he found himself hot and unable to sleep. He frequented the vestibule at the end of the car where he'd open the top half of one of the double windows, allowing in a cool breeze. As he thought of all the bloodshed he had seen during his time in Mexico, tears came to his eyes.

"You okay, son?" he heard. An older fellow with a bushy mustache and only one arm was leaning against the opposite wall, puffing a corncob pipe.

"Yeah," Paul replied, wiping away his tears. "I'm just glad to get away from all the fighting below the Rio Grande." He didn't have any more to say.

"Son, I'm seventy-seven," the fellow said with a Southern twang. "Fifty years or so yonder, when I was about your age, I was a soldier for the Confederacy, and I don't mind telling you that this entire area we're passing through, and all the young men in it, well . . . you're passing through the land of the dead. You just couldn't imagine ever recovering from so much loss, and yet you do."

Paul responded politely and excused himself.

After four more squalid days without even enough money to eat for the final stretch, Paul arrived in New York's Pennsylvania Station. With a bundle of filthy and torn belongings under his arm, he walked up to his parents' home on 46th Street. When he rang the bell at 11 o'clock, Maria answered and let out a shriek upon seeing the bearded, wild-eyed scion of the Moses family.

Bella appeared at the door and immediately started yelling. "Didn't I warn you! Did I not say that a woman like that is only out for herself? Did I tell you that or not? Answer me!"

"You told me."

"And did you listen?"

"No, I didn't listen."

"And what happened? Months and months of your life wasted! You might as well have been in prison. Not to mention the fact that you could've very easily gotten yourself killed."

"I'm sorry." He wasn't about to share the risks he had taken and the murders he had committed.

"What sense is any of this? A Jewish boy getting himself killed fighting for . . . for what? Tar babies and jungle heathens? Why?"

Suddenly, Paul collapsed. Maria and his mother helped him to his feet, then washed him, fed him, and put him to bed.

The next afternoon, after having slept for more than sixteen hours, Paul came downstairs for a big brunch of matzo ball soup, whitefish salad, fresh bagels, and orange juice. Bella sat with him as he ate.

"What do you want to do now?"

"Just finish my degree," he said quietly.

His grades, his extracurricular activities, his attendance and conduct had all been excellent—it was August, and with a little luck (and his family's connections), he could get back into school in time for the fall semester.

Inspired by Thomas Alva Edison's breakthroughs in electricity, Paul believed that technology could somehow level society's playing field and help foster true justice. He had learned that only a tiny percent of the population in Mexico was literate, and he couldn't help thinking that if all the little villages had access to electricity, groups would be better able to assemble and share ideas. Individuals would be more compelled to learn how to read, and education made people more politically alert.

That night, in the sumptuous luxury of his parents' house, as he was drifting off to sleep, he felt once again as though he were drowning.

Bolting up, he turned to flip on his bedside lamp, only to realize he was naked and floating in warm black water, gasping for air. And he wasn't Paul; he was someone named Uli. Desperately clawing at some kind of thick fabric wrapped tightly around him. A helmet chin-strapped to his head.

Feeling about, he found a small hose secured near his mouth. He sucked on it, hoping to draw oxygen . . . then remembered. Clenching his diaphragm to keep from choking, he nervously fingered the hose into a tiny tank attached to his naked back. He turned the tiny knob on top and a jolt of oxygen shot down his throat like a snake. Awkwardly, he gulped down several deep breaths, then turned the knob off to conserve his air supply. *Where the hell am I? And how do I get out?* He closed his eyes and tried not to panic. Strangely, the Mnemosyne, the drug he had been injected with to keep him alive in the black water, was still working. His eyes still shut, he took it all in, almost like a song playing in the background: someone named Paul, years ago. He was simply unable to stop the images rushing through his head.

8

Paul spent the new school term studying physics and electronics and began his thesis on Maxwell's unified theory of electromagnetism.

Each day in class, Paul's thoughts returned obsessively to poor Millie and the hardships she must be suffering. He'd start scribbling letters to her, filling them with his testaments of love and regret, but invariably he'd tear them up recalling what he regarded as her betrayal. He tried desperately to reroute all his grief and heartbreak into electrical engineering.

Several months after returning to Princeton, Paul opened the paper one morning to find an article about a bombing of a courthouse in lower Manhattan, allegedly conducted by anarchists. Other bombings followed. He began to fear that Carlo and his band of Italian revolutionaries were responsible; after all, they had claimed to have agents in America. Courthouses, churches, police stations, and even the homes of politicians came under attack. Paul considered placing an anonymous call to the police department, but he wasn't sure what he'd say. He only had a few names, and he didn't know any locations or plans. Ultimately, he feared that his own identity would be revealed and he'd come under suspicion, so he kept silent and hoped the attacks would cease.

While Paul was down in Mexico, his brother had married his girlfriend and completed a graduate program at Oxford University. Using his mother's connections, he had gained admission to the prestigious new Training School for Public Service, the first of its kind. Young Robert Moses was promised a job with the Bureau of Municipal Research—the organization that had founded the school.

Bella was impressed with Paul's determination to catch up. When he finally graduated from Princeton, his mother said she wanted to help him build some financial security so he could begin thinking about a family. "Opportunity is where you find it," she told him, "and except for Edison, I've never heard of anyone getting rich in electricity."

She invited him home for a big dinner to be thrown in his honor. Naturally, Mr. Robert was too busy to come. When Paul arrived early at the Midtown manor several days later, he followed Maria into the kitchen, still disgusted by the latest news he had read on the train to the city. The families of the victims in the recent Triangle Shirtwaist fire, after having filed a civil lawsuit against the owners, had been awarded the insulting settlement of seventy-five dollars for each of the 148 young girls who had been burned or fallen to her death.

Maria interrupted Paul's train of thought, mentioning that his mother had arranged a surprise for him that he wasn't going to like.

"Who's this princess?" Paul asked, spotting a pretty little girl peaking out at him from behind a curtain.

"Lucretia, come here and say hi to Paul."

Paul curtsied, asking, "Are you the Duchess of Ferrara?"

"Who?" the little girl asked.

"Lucrezia Borgia, Duchess of Ferrara," Paul replied. "She had a ring with a secret compartment in it, through which she could easily poison her unsuspecting adversaries."

"Well, I never poisoned no one," the girl said, then dashed off.

At that moment, Bella shouted out Paul's name from the living room, so he said goodbye to Maria and her young daughter. They were served drinks and sat talking for half an hour until Paul's father and sister arrived, then they all moved into the dining room.

Maria had prepared a fabulous red snapper dish. When they were finished with dinner, Bella announced that with Emanuel's help she had arranged for Paul to get a great job where he could make excellent use of his mathematical skills.

"It's in banking," his father quietly added.

"Kuhn & Loeb," Bella elaborated. "David Loeb himself secured you the position. You start in two weeks."

Paul sighed.

"It's a very prestigious firm," Emanuel said. It was obvious that Bella had put tremendous effort into orchestrating this. Usually his father didn't make a peep.

"Mom, I'm grateful for the offer, but I'm just not a banker. I want to—"

"Paul, you're still young. Why don't you just give this a chance?" Bella pushed. Paul smiled, not wanting to make a scene. "Just try it for six months and—"

"I told you repeatedly that I want to work in the public sector and I want to be an electrical engineer."

"Well, that's admirable, son, but . . ." his father began.

"What the hell do you know?" Bella bursted out. "You're a damn kid who just got home from Mexico. We paid a truckload of money for your college degree."

"I don't even like bankers! You just don't listen!"

"Paul, please," his father said.

"Robert was right," Bella said. "I've turned you into a snot-nosed brat. You won't even try this before turning it down."

Paul rose, grabbed his coat, and hurried out as his mother continued yelling about his wasted time south of the border with Señorita Obnoxchez.

Paul awoke that night with the blanket pulled over his head, and he was once again unable to feel his arms or legs. He could sense an air pocket forming along the top of the blanket, but then he realized it wasn't actually a blanket.

He was having a nightmare of being trapped in a bag filled with water.

But it wasn't a dream—and he wasn't Paul. He shook his limbs until sensation started to return.

I got to find some way out of here before I drown.

Reaching around, he twisted the knob on the top of the oxygen tank and took another injection of air.

Focusing on regaining his calm, Uli remembered that he had been inserted into the sleeping bag for protection. A string loosely sealed the top of it. With minimal struggle, he was able to snap the string and pull the bag over him. It was immediately sucked away and he found that he was entangled in a series of crisscrossing lines of some kind. A faint ray of light from above allowed him to see that he was snared in a network of loose cables, like a big fishing net. He was still in the large sewer pipe he had been swept down. His helmeted head was being pushed into a pile of boulders that seemed to be holding down the base of the netting, preventing him from continuing onward. He remembered having read that the average person needed a breath every three or so minutes, but it felt like it had been at least five since his last one: The chemical injected into his system seemed to have lingering effects. He took another gulp of air, then realized he had to break through these ropes to have any chance of staying alive.

9

Uli wondered if the current of water pushing him against the net was powering some massive generator. He remembered Nikola Tesla's famous hydroelectric generators at the Adams Power Station, powered by the mighty waters of the great Niagara Falls. Their boundless megawatts of electricity were channeled down high-tension wires, bringing fifty thousands volts across New York State to the city.

Apprenticing as a field engineer with the Consolidated Edison Company of New York, Paul had personally inspected a great deal of the system. He had joined the ranks of the linemen in jumpsuits and had climbed up the poles and seen thousands of miles of powerlines racked side by side. He had also descended into the many semiflooded manholes, checking the countless transformers where voltage was stepped down to 220 and routed into households throughout the five boroughs.

Just a quick glance at the sprawling electrical grids that supplied the various communities of the perpetually expanding city—it was evident that a dramatic power shortage was looming. The mouths of ever more babes were suckling at the same fixed row of nipples. Multiple feeders rerouted electricity further and further away. It made Paul realize they didn't simply need more generators in New York; new ways of moving the turbines were also required.

Uli tried to hold onto the thoughts, but marinating there in the giant pipe, he now recalled the submarine that fired torpedoes into the luxury liner *Lusitania*. Over a hundred Americans had been killed.

Woodrow Wilson demanded that Germany cease its attacks on passenger ships. They complied. Still, domestic pressure increased and blowhards like Teddy Roosevelt denounced Wilson as a coward.

In April of 1917, the United States finally joined the war. After hearing Wilson's speech about making the world "safe for democracy," Paul, who had been working as an engineer for two years but still hadn't risen to the upper echelons of Con Ed, decided to quit his job and follow his president's call.

He telephoned Robert and said, "Now it's *our* country at war, not Mexico. I'm enlisting. Will you join me?"

"Does Mom know you're doing this?" Robert asked cooly.

"Not yet."

"Tell you what," Robert said. "If she gives you her blessing, I'll seriously consider joining with you."

Paul replied that he would take his brother up on that.

The next day, when Paul visited his mother to tell her that he was intent on joining the army, she screamed, "What, did you meet another girl? Whenever you get horny, you want to go invade some country! Who's the woman this time?"

"Lady Liberty," he quipped.

Bella argued that he had already gone through one war, which was more than enough.

"I'm still of draft age."

"No one's going to draft you. I'll see to that." Then, taking a breath, she calmly informed him that if he joined the army, he should never contact her again.

Paul hugged his mother, who didn't budge, and then left the house.

Later that week, when he told the recruitment officer that he was an engineer well-versed in electrical circuitry, the man's eyes lit up. He said he had been waiting months for someone with half Paul's qualifications. Paul had been partly hoping to get sent to boot camp and fight overseas. Instead, he was immediately commissioned as a first lieutenant and sent to some vague assignment in Washington, D.C. There, he found himself working at a desk in the Weapons Malfunctions Report Unit—the WMRU—reviewing incidents of battlefield equipment breakdown. Initially it was only about half a dozen incident reports per week. Machines guns jamming. Grenades failing to explode. Trucks and jeeps malfunctioning in the heat of combat. Soon after starting, Paul explained to his commander, Colonel Gibbons, that he had no experience in weaponry, and asked to be transferred out.

"I'm drastically undermanned as it is. Reynolds doesn't even know how to hold a damn gun, much less assemble one. And Lindquist is a bloody pacifist. But you've all got great minds and you're quick learners. Transfer denied."

Paul's job was to assess if a weapon had failed for a unique reason or if there was a manufacturing flaw. A key focus was identifying makes or models that required modifications or recalls.

As America's involvement in the war heated up, reports started pouring in. Paul was promoted to captain and put in charge of all field artillery reports. Soon, however, the work fell into routine drudgery and he began daydreaming about the great struggle happening a quarter of the way around the world. Reviewing reports of the carnage, he found himself recalling his days in Mexico. There was little romance in planting sticks of dynamite and running like mad. Though he had seen dead bodies—and was even shot at once—he had never witnessed combat on the front lines. Most of the men in Mexico barely had guns, let alone uniforms.

His mother never wrote, but he did receive letters from his sister Edna once a week, and on occasion Maria would drop him a postcard updating him on life back home. Sev-

eral times she enclosed pictures that her daughter Lucretia had drawn at school. And it was through Maria that
he learned that Mr. Robert had finally gotten his first big
break, an appointment in the Municipal Civil Service Commission under the "boy mayor," John Purroy Mitchel.

10

As Uli wrestled with the various squares of netting and tried to shove through, he thought, *A tank could tear right through this like wet toilet paper*. With its steel caterpillar wheels, it could roll right over mines and through waves of enemy fire. The common belief was that it would quickly end the war.

America needed to develop the basic models for a big tank and a small one, the Renault, and this required a complex compromise between British and French designs, as well as the work of over seventy subcontractors and five different manufacturing plants for final assembly.

The entire process was taking so long that no one thought any of the tanks would actually see action during the war. Before the first American tank even rolled off the assembly line, the Germans managed to seize a British one; with their own modifications, the Germans started assembling their own battalion. Soon, the few American tanks in action began breaking down and Paul found himself sifting through stacks of incident reports late into his nights.

A recurrent malfunction quickly became apparent during a spring offensive. The men inside the tanks were getting killed when mines exploded right through their floors. In the space of three weeks, eighteen tanks had been destroyed in the same way, killing more than thirty doughboys. Paul immediately requested to see the blueprints of these particular tanks.

The outer metal skin of the tanks was supposed to be five-eighths of an inch thick, yet the actual thickness varied in four different reports, and two of the torn hulls measured as thin as a quarter of an inch.

He contacted the military attache at the Byrd & Hale assembly plant in Cleveland, Ohio, and asked for confirmation of how thick the hulls of their tanks were. He was told they'd need three days to research that information.

The next day he got a phone call from one Samuel P. Bush, who introduced himself as a government contractor.

"How can I help you, Mr. Bush?" Paul asked.

"I'm Chief of Ordinance, specifically small-arms munitions."

"You probably want Captain Reynolds. He's the case officer who handles small-arms malfunction reports."

"No, I want to speak with you."

"About what?"

"I just thought maybe I could stop by and we could talk."

"Fine."

At 5 o'clock, just before Paul was about to leave for the day, a swollen-looking man with a thick bushy mustache and a bowler showed up and introduced himself as Samuel.

"So you're a Yale man?" Samuel asked.

"No, Princeton. How about you?"

"Stevens Institute, but both my father and son went to Yale."

"Were you hoping to raise some money for the alumni? Cause I can give you my brother's phone number, he went there."

"No," the older man chuckled. Looking around the stuffy basement, he said, "Listen, I'm starving. Would you care to join me for a bite? I know a place near here that has great chops—Dutch's."

Paul said what the heck, he was about to leave anyway. As the government contractor led him outside to his car, he explained he was there because of the phone call Paul had made to the Byrd & Hale assembly plant.

"Oh, yeah, about the thickness of the hull of their two-man tanks. Why, did they contact you?"

"Not officially, no. It's just that I work with them a lot, and Shane Richards asked me what was up."

By the casual, unassuming way Bush drove as he talked, Paul's first instinct was that the man was there on behalf of some higher-ups in the War Department who were launching their own probe. When they entered the restaurant, the maître d' immediately recognized Mr. Bush and showed him to his "usual table."

In another moment, a fine bottle of French wine was uncorked and poured. Bush ordered two plates of filet mignon—both medium rare—then offered Paul an expensive Cuban cigar. Paul politely refused. That was when he first considered that the man might be representing corporate interests. Almost as soon as he thought this, Bush said, "The reason I'm here is because a group of us got heavily involved in America's new tank project and, well, we think of it as our own baby."

"Success has many fathers, and failure is an orphan," Paul replied.

"Exactly, but success doesn't come as quickly as we'd like. We're trying to get this thing on its wobbly little feet without any problems, and at this stage, if any little thing comes up, it can have a big effect on the war effort."

"Doesn't it help the baby if we heal it when it's sick?"

"We already know the hull is too thin. We've doubled the size of it, but we're trying to keep it a little on the hush-hush."

"I read that the thickness was supposed to be five-eighths of an inch, but some where measured at a quarter-inch, and if you multiply that discrepancy by the four thousand tanks which the government commissioned, that's a whole lot of clams saved."

"The tank in question, as you know, was put together

from several different blueprints from French and English designs. So where exactly would you lay the blame?"

"Which company manufactured the hull of the tanks that blew in and killed over thirty young American soldiers?" Paul asked coolly.

Bush smiled and just stared at him as though he were a child. In the course of the next twenty minutes, as the subcontractor rattled off statistics to put the facts in a context that made them seem trivial, Paul's food was taken away uneaten. Bush ordered a Baked Alaska and brandy, and then more brandy. Other patrons stopped by, shook Bush's hand, and left.

"You know, these tanks were finished way ahead of deadline. No one even thought they'd make it out onto the battlefield in time. Do you know how many infantry soldiers they have saved?"

"They're death machines for the two men inside."

"And we've already taken measures out on the field to have the tanks reinforced with one-inch plates riveted to their undercarriage."

"Then that should be made public too."

"Maybe it will soothe your mind, Captain Moses, to know that all this has already been brought to the attention of everyone from the attorney general to the inspector general's office."

"Then why are you taking me out for dinner?"

"Because, frankly, there is enough stuff here to start a congressional investigation, though that in itself doesn't worry me. There are plenty of parties who can shoot smoke in all directions. What saddens me, and the reason I'm here spending my own dime and time, is the fact that this investigation could hurt our nation's new tank project." Some suited older man came over and gave Bush's hand a shake. Bush shook back without even pausing. "And I think a delay would put America at a strategic disadvantage that could affect us for the next fifty years."

"You're very popular," Paul pointed out, referring to all the handshakes.

"That's how deals get made."

At this, Paul stood up and said, "If you can prove to me that these mistakes have been corrected and I don't see any more reports of this type, I'll consider sitting on it."

Bush said that he'd send Paul documents detailing all the changes underway as well as the new procedures they were using to temper the steel. "By the way, I'm very impressed by your credentials," he added. "I don't know if you'd be interested, but I can make great use of someone with your qualifications."

"I'm not a weapons inspector," Paul said. "I sort of got sent here by mistake."

"I know. You're an electrical engineer. I happen to sit on the board of several companies that are looking toward electrical expansions. They could make good use of your talent, sir."

Though he was indeed greatly interested, Paul feared that this was a veiled bribe and said that he was already committed to working at Con Ed once the war was over.

"Well, let me ask you this: Would you consider doing some freelance work for me?"

"What kind of freelance work?"

"I'll send you diagrams and you tell me in layman's terms how they work."

Paul said he'd be glad to try to help the contractor.

Three days later, Paul received a package with Bush's return address. Inside was abundant documentation from Byrd & Hale proving that the floors of tanks were being more heavily reinforced, along with a diagram of a simple artillery gun and a self-addressed envelope. The artillery piece in the diagram wasn't new, and after researching some data in various manuals, Paul wrote a letter describing the range of shells it fired and mailed it to Bush. A week later, he received a sealed envelope with three crisp hundred-dollar bills and a folded piece of paper that said, *Consultant Fee*. After wondering what to do, Paul simply put the money in the bottom drawer of his desk.

Over the course of the next six months, he received a new design of some weapon every four weeks. Most of them were simple artillery pieces, weapons that anyone could research during an afternoon in the military library. Each time Paul wrote a report and sent it to Bush, he'd get an envelope with three hundred dollars. Initially Paul found it amusing, never spending the fee. Before long, however, he started feeling a little insulted. Was this something that Bush hoped to extort him with? On the other hand, the incident reports regarding the hull of the new American tanks had abruptly stopped. The problem appeared to be corrected.

That December, Paul received an embossed invitation to an upcoming Christmas party at the Eldridge, a swank hotel in Washington. It turned out that two other officers in the WMRU had also gotten invites and were planning to share a cab to the hotel.

"Do you guys all know this Bush fellow?" Paul asked during the ride to the party a week later. They didn't. As Paul listened to them, it turned out each had been approached by someone in the War Department who introduced them to "how things get done here."

"I was told I had sent the wrong report out," said Captain Reynolds. Paul wondered if they too had been overpaid for minor consultations, though he sensed that the two guys didn't really want to discuss it. But thinking about it, he had never heard either man complain about money, unlike most others he served with.

When they arrived, at least a thousand men, most in uniforms, were crowded together in the grand ballroom of the Eldridge. Next to a forty-foot Christmas tree, an eight-piece band was playing "Auld Lang Syne." A large banner hanging from the ceiling read, *Merry Christmas—The Last Year of the War Thanks to You, Our Heroes in Uniform!*

Paul realized that the three of them from the WMRU were vastly outranked. Generals and admirals from all branches of the armed services flanked the four bars. Waiters served hors d'oeuvres.

"No girls here," said Reynolds to Paul and Lindquist, holding a roasted chicken leg in one hand and a gin and tonic in the other. "After I fill my gullet, I'm skedaddling."

Paul made no objection. He simply drank soda water and walked around looking at the other revelers. After thirty minutes or so, he heard someone shout, "Peter!"

Turning around, he spotted a tuxedoed Samuel Bush wearing a newspaper folded into a commodore's hat. The contractor squeezed out from a group of generals. Paul assumed he was addressing someone else until Bush grabbed his arm.

"Pete, how are you doing, pal?" he slurred.

"Fine."

"You did a great job with that last report—did you get my little honorarium?"

"I'm glad you mentioned that," Paul said. He reached into his pocket and handed Bush the six envelopes of cash he had received thus far. "We both work for the same government, so I really don't think you should have to pay me."

"Oh, don't worry about it," Samuel Bush replied with a big drunken smile. "Buy yourself a nice Christmas gift."

"I'm Jewish, we don't celebrate Christmas."

"Suit yourself," Bush said, tucking the envelopes of cash into his crest pocket. "You know I like you, Peter, you're honest and straightforward."

"Thanks."

"But let me ask you something. What exactly does an electrical engineer do?"

"Well, instead of wiring machines, for example, we can assess how much electricity is needed in a region, and we can map it out. In effect, we can wire an entire landscape."

"Why would anyone want to do that?"

"Areas with comprehensive power coverage display vast improvement in all major quality-of-life indexes, impacting everything from the economy to education and even crime rates. Numerous studies and reports have shown that—"

"Can you explain to a group of politicians why they might need things like new power plants or additional power sources?" Bush suddenly seemed to sober up.

"I suppose I can," Paul answered with a smile.

"And diagrams and all that technical stuff, you can make heads and tails of it all?"

"I suppose so. Why?"

"This war is going to end soon and I need someone with your skills." Bush didn't seem to remember that he had already offered him a job.

"It sounds like a great opportunity for someone," Paul replied, "but I'm looking to *do* electrical engineering, not just pitch it."

"Well, if you were to take the job, I'd do everything in my power to see that you'd actually carry out some of the work. How does that sound?"

"I'm looking for something a little more civic-minded—I really want to work for city government. But I can recommend a dozen sharp engineers to you."

"No," Sam Bush said, "I want *you*."

"Why me?"

"You're an honest man and people sense that."

"How many people did you give the envelope test to?" Paul asked.

Bush smiled. "The job pays better than anything you're going to get in the public sector."

"Tell you what," Paul said. "Let me think about it."

Bush gave him a business card and they parted ways.

Take the damn job! Uli thought, then pinched himself through to the moment. The upper part of his body had squeezed out of the underwater netting, but the oxygen tank strapped to his back had gotten stuck in the ropes.

When he turned to free it, it snapped loose and shot forth into the dark pipe. He needed to breathe. There was only one way to go—up. Fighting against the water pressure pushing him forward, he hauled himself up along the netting toward the circle of light.

11

An oval of dull light overhead was like a message coming closer: *Your friend Carl from Mexico called to say he is in Washington but can't be reached anywhere by phone. He promised he would call back at the end of the day.* It was a note from the switchboard operator.

How the hell could he have tracked me down here? Paul wondered. He realized that his old comrade from Mexico must have passed through New York. Without even registering that he hadn't spoken to his mother in months, Paul immediately called her.

"Did you get a phone call from someone named Carlo?" he asked tensely.

"Paul?" she replied. "Is that you?"

"Yes, Mom. I'm sorry for being abrupt but—"

"You run off, join the army, then you call me one day hollering?"

"I'm sorry, Mom, I'm just a little tense."

"Since you left, I haven't had a full night of sleep. Every day I'm reading about young boys being sent to slaughter."

"The only way I'm going to die is if I get bored to death." He knew his sister had already told her, but to regain some good will he explained that he had a comfortable desk job in Washington.

"Well, I know I usually only say this about your brother, but to be honest, son, I'm proud of you."

"I haven't done anything to be proud of."

"People say Jews aren't fighters, but it makes me proud to say my son joined and he's an officer in the United States Army."

"Thanks, Mom. But listen, I need to know, did someone named Carlo Valdinoci call you?"

"I don't remember the name, but someone did call and say he knew you through Princeton." It sounded clever, like something Carlo would do. He knew that Paul had attended the university.

"What did you tell him?"

"I think your father said you were stationed in Washington and told him how to get ahold of you. Why?"

"No reason," Paul said, sighing. "I was just surprised to hear from him is all."

"You're a bright boy. Is it any wonder people would want to be friends with you?"

"No, Mom."

"I'm not ashamed to say that this sharp brain of yours is what has probably spared you from being killed like so many others in France."

"Truth of the matter is that I wish I was over there."

Bella abruptly changed the subject and went on to say that his father and sister were both doing well.

"How's our dear Mr. Robert?" he asked.

"He's gambling his future on something that could make him quite electable."

"What's that?"

Over the past thirty years, she explained, when a local political leader delivered a precinct to some Tammany Hall boss, his idiot nephew or illegitimate son would get hired in return as an elevator operator or some other post. The city's payroll had become swollen with countless half-wits and useless employees.

Now, under the new mayor, Mr. Robert had dreamed up a complex scheme to grade the massive army of civil servants who had been haphazardly brought on over the years. This was becoming a key feature of Mayor John Purroy Mitchel's attempt to reform city government and save millions of dollars. The scheme, Bella continued, was called

Standardization. It would take years to implement, but first Robert had to campaign for it to pass. "Your brother could run for mayor himself if he pulls this off."

At that very moment, Paul decided to accept Samuel Bush's offer. After all, it might similarly kickstart his fledgling engineering career.

Paul waited by his desk until 5 that afternoon. Sure enough, his phone rang just as he was about to leave.

"Capitán Pablo!" he heard Carlo's distinct accent. "How are you doing?"

"Good," he said curtly.

"You know, that address you gave me wasn't where you live," Carlo said provocatively.

"Carlo, you and I really don't share the same politics."

"This saddens me greatly," Carlo replied. "Someone with your skills fighting to help the peasant class would make a big difference in the struggle."

"I am committed to helping the poor, but I don't believe in violence. I don't approve of all the bombings I've been reading about. And I think our system of government can repair itself."

"Allow me to explain that mankind is in the fight for its life between the greed of the very rich and the rest of us. If we lose that fight, we will all be at the mercy of the rich forever." Carlo sounded far more articulate than the playful youth he remembered in Mexico.

"I disagree," Paul said. "But you don't have to worry about me going to the authorities, I simply ask to be left alone."

"Viva la revolución," Carlo said, and hung up. Paul hoped this was the last he'd hear from the guy.

On a positive note, the call to his mother seemed to have reestablished their relations. She began teasing him with the title *Captain Paul*. She also gave him constant updates about his younger brother. Mr. Robert was attending dozens of municipal hearings, pitching the beauty and equity of his great Standardization Plan. *"It values competence over seniority, meritocracy over cronyism . . ."* Bella loved mimicking her youngest son.

Soon after Paul's phone enounter with Carlo, Samuel Bush requested a meeting with him in one of the Senate office buildings. When Paul arrived, he found the contractor huddled with a small group of men outside a Senate Armed Services hearing.

Instead of saying hello, Paul simply approached the contractor and asked, "Who exactly will I be explaining these engineering plans to?"

"These fellas right here," Bush said, pointing toward the hearing room. "You might be doing some public relations work with them as well."

"And if I take the job, you'll eventually get me signed on as the electrical engineer to some of these projects?"

"I'll try my damnedest," Bush replied earnestly.

Paul's stint in the army was almost over, as was the war. With no other immediate prospects, he accepted the offer. His formal title would be lobbyist/consultant for Byrd & Hale.

His first task was assisting Bush in trying to persuade a congressional delegation from depressed areas of the country to promote legislation that would develop electrical systems in their districts. A big region that the subcontractor had targeted for development was down in Appalachia.

Several times, drawing on Paul's credentials as a former weapons incident report writer, Bush asked him to give testimony in congressional hearings to encourage further funding for tank development and more sophisticated armaments.

While spending time with Bush, and seeing up close how lobbyists could legally bribe politicians, Paul found himself growing disgusted with his job. Much of Paul's challenge here was to find ways that the congressmen could pitch these pork-barrel projects so that their constituents didn't think they were driven by private interests. But Samuel was right: Paul's intelligence and sense of social purpose immediately appealed to people. Reporters used lines lifted directly from his press releases in articles and editorials. Politicians often supported endeavors that he pushed. Each time he talked about quitting, Bush assured him that if he just stuck it out for a few years, he could surely set Paul up with an ideal civic engineering project right here in Washington, D.C.

The sudden reek of shit woke Uli just as he broke into the oval of dull light. Gasping for air, he climbed up the rigging of ropes along a three-foot ledge leading toward a dark, open expanse. He could hear a strange mix of weeping and chanting.

Exhausted, he pulled himself onto the stone floor in a giant unlit chamber. It looked like a large train terminal, like Grand Central Station. In the faint flickering of dozens of little fires, he could make out a vast group of people encamped on the wide floor; most appeared to be semi-naked.

"Casey? Is that you, son?" said a soft female voice beside him.

"No," he mumbled back, as he lay down exhausted and dripping on the floor. Popping off his helmet and dropping it, he peered up at the large vaulted ceiling. Slowly catching his breath, he heard a periodic *boom . . . boom . . . boom . . .*

"Casey, what's the matter?" she asked. "You okay?"

12

. . . Uli thought he was hearing the far-off blasts. A series of bomb attacks throughout the U.S. in 1917 had been orchestrated by anarchists following in the footsteps of Luigi Galleani. Russia had just revolted and these radicals believed that America, too, was on the brink. He remembered Vladimir Ustinov's declaration that the U.S. just needed a little push to set it off.

Legislation passed quickly in Congress allowing for a stiff crackdown on these radical saboteurs who were terrorizing everyone. A series of anti-immigration and anti-anarchist laws followed.

By June 2, 1919, when a bomb detonated prematurely and damaged the home of the newly appointed Attorney General Mitchell Palmer (and killed the bomber), all of America was horrified. Eight days later, sitting in his office at Byrd & Hale, Paul read that the identity of the bomber had been revealed as none other than Carlo Valdinoci—his second-in-command in Mexico.

Coming home from work one night a couple of weeks later, Paul felt his stomach churn when he saw that a memo from the United States Attorney General's Office had been slipped under his door. The letter requesting that he pay a visit tomorrow afternoon was signed *John Hoover*.

Paul took a taxi the next day to the Attorney General's Office, a drafty old nineteenth-century building. Inside the lobby, he located Hoover's name on the building's directory. Marching up into the office, Paul passed a middle-aged secretary and stepped up to a handsome young page to ask if he knew where he could find John Hoover.

"I'm Hoover," the kid said.

"You're the person who left me this note?" Paul asked, arching his eyebrows in annoyance. Hoover rose silently and led him into his office and closed the door.

"Did you know one Carlo Valdinoci?" Hoover began.

"You mean the fellow who bombed the attorney general's home?"

"I'm not going to pussyfoot around, Moses. I know you served honorably here. I know you work for Byrd & Hale. And I know you fought in Mexico alongside this wop. I'm not after you. We got the entire anarchist mailing list. We know who's who and what's what. Now, I don't care if you fought against Porfirio Díaz, but I want some names and I want them now."

"I have to speak to my attorney first," Paul replied, feeling only resentment toward this oily kid.

"Mr. Moses. Either cooperate with us right here and now or, so help me God, the Attorney General's Office will be the worst enemy you've ever had."

After a long pause, Paul exhaled and said, "I didn't catch most of their last names. They were Italians. But I never even joined their fight."

Hoover took a legal pad and a fountain pen from his top desk drawer. "I'd like a complete timetable of when you arrived there. What missions you were on right up until you left. Then I want a list of first names or monikers of your confederates and basic descriptions of what they looked like and what they did."

Paul sighed and asked if he could have a few weeks to provide this information.

"I want it right now or you're under arrest. And if I feel that I'm getting anything other than the absolute truth, I'm going to press charges against you, and I guarantee I'll make them stick."

"I did nothing wrong."

"The attorney general of this great republic was attacked a few days ago at his home. We are in the grips of terrible times, Mr. Moses."

"I'm truly sorry about that, but—"

"Foreign agents have brought a war onto our shores and some of these bastards worked with you. I'm willing to overlook the possibility that you might very well be one of these sons of bitches, and I'll give you the benefit of the doubt that you are no longer in cahoots with them—*if* you do everything you can right this moment to help us find them." Hoover stared at Paul intensely.

Paul let out another audible sigh. Reaching across the table, he took the pen and paper and slid them in front of himself. Only when Hoover rose did Paul realize that another, larger man was standing behind him. Over the next four hours, Paul drew up an approximate timetable of missions, along with a list of places where they occurred and others he had worked with, deliberately lying about the names of those who he knew were harmless. By the time Hoover's assistant brought him a dry ham and cheese sandwich for dinner, Paul had come up with fourteen names, mainly Italian and Spanish, and one Russian—the late Vladimir Ustinov. By 10 o'clock that night, hours after Hoover had left, he was allowed to leave provided he return first thing the next morning.

Paul came back at 9 a.m. and sat across from young Hoover, who reviewed all the facts and figures he had written on the legal pad pages.

"Right now," Hoover said, "I really have only one question."

"What's that?"

"What the hell prompted a young man, someone who was an A student at Princeton, who comes from a position of wealth and privilege, to toss it all aside and go to Mexico to fight in some pointless wetback war?"

"Well, to be honest with you," Paul replied awkwardly, "I was in love with a girl and she brought me into it."

"I sensed that might be the answer," Hoover said with a smile. "The only woman you can ever trust is your mother."

Paul smiled back, just wanting out.

"All right, here's the deal. A contingent of these foreigners who you broke bread with got munitions training south of the border and now they're using it up here. If everything you told us checks out, no charges will be filed against you." Looking Paul in the eye, Hoover pulled his seat forward and added, "But frankly, I'd like you to leave this city."

"I live and work here."

"Look, you've come here with a group of terrorists."

"I have no connection with any of them!"

"That might be the case, but we're planning on rounding them all up and tossing them out of the country. You were born here so we can't do that to you. But I'll sleep a lot easier just knowing that you aren't around."

"I work for a major corporation."

"Tell you what," Hoover said almost sympathetically. "I'll give you two weeks, so you can turn in your notice today."

"I've been absolutely honest and direct with you and I don't think this is fair."

"Mr. Moses, if I didn't think you were honest and if you didn't serve honorably in the military and attend Princeton, I guarantee I'd have you in jail serving at least three to five years."

"For what?"

"For my peace of mind."

As Paul left the old building and tried to hail a cab back home, he thought maybe this was all for the best. He was getting sick of Washington and he missed New York. Upon arriving home, he promptly contacted Bush and delicately explained that it was time for him to head back to New York. He was giving his two weeks notice.

"Paul, you're throwing away a very promising, lucrative career here."

"It's not a money issue."

"You want to do design work, I promise I can—"

"It's not that, it's just that I've always wanted to work in the public sector in New York," Paul said, trying to find a comfortable excuse.

"Look, I don't want to make promises I can't keep, but we've donated a lot of money to the Harding campaign. I might be able to arrange a nice administrative appointment."

"I've decided I want my old job back," Paul lied, and thanked Bush for all he had done.

Paul had been using his spare time in Washington, as well as the data he had access to, working on a paper that examined New York City's power system losses and transformer tap settings. The gist of the study was that the metropolis could acquire electricity more efficiently by installing hydroelectric generators along the St. Lawrence River. When he showed his plans to an old colleague who had become an executive at Con Edison in New York City, he was quickly offered a job as a property assessor.

Meanwhile, Mayor Mitchel had abandoned young Robert Moses and his notorious Standardization Plan in an effort to regain some popularity. But it had made little difference, and in 1918 Mitchel lost his reelection bid to John Francis Hylan, "Red Mike." Bella said she had never seen her youngest son so crestfallen as he had become since losing his job. In addition, Mr. Robert had been stigmatized in the press as a privileged rich kid, an enemy of the working man.

Bella told Paul how his brother had been contacting everyone he knew and was going out on every job interview he could get. It was then, almost as if their fates were inversely related, that Paul got accepted into a prestigious new executive program at Con Edison—just the break he had been waiting for. He was now in line to move up the ranks and make some real policy decisions.

Seeing these developments as an opportunity to bridge a gap that had widened between them over the years, Paul decided to pay an unannounced visit to his brother. Robert's new wife Mary invited him in, but told him that her husband was out looking for work. Robert called him back that night and explained apologetically that it was a bad time for him to see people.

It was kind of like the opposite of going to a dentist's office: Uli found that if he concentrated hard on something painful, he could remain in the moment. He pinched himself and counted at least thirty small fires illuminating the wide underground encampment. A group of people were kneeling by a wall under what appeared to be a series of large, sealed sluice gates. Uli realized that this vast space had probably been some kind of dried-out, obsolete catch basin. It appeared that water had once drained down into the sewer pipe he had just climbed out of. Clusters of groaning people huddled around the huge, flat cement bottom of this empty reservoir. The walls of it sloped upward at about a forty-five-degree angle. All appeared filthy, most of the men in rags and loincloths and sporting beards of varying lengths. Several had no clothes on whatsoever, which made Uli feel less self-conscious about his own nudity.

"Are you sure you're not Casey?" asked the middle-aged woman with short auburn hair.

"No, I'm pretty sure I'm Uli . . . though I might be Paul."

"You didn't see my son? We were together and—"

"I didn't see anything other than that damn net down there. It blocked my escape."

"No one can make it all the way down that pipe," some long beard called out. "People were drowning."

"How do you know?"

"Know what?"

"That you can't make it out?"

"Some guy told me."

"Who?"

"The black dude we elected leader. He was the one who set up the netting to try to rescue anyone who was flowing through."

"Where is he?" Uli asked, glancing around.

"Who?"

"The leader!" Uli snapped.

"Oh, he vanished into the Mkultra years ago," the bearded man replied, and then as if to emulate the leader, he too wandered off.

13

The large chamber looked to Uli like some kind of vast primordial internment center. He remembered the roundups and deportations in 1920, including all the suspected anarchists that Attorney General Palmer and his boy, J. Edgar Hoover, had tracked down. A ship full of suspects had pulled away from Manhattan, deporting all the Red troublemakers back to Russia.

Just thinking of Hoover's lumpy old face, Uli felt a mix of loyalty, friendship, and despair—he wasn't sure if this was coming from himself or Paul. Uli vividly remembered him at the height of his power in the 1960s: Hoover, the stodgy authoritarian, shouting commandments down from high. He didn't know why, but he could also envision the short pudgy man wearing a woman's corset and garter belt, sitting on the edge of a bed. In another moment, as Paul's memories came back into focus, he saw a different Hoover, slim and dapper, an ambitious young man who had secured his post in the Attorney General's Office through his mother's cousin. He could just as easily have served in the Department of Interior, like his father had, or worked in any other sector of government bureaucracy, like many of his other Washington relatives.

That year, Bella invited all three kids home for Rosh Hashanah. As soon as Paul showed up, she told him how Robert had recently traveled all the way to Cleveland for a minor bureaucratic interview, only to get rejected again.

When Robert and Mary arrived with their two baby girls, his sister and parents greeted them at the door. Emanuel shook hands with his youngest son and tried to utter some encouraging words, while Mary complained to Bella and Edna about how their apartment on the Upper West Side was getting too tight with the birth of their youngest daughter.

"Well, you've just got to find a bigger place," Bella said with a big smile.

"Robert!" Paul called out, coming down the stairs. "It's impossible to get ahold of you, brother."

As Paul approached his sibling, Robert replied, "You dumb son of a bitch, you've ruined my life!"

"Robert!" their father snapped.

"You can't talk to Paul that way!" Edna added.

"What the hell's the matter with you?" Paul asked.

"When Mayor Hylan took office, some little creep approached me and said that if I ever poked my big kike nose in City Hall again, he'd make sure the papers got wind of my Bolshevik brother."

"What?" Edna cried out. "Who said such a thing?"

"Evans, a Tammany Hall boy who they hired to get rid of me because of my reforms. He got the information from some muckety muck in Washington. Why don't you tell them yourself, Paul: What was the real reason you quit your big Washington job?"

"What are you saying?" Bella asked.

"I'm saying that your eldest son became best friends with every bomb-throwing Commie in North America."

"They weren't my friends. I told the government everything I knew about them."

"It was that damn Mexican girl."

"Watch it!" Paul warned.

"If you want to rub Mom's face in crap all her life, that's your prerogative—"

"Robert, that's an awful thing to say!" Bella interrupted.

"—but I'm not as forgiving as she is!"

"My relationship with Mom is none of your business," Paul fired back.

"You gave your boy an Ivy League education and in re-turn he's become an enemy of this country."

"Just stop it!" his mother gasped.

"When are you going to get it?" Robert asked. "He hates us!"

"Shut up, Robert, I'm not saying it again!"

"She and Dad worked so hard to get you that interview at Kuhn & Loeb. Everyone knew about it."

"That's enough, Robert," Emanuel said.

"You thoroughly embarrassed her," Robert jabbed.

"I appreciated what you did," Paul said, turning to Bella. "I just didn't want to be a banker, Mom!"

"Instead, you became a goddamn lobbyist for an arms manufacturer," Robert said.

"Byrd & Hale owns a number of companies, one of which is munitions. They promised that if I did lobby-ing work, they'd reward me with an electrical engineering job," Paul explained to Bella.

"And you couldn't even do that, could you? Your past caught up with you and you had to quit," Robert continued. "Well, you ruined your career and now you've hurt mine too!"

"Look, Robert, I'm truly sorry," Paul said. "Yes, I knew some unsavory types down in Mexico, but I had no in-volvement with any of this stuff."

"I don't reward people for screwing up my life. I pun-ish them!"

"I never meant to embarrass you."

"I think you should apologize to Paul," Bella said.

"I've spent my life carefully avoiding situations like this," Robert added, "and when I find out that my family has to pay the price because my brother wants to get in the sack with some hot little tamale—"

Paul slapped Robert, who nearly fell to the ground, remaining bent to one side for several seconds.

"Oh God!" Mary screamed. Her little girls shrieked. Even Edna covered her mouth.

"That's enough!" Emanuel shouted, stepping forward between his two taller, broader sons. But he didn't need to, neither brother was going any further. Uli knew that something irrevocable had just occurred between them.

When Paul grabbed his coat, only Maria, standing in the foyer, tried to stop him. He hurried out of the old brownstone, slamming the door behind him.

On his way home, Paul angrily assessed the full magnitude of his fight with Robert. For the first time, Paul had actually seemed to be in a superior position, and his brother must have decided that this calculated act would turn their mother's opinion around. Robert wasn't a failure, just a victim of his brother's cavalier behavior. And Paul—who was finally doing well—was the clear cause of Robert's recent bad luck.

Further proof that this was a premeditated act, Paul noted, was the fact that he had repeatedly tried to meet with Robert in recent weeks to offer his support. Now it was clear that Robert had just been biding his time—all for this ambush. Some peon had probably revealed his meeting with that snot-nosed Hoover kid in Washington. Instead of approaching Paul and conveying his anger and frustration, Robert was using it as capital, exploiting this embarrassing development for all to see.

By the next morning, though, Paul decided he was being unfair, even paranoid. There's no way his younger brother could be this strategic or diabolical. He simply lacked the guile. Paul began to feel guilty for even thinking such a thing.

Over the ensuing days, the more he thought about it, the worse he felt about what had happened with Robert. His brother was a young father of two, and just when he thought he had reached some station of security—a plum assignment from Mayor Mitchel—it was pulled away in the most humiliating fashion. All the rage and frustration of being dismissed by the boy mayor and then being snubbed by Hylan and Tammany Hall and so many others—Paul could hardly blame Robert for losing his temper.

About a month later, Paul received a call from Bella with exciting news. Due to the blessed intervention of some politico's wife, Robert had just had an encouraging meeting with the newly elected governor, Al Smith. Great things were on the horizon. A week later, she called Paul again to announce that Robert had been appointed Smith's chief of staff. He was placed on a commission addressing the reorganization of the state government, something very much akin to what he had been feverishly trying to do for the City of New York.

Paul decided to call Robert at home, hoping to congratulate him on the news. Mary picked up to say that Robert was still at the office. Paul told her that he was truly sorry for their spat, and that he wanted to apologize for his behavior.

That weekend, when Robert still hadn't called, Paul tried again. This time, Mary said that Robert had gotten his message but was too busy to call back. "He told me to say thanks. When things calm down, he'll call you."

Paul asked for his brother's work number, but Mary just giggled nervously and said that even she didn't know it yet. It was clear that despite Robert's reversal of fortune, he was not yet ready to forgive Paul.

In mid-September, just as Paul was getting up the nerve to pay another unannounced visit to Robert at his New York City office, the unthinkable occurred: A horse-drawn wagon approached a lunchtime crowd at 23 Wall Street and detonated a hundred pounds of explosives along with five hundred pounds of cast-iron slugs, leaving scores maimed and dying. Thirty-eight people were killed and over four hundred were wounded. A note found nearby said, *Free the political prisoners or it will be sure death for all of you!*

Once again, a pair of officers from the Department of

Justice paid Paul a visit, this time at his Con Ed office on 14th Street. They deliberately embarrassed him by pulling him out of an important committee meeting.

"We find it mighty strange that Hoover tossed you out of Washington and the bombings stop there," said one of the investigators. "Then you come down here and they follow you."

"I swear, I don't know a thing about it," Paul replied nervously. Things were going well at Con Ed and he feared that they were now going to ask him to leave New York.

"You don't remember anything else from Mexico, do you?"

"Absolutely not. I told Hoover everything," he assured them.

Paul did not lose his job, and after six months at Con Ed, he became a chief consultant and had earned enough respect to finally be put in charge of his pet project, a large feasibility study on the energy generated by a dam on the St. Lawrence River.

No electricity down here, Uli thought as he roamed naked along the wide floor. Small votive candles lined rows of crooked walkways. Most people sat or laid upon clumps of papers. Office items appeared to have been modified into primitive tools: staplers were hammers; trash cans served as toilets; an old Underwood typewriter, caked with what appeared to be blood, may have been used as a weapon.

Uli heard occasional groans set against a constant chorus of weeping, and as he walked onward, they morphed into a kind of forceful chant. Uli spotted a group of the worshippers kneeling in lines, all facing the rear wall where the sluice gates were. One man stood in front, leading the group like a minister. The guy was holding what appeared to be homemade rosaries.

"How many people are there down here?" Uli asked the lost mother, who was moving along with him.

"I don't know. A bunch went into there." She pointed to a hole in the wall.

"What is this place?"

"They call it Streptococci River cause it's supposedly infectious, but everyone drinks the refiltered water."

"What are they doing here?"

"Whenever people wander into the Mkultra they vanish, so the leader told us to wait until he finds a way out."

"Who is the leader?"

"A great memory man," some old beard passing nearby piped up.

"This is my boy Casey."

"I'm afraid not," Uli reminded her.

She suddenly turned angry. "What the hell did you do with my boy?"

"He escaped," Uli lied. "He made it all the way through the pipe."

"Thank God!" She put her hand over her heart.

Uli sat down. It was getting harder for him to focus. Paul Moses's life was pushing back through.

14

Paul moved quickly up the Con Ed executive training program, but he worked almost constantly. His mother invited him to various society functions, hoping he would meet a future wife. It was at one of these parties that he was introduced to a sexy divorcée named Teresa. She'd had two kids with her husband before leaving him for chasing every skirt that crossed his path. After five dry martinis, Paul confessed that while he had been with a number of women, few seemed to truly enjoy sex.

"Then I guess I'd be your first," she boldly said, downing her drink.

Uli found himself thirsting for water, so he took a sip from a rusty old water pump, but spat it right back out. The dark liquid tasted like shit.

"You better learn to like it if you have any hope of surviving down here," said the lost mother.

He found an empty cardboard mat and lay down.

Paul was surprised that his brother was actually learning to play the game of politics and had succeeded in pushing through his massive overhaul of the state government. This involved an extensive consolidation of ragtag agencies and slapdash departments into a handful of more efficient ones. The money saved in eliminating redundancy alone was considerable. The restructuring earned Governor Smith such good press that editorials began suggesting he'd make a good president. He rewarded Robert by elevating him to New York's secretary of state.

"This puts my *bubala* in line to run for governor himself," Bella speculated, adding that this was exactly what Robert had been hoping for.

Through the aggressive campaigning of both parents at dinner one evening, Mr. Robert finally forgave Paul with a firm handshake. Relations, though never warm, became cordial. Neither brought up the anarchist charge nor the slap ever again.

For his part, Paul began overseeing other feasibility studies for Con Ed throughout the northeast. One day, a dear friend from his time in the army, Colonel Stuart Greene, who was now head of the Department of Public Works in Al Smith's administration, called to say that Paul would be perfect for a top engineering post in his department.

"Oh my God," Paul said to his new girlfriend, Teresa, "it's exactly what I've been waiting for!"

He thought about calling Robert to see if he could put in a good word, but Greene said that it wasn't necessary— the appointment probably wouldn't require the governor's approval.

Paul shared the good news with his parents instead. The appointment would earn him the recognition he had always wanted. And since there weren't a lot of qualified men in electrical engineering willing to work at a government rate, he was sure it would lead to some prestigious appointment. The colonel had told him that the only drawback was he'd have to commute regularly up to Albany.

Two days later, however, Greene called to say the appointment had fallen through. There was no explanation as to why.

"Where exactly does that go?" Uli asked as they passed the only hole in the chamber.

"Leads to a fallout shelter," the mother replied. "They found gas masks and old body-protection suits and stuff like that." She pointed to the black hose tracking up from the large sewer pipe into a corner where five large metal oil drums periodically spat out recycled water into a giant wooden barrel.

"And what does everyone eat?"

"Crates and crates of C-rations."

"How long before the food runs out?"

She shrugged.

"If this is a shelter, there must be an exit somewhere."

"They're all sealed," she replied. Casey's mom brought Uli over to her corner, where a bunch of dirty, crumpled papers were scattered on the ground. He collected some into a small pile and lay back down. The place was a massive echo chamber, and above the nonstop prayer-a-thon in the back he heard low moans that sounded distinctly sexual.

15

Teresa's father steered Paul toward a promising investment: It was a popular swimming club called Llenarch in Upper Darby, Pennsylvania, near Philadelphia, and its central location appealed to the affluent locals. The previous owner had died and the family needed to unload it quickly to avoid what was shaping into a major probate battle.

Paul's father, a savvy businessman in early retirement, looked over the books and was duly impressed. It was a solid investment with a steadily growing membership.

"The secret is," Emanuel imparted, "if it's not broken, don't fix it. This place will keep earning you a profit as long as you don't push it."

"It looks a bit run-down," Paul said. "Maybe I'll just give it a paint job."

His father gave him a check to cover the cost of the down payment. Two weeks later, before Paul could even bring his dad up for a weekend, Emanuel Moses suddenly died of a heart attack. Paul soon learned that he had left every cent of his fortune to his wife, Bella.

Finding a long strand of wire on the ground, Uli tied it around his arm so that a constant yet minor pain would keep him fully conscious. He figured that whatever was causing the visions of Paul Moses must also be afflicting all these other people. He remembered his sister Karen injecting him with a strange drug to keep him alive in the sewer tunnel. He also remembered that crazy pseudo-Indian hippie Tim Leary inserting two additional hypodermic needles for him in the cushions of the helmet he had discarded earlier.

Uli heard a thumping sound and feared another intrusion from Paul's world. Peering up into the hole in the wall, he glimpsed a scrawny man with bony knees using a rope to carefully lower an overloaded hand truck down the forty-five-degree incline. Once safely level, the man wheeled over to the barrel of refiltered water where a dozen empty trash baskets were stacked inside each other. A group of men came forward, each one taking an empty basket. Bony Knees passed out boxes of C-rations, which turned out to be nothing more than crackers. Each of the men crushed the crackers in their garbage can, then filled them with the awful water. They stirred their buckets until the crackers became a thick paste. People from different parts of the dark shelter began shuffling forward like zombies, holding out metal cups. Each person moved into one of twelve lines as the men ladled out gruel from their garbage cans.

"Suppertime!" Casey's mother announced, handing him a filthy cup. Uli got in line with the woman, who was once again entering her joyous cycle of believing Uli was her son.

Uli was famished and gulped the muck down. He hadn't eaten since escaping from Rescue City—that bizarre replica of New York concocted as a refugee center, which now essentially served as a giant prison in the middle of the Nevada desert. When he rose to get in line for a second cup, he spotted a tall brawny man wearing his discarded helmet.

"Mind if I see your headgear for a moment?" Uli asked nervously.

"Mine," the guy replied, his face covered with muck. Quickly and gently, Uli slipped the helmet off the man's skull. From between the insulating cushions in the top of the apparatus, Uli removed the two syringes that Leary had taped there. The large man's hand slowly rose, so Uli carefully fixed the helmet back on the guy's head. Uli then went over to one of the bonfires and located a dark vein in his right arm. He injected himself with both syringes, then tossed the needles into the open sewer hole. Near the barrel of refiltered water, Uli found a bag that had been made from an old shirt. He slung it over his shoulder and discreetly slipped an unopened box of C-rations into it.

"Is there any way to get some clothes?" Uli asked Casey's mom.

"Shub had no right!" she said. Her thoughts had shifted elsewhere.

"Look what he did to us," another lost soul roaming nearby joined in.

"By any chance, is anyone else thinking about someone named Paul Moses?" Uli called out into the large empty room.

"Moses, Charlton Heston," someone free-associated.

"Best clothes are on the dead," said some shorter beard, responding to Uli's first question. "But you have to get them before they start rotting."

"Where would be a good place to find some?"

"In the Mkultra, it's loaded with dead bodies. Just don't go too far or you'll never find your way out."

Coming across some shredded cardboard and frayed twine scattered among the litter, Uli fashioned himself a pair of basic foot protectors. It was difficult to walk more than ten feet without stepping on hardened human excrement.

"Does anyone know what's down there?" Uli asked, pointing toward the hole in the wall.

"The first floor of the Mkultra is called the Lethe; it's made up of secretarial pools," the short man replied.

"What the hell is the Mkultra?"

"Subdivisions and sections of some government agency.

Our leader learned those names from documents he found. He's in there looking for a way out."

"He's probably lost or dead by now," someone else lamented.

"Anyone know what this guy looks like?" Uli asked.

"Black—he's black all over," a voice replied.

"Anything else?"

All were silent.

"Does anyone remember his name?"

"Blaster!" someone shouted out.

"No, not Blaster—Bomber, cause he bombed that hole!" someone else said, pointing to the jagged hole that led to the Mkultra. And he had caring people with him."

"Caring people?" Uli asked. "You mean like a family?"

"Yeah, a wife and a kid, I think."

"Fucking Shub ruined all our lives!" another lamented.

"Can anyone tell me who this Bomber leader is, or where I can find him?" Uli was becoming increasingly exasperated with the filthy, mentally impaired congress around him.

"Who's this new voice inquiring about the leader?" A long-bearded man shuffled up to Uli. In the dull glow of a distant fire, Uli could see that in place of eyes were dark empty sockets.

"Here," Uli replied. The blind man delicately touched Uil's naked chin to confirm that he didn't have a beard.

"I remember the leader. He had some strange name like Play Dough. I never saw him, obviously, but I heard he was slim and black. He had a young wife and they had a child here."

"The EGGS epidemic from Rescue City doesn't affect people here?"

"I suppose not. People can still reproduce, but I heard the kid was born with a horrible birth defect—I'd be amazed if he was still alive."

"Why was he elected leader?"

"Aside from his memory and his great positive attitude, he was the only one who could read and make sense of all these forms."

"What forms?"

"If you go in there, you'll see them. Documents are scattered all over the place. Play Dough the Bomber seemed to believe the forms came from different departments and through them he could piece things together. He thought these may have been recently evacuated offices."

"How long after people arrive here do they start to lose their memory?" Uli asked.

"Who knows? This disease affects some people faster than others. I also know that here in the Streptococci River we look out for each other. This is your best bet for surviving until he rescues us."

"But suppose he doesn't. I stopped putting my trust in leaders when I woke up in a detainment center that they had the gall to name *Rescue City*." In a loud voice, Uli called out, "If anyone has any advice on the best way out of here, I'd love to hear it."

"Across to the Sticks!" someone shouted back.

"What's that?"

"Some place filled with caves where people are trying to dig their way out."

"Where is it?"

"All I know is that it's called the Sticks cause it's out in the sticks."

"But where exactly is it?"

The man smiled and shrugged. "Never been there, but I heard it has several levels. And some levels are more dangerous than others."

"Dangerous how?"

"I heard there are warring gangs and ferocious animals in there."

"What kind of animals?"

"I don't know."

"Are there any sources for food or water?" Uli asked.

"There are several caches for food," the blind man explained, "but we don't know where they are. And there are the drips, places leaking with water. People usually put containers down to collect reserves."

"And if you find a way out," someone else called out, "please don't forget about us."

Uli said he wouldn't and thanked them.

Climbing up along the slanting side of the huge basin, Uli reached the jagged hole roughly three feet in diameter. Up close, it looked like someone had roughly hewed through the concrete. After crawling twenty feet in total blackness, scratching his back and belly in the process, he arrived at another large room. A tall, powerful man extended his hand and helped Uli inside, letting him pass. The bony-kneed guy and several others were standing about idly. As Uli walked past, he came upon dozens of stacks of empty wooden crates. He realized this must be the rations depot.

As he passed through the back of the depot into a dank corridor, he found himself completely alone. He followed a distant, unsteady light out to an even larger space with a vast oak floor—presumably the Mkultra. Inside, he quickly discovered that the only sources of light were the flickering tips of several distant fluorescent tubes. Moving slowly through the silent darkness, Uli found his focus dissipating.

16

In the spring of 1928, Paul's mother fell ill and no one could figure out what was wrong with her. Paul told her maid Maria that he suspected it was just Bella's relentless desire for attention.

But the woman became even sicker and increasingly cantankerous. Paul tried to be patient, but she began mentioning "that bitch Millie" and his "wasted years in Mexico," and when he refused to react, she called him "another one of those goddamned bomb throwers who should've been shipped off to Russia."

"She's just feeling angry and threatened," Maria told him, but he knew that she was simply disappointed in him. And she continued badgering.

Hard as he tried to resist, he was eventually drawn in, at one point declaring that Millie was more compassionate than she'd ever be, and fighting in Mexico against oligarchs like her was the noblest thing he had ever done. When Mr. Robert saw what was happening on a mutual visit, he started taking his mother's side.

"Why do you always have to fight with her?" Robert yelled at him.

"This is between us," Paul shot back. "Don't butt in."

Robert, who had just lost his coveted position as secretary of state when Franklin Roosevelt was elected governor of New York, refused to be swept aside. "I know she can be annoying, but she's sick. Can't you just be decent once, goddamnit?"

"It's not a matter of decency," Paul replied. "This has always been our way of communicating."

"Oh, spare me the bullshit!"

"It's not bullshit. I'm telling you, she does this to stir our feelings."

But Robert would hear none of it.

Soon, Bella grew too weak to remain at home and was transferred to a private room at Mount Sinai Hospital. Paul escorted her there, along with Maria and her twelve-year-old daughter Lucretia. Initially the visit went nicely, but before long Bella made an obnoxious comment about the young girl not being dressed appropriately for a hospital.

"Mom, don't worry about her dress not being expensive enough. This isn't a social."

"If it were up to you, we'd all be in rags," Bella accused feverishly. Her face was ashen.

"Not everyone inherited a fortune."

"You don't need a million dollars to dress well!" she rasped, and started coughing.

Maria waved for Paul to calm down. While the little girl sat with Bella, Maria took Paul outside and said, "Go have a cigarette and cool down."

"She's so annoying!"

"She's dying, Paul. There's no need to fight anymore."

The next shift of nurses arrived and helped Bella use the bathroom. As they prepared to give her a sponge bath, Lucretia, Maria, and Paul said goodnight and headed out. When Paul realized the maid and her daughter were walking to the subway, he offered them a lift.

"We're all the way up in the Bronx," Maria said.

"I don't mind. In fact, I insist," he replied. So the three got into his car and drove up to East Tremont in the Bronx. Once there, Paul commented on how nice the houses were. He had imagined them living in more of a shack.

"The place is great, but it needs work."

"What kind of work?" Paul asked.

"That's the thing, I don't really know."

Paul, who had accumulated a wealth of knowledge

about construction during his engineering career, offered to take a quick look.

Maria and Lucretia made dinner for him as he changed into dungarees and an old shirt that he dug out of his trunk and crawled under the house. Next he went up to the attic, inspecting the load-bearing walls and integrity of the building.

"Well, the good news is, you have a nice old place that looks fairly sound," he explained half an hour later. "The bad news is it can use a lot of little repairs." When Maria expressed a look of concern, Paul said, "Maybe I can come by and help."

"No, Paul, you've been kind enough."

"You've helped me so much with my mother and I'd really like to repay the favor."

She thanked him politely and he left. Over the next few months, when Paul would bump into Maria at the hospital, she had a calming effect on him. When Bella would make a nasty remark, she'd step in before things could escalate, giving him a chance to cool off. By the end of 1929, just months after the stock-market crash, Paul's relationship with his mother had improved to such a state that Bella began consulting him about her business affairs.

Uli knew this would be the beginning of the end for Paul. The Depression of the 1930s was just waiting for him. He wished he could find some way to impart this information—*Dump all your stocks and make peace with your dying mother!*—but it was as if he were picking up a radio transmission from fifty years before; all this was long behind him.

Just as he had been told by the blind beard, the first floor of the Mkultra—the Lethe—seemed to be made up of nothing more than large rows of desks extending on and on, secretarial pools occasionally interrupted by waiting areas or conference rooms. As Uli traveled further outward, he encountered large executive suites lining the edges of the massive floor. Warped and buckled parquet wood covered everything. He didn't see any staircases, but from time to time he'd come across gaping holes smashed through the ceiling into an upper floor. He'd shout up, but hear nothing back. When he found something that resembled a rope dangling out of one hole, he grabbed it and started climbing. Before he could make it very far, however, he heard a frantic whispering above him. Fearing an ambush, he slipped back down and stayed on the Lethe level.

Uli periodically called out, "Play Dough!" in hopes of finding this mysterious leader. As his ears adjusted, he began hearing a variety of little clicking and scuttling noises. Some of the sounds were from the leaks, as people had strategically positioned trash baskets to catch the drips. But it wasn't until he saw the first rat with its bright white hair and beady pink eyes that he realized what accounted for the constant scampering he was hearing. Soon, he started spotting them all over—the Lethe was infested.

After an hour or so he saw his first human, a form moving about in the distance. Uli watched as the dark figure picked up one of the many drip-catching buckets and drank from it.

"Play Dough?" he called.

When the figure dashed behind a pillar, Uli remembered that he was in a hostile environment.

If there was some pattern to the vast layout of the Lethe, Uli didn't recognize it. Occasionally a barricade of desks and chairs forced him to create new paths. Several lines of phosphorescent paint ran along the floor in different directions. Uli followed one until it dead-ended at a wall. At another point, he thought he felt a breeze. Looking up, he glimpsed a hole in the ceiling with large metal rods bent downward as though a small meteor had crashed through. He decided to investigate. Pushing a desk below it, he was able to jump up and catch one of the rods. He pulled himself up through the hole to a cracked wooden floor, where he had to carefully avoid getting splinters.

On this new level he found a series of laboratory counters. Broken glass littering the ground worried him since the old cardboard over his feet was not very thick. Inspecting the shards, he discovered they were shattered test tubes and beakers. *They must've done animal testing here,* he thought, noticing open cages of varying sizes scattered throughout. He wondered if there had been any germ-warfare testing, and if any pathogens were still airborne.

17

Uli covered his ears; for the first time, instead of resisting he tried to engage the Paul visions. They were the only distraction as he walked, the only place to hide from everything around him. He remembered Paul building a large empty space like the one before him. It was a dance hall. And if people were coming for romantic evenings, Paul thought, they should have a cocktail bar. "Go the whole way," his girlfriend Teresa advised, encouraging him to add a restaurant, a nice place where a guy could drop a chunk of change on his gal. But while visiting one weekend and seeing so many blue-collar Joes eating sandwiches in their cars, Paul decided to add a diner. Then he figured a bowling alley would really tie the knot. He got in touch with a contractor, showed him the plans, and the construction soon began.

At the end of the year, though, Paul was drained. Despite the fact that the swimming club had had a profitable summer and he was drawing a good paycheck from Con Ed, he still couldn't cover the expansion. For the first time, due to the Depression, the income that had been consistently coming in since he bought the place started slackening. With bill collectors knocking, he broke down and asked his mother for an "advance" on his inheritance.

"Your brother just asked me for a twenty-thousand-dollar loan to build some goddamn highway to his Jones Beach place and now you want my money to add more water to your swimming pool?"

"Mom, the taxes from the people of New York should be paying for their highways. I'm building a family business that will soon be the most successful club in central Pennsylvania. Hell, I think it can attract people as far away as here in the city."

Lying in her hospital bed, Bella took a deep breath and rolled her eyes. "Are you a moron? Who the hell is going to drag their family three hours out to Pennsylvania to a swimming pool, when your brother has given them an ocean-front resort for free?"

"For your sake, I hope there's no hell, cause you aren't long for this world!"

A few days later, when he finally got up the strength to reconcile with his mother once again, she refused to take his calls. Over the course of the next two weeks, he'd listen to her phone just ring and ring. He didn't understand why she was so angry. They had always fought. This time was no different. He couldn't even remember what he had said to her. It didn't matter, he needed to stay at Llenarch and do everything he could to try to bring it up to speed.

He called Edna to seek her advice.

"You should just go down and visit her. She's not doing well."

"I'll try," Paul replied. Then, as an afterthought, he asked how Robert was faring.

"All last week, Robert kept talking about running for mayor on the reform ticket."

"Mayor?"

"Yeah, but the plan quickly fell through when he realized he couldn't get the support."

"I wish I had problems like that," Paul said.

"He just endorsed the new reform candidate."

"Who is it?"

"Some little Italian guy, a congressman from Harlem. If the guy gets elected, Robert's hoping to get in his cabinet."

"Maybe he'll be the next chief of police," Paul kidded.

"No, he's secured appointments on several commissions, so he can't work full time."

"I guess there's not much left after being secretary of state." Paul was glad that his bastard brother had been taken down a couple notches.

One Friday, after getting news that a businessman was interested in meeting with him on Monday to possibly buy a percentage of the club, Paul felt so exhilarated that he drove straight into New York to tell his mom the good news. Upon entering her room, he was surprised by what he saw. Nearly yellow from kidney failure, she looked awful. Flesh was just hanging off of her, and she was trembling with sweat. He gently woke her, but she was dosed with painkillers. Her eyes fluttered, she smiled a bit and muttered, "Hi, Paul."

"Hi, Mom." He tried to keep from crying.

She closed her eyes and resumed sleeping. The woman he had known all his life—opinionated, strong-willed, and intrusive—had shrunk down to this dying little old lady. He sat next to her bed for three hours, until the nurse came by to help her with a bedpan.

"I'll come back first thing on Tuesday," he vowed, and gave her a kiss on her sweaty forehead. That afternoon he drove back to Llenarch through a rainstorm.

On Monday morning he received a phone call from Edna at his Pennsylvania office. Their mother had just passed away in her sleep. "Why the hell didn't you stay with her?"

"My business is on the verge of going under. I had a crucial meeting with a potential investor this morning."

"We were all here except for you. Even Robert canceled his appointment with Governor Roosevelt."

A week later, gathered with his brother and sister in the office of their family lawyer, he listened as the will was read. Paul expected to hear that her estate, including what their father had left, would be divided evenly between the three children. Instead, the lawyer announced that it would essentially be split between Robert and Edna. Paul had been left the interest from a principal of one hundred thousand dollars—he had been cut!

Upon hearing this, Paul looked over at his siblings, believing they would share in the indignity of it all, but neither of them returned his gaze. As the full magnitude of his mother's cruelty hit him, he felt as if his fate were sealed. Despite their many fights, he had always believed she loved him. He knew he had never stopped loving her.

"I can't believe this," Paul said, and asked the attorney if he could look at the will. Doing so, he immediately realized that the document had been rewritten in just the last few weeks. It was brand new, not the one he had seen when she first became ill.

"Paul, we talked with Mom . . ." his sister began.

"Edna, please let me handle this," Robert said. "Paul, this isn't about any of us. This is Mom's will, both literally and legally, and we plan to honor it."

"I can't believe she'd do this to me."

"What are you saying, Paul? That *we* did it?" Robert asked.

"I'm saying that this is insane. And I can't believe that you two—"

"Goddamnit, Paul, I spent years, *years* telling you not to fight with her! I begged you—"

"No one is going to tell me how to live my life!" Paul shot back.

"Oh, give it a break," his brother said. "No one's ever told you what to do with your goddamn life and you know it! This is about you constantly riling Mom."

"When I get attacked, I respond!"

"And this is what you get for it."

"This is unfair. Some of that money belonged to Dad and—"

"Paul, she didn't cut you out," Edna countered, "she simply didn't give you an even share."

"I can't believe you two are going through with this."

"This is her last will and testament and, like it or not, we've agreed to stand by it," Robert said.

Even Uli hadn't expected Paul to be cut out of his mother's will—and though the two brothers weren't close, he never suspected a doublecross. Uli's thoughts were accompanied by the persistent scuttling and squeaking of rats.

Large laboratory counters, chairs, and tables had been pulled apart and rearranged to section off areas of the vast wooden floor. It appeared almost as if organized battles had taken place here—but where would the bodies have gone?

At one point he spotted the faint flickering of a small bonfire. Uli cautiously approached a small group huddled before the flame. As he got within a hundred feet, however, they noticed him and scattered.

"I just want to talk!" he shouted, to no avail.

Soon, he began spotting corpses. He inspected each one he came across, but the state of decomposition always made scavenging impossible. While carefully making his way beneath a massive obstacle course of broken desks, Uli reflected that the entire space felt like some giant skyscraper that had collapsed into just a few levels, spilling every which way.

Whenever he passed an upright desk, he scrounged through its drawers for supplies. In one drawer, to his delight, he found a small working flashlight. In another were two mercury dimes. Besides these items, he found little else of use.

Proceeding through the darkness, he began hearing distant screams. He cautiously followed the cries for about five minutes until he saw what appeared to be a pool of light in the distance. Next to it, an older man was lying on his back. Flipping on the little flashlight, he saw that blood was running from fellow's neck into a puddle of phosphorescent paint that had spilled from a bucket. The man had apparently been attacked while painting the lines that Uli noticed earlier. A small incision ran across the guy's neck—he was still breathing.

"What were you painting?"

"Lines for Plato."

"Why? Where to?"

The man winced in pain.

When Uli confirmed that there was nothing he could do, he asked, "Who did this?"

"Fucking miner," the man sputtered. "Stole the vest Plato gave me. Had a stripe on it . . ."

Uli remembered hearing about the miners in the Sticks. "Where'd he go?"

The man pointed with his eyes toward his feet. A moment later he stopped breathing. Uli delicately undressed him—his ragged yellow tennis shoes, torn pants, and blood-soaked shirt, all probably recycled from earlier victims. He left the unfortunate man in his underwear. None of the clothes fit Uli but at least they stayed on.

He headed in the indicated direction for about twenty minutes until, much to his surprise, he saw it: a small stripe bobbing in the darkness. It was the murderous miner wearing the stolen vest, walking about five hundred feet ahead of him. For the next hour or so, Uli followed at a generous distance—down holes, across vast spaces, and through other ruptures in the ceilings and wood floors—until he finally lost the killer.

18

The notion of dying in this place, with all the rotting corpses around him, terrified Uli. Even Paul had friends. Yet other than Teresa and her kids, the only people who consoled him at his mother's funeral were Maria and her daughter Lucretia. Apparently, everyone believed he had neglected his mother during her final days. Mr. Robert and Edna stood near her coffin.

As the oldest, Paul spoke first. He eulogized his mother respectfully, explaining that depite the endless spats between them, their love had only increased over the years. Robert then spoke eloquently about her zealous philanthropy and eternal wisdom. Edna said that Bella had been both her mother and her best friend. They made their moody parent sound like a regular Florence Nightingale. Afterwards, none of Paul's aunts, cousins, or close family friends seemed to even notice him unless he approached them directly.

Two weeks later, the family lawyer verified that Paul had been left with whatever interest could be generated from a hundred-thousand-dollar trust. Furthermore, that trust was to be administered by Mr. Robert and Wilfred Openhym, a cousin. The final humiliation was a clause stating that if Paul ever contested the will, he'd forfeit every cent. This had all the fingerprints of his dear brother.

Around this time, Paul started noticing Robert's name in the paper again. He had just been appointed as the first citywide Parks Commissioner of New York. Small articles began appearing, announcing ribbon-cutting ceremonies at small parks throughout the five boroughs. Soon the son of bitch seemed to be pulling playgrounds and swimming pools out of thin air. "Vest-pocket parks," they were called, unused city property that Robert snatched up and converted into recreation space. Then it was announced that after years of neglect, Central Park was being extensively renovated. A new restaurant, Tavern on the Green, was being built in a former sheepfold near the Great Lawn, which was being re-sod and seeded.

Paul called Robert at his office one day, and when the secretary asked his name, Paul facetiously explained that he was a reporter intending to write a puff piece on how Robert Moses tamed Central Park. He was surprised when the call actually went through. As soon as Robert picked up, Paul said that he was sorry about the way things had turned out between them and that he had made peace with their mother's will.

"All I hope," Paul said, "is that maybe we can bury the hatchet and be brothers again."

Robert listened patiently. When Paul asked if he could secure a short loan for his business, Robert said that with his own mounting expenses, he simply couldn't afford it. Paul had already asked Edna and she, too, had claimed that her money was tied up and that she couldn't help him. The Depression was taking a toll on everyone.

Meanwhile, membership at Llenarch was slowing down, so Paul began working around the clock at Con Ed to try to keep up with his growing debts.

19

U li felt a strange sense of calm when he thought about Paul's relationship with Teresa. They worked really well together. And he took an immediate liking to her two kids. When she learned that he had moved out of his place to save money and was living in his Con Ed office, she insisted he move in with her.

One afternoon she popped in for an unannounced visit at his office and learned he hadn't come in at all that day. Teresa had divorced her first husband for cheating on her; for this reason, she'd been discreetly checking on Paul every once in a while. Usually he was at work, but occasionally he would simply vanish. When he'd come home, he always seemed quiet, even contrite.

She started suspecting the worst and hired a private investigator. After a month, she learned from her gumshoe that Paul had attended ribbon cuttings for five new city parks and even the Triborough Bridge. The PI further reported that Paul would always stay in the back of the crowd and remain long after everyone else had left.

One night over dinner, she delicately confessed what she had done and apologized for it. He didn't say a word.

"Paul, you have to push your brother out of your head. The feeling of betrayal will eat you alive. I know cause I went through this with Mike."

"Envy, jealousy . . . that's only a small part of it. When I see Robert and all he's doing with his life . . . well, it's the life I expected to live. His very existence is a monument of my failure."

Driven by Paul's growing despair, Uli became even

more intent on making his own mission a success and find-ing some way out. As he moved in the direction where he had last seen the murderous miner, piles of stones started appearing in wooden boxes, which turned out to be desk drawers. They covered the ground, though there was not a soul in sight. He kept walking until he eventually came to a corner doorway that opened to a long, narrow corridor.

Inside the passageway, a massive hole had been cut right into the cement wall and the hard stone behind it. A stale aroma of concrete dust and decay vented out. The hole forked off into three different directions; with his flashlight he could see that two of them were dead ends. Following the third channel and passing by several dark caves, he could hear faint snoring and movement. Peering into one of the caves, he realized he was in the presence of sleeping bodies—this was some kind of dank, narrow bunk room. Uli tiptoed away, fearful of waking them.

He eventually counted six tunnels that went varying distances into the earth. The opening of one foul-smelling cave in a particularly remote section of the tunnel system was covered by old sacks hanging from the low ceiling. Pushing through and flicking on his flashlight, Uli could make out dozens of shriveled feet; bodies were piled side-ways like cords of wood.

As he ventured forward, he heard more moans and a constant shuffling of feet. The tunnel pitched downhill at a sharp angle for about a hundred feet, then opened into a larger area that seemed to be another supply depot. In fact, it turned out to be a treasure trove of stock. Stacks and stacks of wooden boxes, presumably food, and green metal barrels marked FRESH WATER were piled to the ceiling.

To Uli's horror, he discovered that what he had been hearing was a chain gang, a paddle wheel of filthy men and women—not particularly old, all nearly naked—shackled together at their wrists and ankles. Their lower quarters were spattered in dirt and excrement. They held wooden boxes and desk drawers loaded with stones and dirt. Uli watched them dump the contents of their boxes into a large pile in the depot area, then one-by-one loop back down into the same broad tunnel they had just exited—a human conveyor belt.

Strangely, though, there seemed to be no guards monitoring the activity. After twenty minutes, Uli stepped boldly into view. "Excuse me!" he said to one and all.

Some looked up as they passed, but no one said a word. They just continued dumping rocks and shuffling back into the service tunnel.

"Who's in charge here?"

None replied.

"Are you being held against your will?"

Nothing.

Drawing closer, Uli realized two things: First, the workers weren't really chained; they were merely tied loosely together with frayed rope. Second, they were all exhibiting some type of dementia or possibly late-stage Alzheimer's. Uli shoved past the two lanes down a short tunnel in search of guards, or at least supervisors. Soon he arrived at a large dome-shaped room, where the tragic chain gang picked up boxes and then turned around. Not a single monitor or guard was anywhere in sight. As best as Uli could tell, each drone worker was simply following the lead of the person in front of him or her.

Uli squeezed past them back up to the supply depot.

Ignoring the human conveyor belt, he headed over to the mountain of stock. Unmarked wooden crates filled the place, much like those he had seen under guard at the depot near the catch basin.

Moving along the far wall of the room, Uli started looking through the crates. Most were filled with C-ration crackers straight from World War II. There were enough survival rations here to feed a small army.

A moment later, Uli tripped over a small pile of dirty

metal rods—digging tools. A large case of candles and a small box of matchsticks were sitting on one of the crates. Uli pocketed some matches, then lit a single candle and rummaged through the stock for food. Aside from the ubiquitous crackers, there were boxes of aspirin, lime juice, and NoDoz. After chomping down two tins of crackers, he popped open one of the barrels of fresh water. It tasted heavenly. At that moment, a bedraggled young woman broke out of the line and grabbed Uli's arm.

"Benny!" she groaned.

Jumping back in shock, Uli could immediately see that the poor woman was suffering from severe dementia. The rope attaching her to the chain gang had snapped. Gently pulling her off, he looked in her eyes and said, "I'm not Benny."

"Where is he?"

"Waiting for you," Uli answered, deciding that deception was kinder than the truth. He pointed her back toward the others and she slowly stumbled away. Uli returned to his crates.

A sudden loud crash was followed by low moans coming from a small utility closet. The poor woman was on the ground—apparently she had wandered inside and climbed up on something which then collapsed. After Uli helped her out and directed her back down the service tunnel from where she had come, he checked out the closet. Turning on his flashlight again, he saw that a large rectangular fuse box had been dislodged and was hanging by a bunch of old cables. The wall next to the utility closet had a stack of crates leaning against it. Moving them carefully forward, Uli discovered that the utility closet serviced an old freight elevator. When he located a pipe and pried open its door, he found that the elevator shaft was packed solid with concrete, utterly impassable.

20

If Paul's mother had left him a hundred-thousand-dollar principal ten years earlier, Uli thought, it would've been a great help, but since it was the beginning of America's greatest depression, there just weren't a lot of good investments. And since Mr. Robert, of all people, had been assigned as the executor of his trust, Paul knew it would forever doom their relationship to one of suspicion and antagonism.

Robert deemed that the best investment he could find for his older brother was in purchasing a loft at 168 Bowery and letting the business that occupied the space pay out a monthly rent that more than covered the mortgage. This investment would be far safer than the stock market and would yield a larger return than any bank or bond. The problem was, the clothing company that occupied the loft was doing no better than the rest of the country. They had cut their staff down to a skeleton crew, and though they weren't going out of business, they were hanging on by just a thread. After the first two years, they were barely able to make their rent. Paul was only seeing a fraction of the money that he expected. When he finally demanded to inspect a financial report of his principal, he was horrified to see that both his brother and cousin—as well as a collection agent—were drawing income from his minuscule profit. Paul convinced Teresa to borrow ten thousand dollars from her father to help pay off his creditors.

By 1933 the Depression was in full swing and to Paul's great dismay, Con Ed terminated his position. But the summer was a scorcher that year, and since he had already closed all the club's side businesses, greatly reducing over-head, the pool actually started earning money again.

One morning in February 1934, Paul opened the *New York Times* to read that Robert was running on the Republican ticket for governor of New York. He closed the paper and shoved it into the garbage can without mentioning a word of it to Teresa. Upon learning the news later that day, she said that perhaps he should contact his sister. But he still felt betrayed by her because of the disinheritance.

"She always liked you, Paul," Teresa argued. "Give her a chance."

When he finally got up the strength to call Edna and ask about Robert's run for public office, she said, "I learned about it in the newspapers just like you."

Exasperated, Paul told Teresa that he didn't want to hear anything more about Robert. Nonetheless, he continued researching his brother's progress. Robert's office published an aggressive campaign schedule to challenge the incumbent, Governor Herbert Lehman, who was trailing in the polls.

"If that son of a bitch gets elected," Paul lashed out, "I'm moving to Pennsylvania!"

"Now just calm down," Teresa reasoned.

"Don't ever tell me to calm down!"

Over the next few days, she found him increasingly difficult to deal with. Paul was in an obvious slump. In the mornings he stopped getting dressed; he just sat around in his T-shirt and boxers staring out the window.

After a lot of thought, Paul decided that this was his lot in life. His younger brother was destined to be successful and he was doomed to live in his shadow. *The sooner I simply accept I'm a failure, the easier life will be.*

"I don't think that's true at all," Teresa said when he shared his pessimistic outlook. "I just think he's having his time in the sun. Think about it: You launched a great business smack in the middle of a terrible depression. Any

other time and you'd have been right up there with Rockefeller. Just wait, you'll have your day."

Feeling as though Teresa was his only rock to stand on,
he finally proposed marriage and she accepted. Not wanting to get another awkward rejection from Robert's wife,
Paul didn't bother to invite his brother, though Edna came
to the ceremony.

With a family to support now, Paul contacted everyone
he knew, trying to reignite his electrical engineering career, but there were only a handful of places hiring someone with his broad expertise. That May, out of the blue, he
got an invitation to have lunch with a mysterious Mr. Paul
Windels. It turned out that Windels was a close personal
friend of Mayor Fiorello La Guardia.

The "Little Flower" had a serious problem and had
asked Windels to help him find the right man to fix it.
He sensed that Con Edison was vastly overcharging the
City of New York on its monthly electricity bill. Finding
a properly qualified person who could prove such a thing
would be a challenge in such a small, tightly networked
profession. Despite this, Windels had been referred by
no less than four different people to Paul Moses. All
seemed to agree that he had the perfect combination of
faith in the public trust and bottomless knowledge of
such particulars.

"So he's looking for a consultant?" Paul asked Windels.

"Actually, he's looking to appoint someone as Commissioner of Water, Gas, and Electricity, but of course it
doesn't pay much considering the vast amount of work the
post requires."

It was the break Paul had been waiting for. He told
Windels that he was very interested in the job regardless
of the salary.

"You probably already know this," Paul added, "but
my brother Robert, who is currently running for governor,
is the city's Parks Commissioner."

"Well, I don't see how that will make a difference one way or the other," Windels replied.

"We're not on the best of terms, which doesn't bode well for me if he becomes the next governor."

"Actually, that might not be true," Windels speculated. "If he does become the next governor, and polls are giving him the edge, he'll have to resign his city post anyway."

That evening over dinner, Paul shared the good news with Teresa. "The job doesn't exactly come with a big paycheck, but it should make me highly employable for future work."

Over the next two weeks, Paul was on pins and needles about the appointment. Several times, he had the urge to break down and call his younger brother to see if he could convince him to put in a good word, but he resisted.

One day, however, Windels called to say that La Guardia had unfortunately chosen someone else.

"Who?"

"Joe Pinelli?"

"Who the hell . . . ?" He had never even heard of the man.

"Welcome to the world of politics. Pinelli is an ignoramus, he's payback to some political boss in the Bronx. I think the mayor mentioned to some bigwig at Con Ed that he was about to hire you. They knew you'd crack down, so they agreed to roll back their rates, provided you weren't hired."

"This is unbelievable."

"Well, it's between us, because I honestly don't really know everything that happened. All I know is that La Guardia picked Pinelli and Con Ed agreed to renegotiate their bill. But listen," Windels added, "if it's of any consolation, I can throw some consulting work your way."

Paul felt cheated again, but he was too broke to turn down anything. Furthermore, he didn't believe Windels had deliberately tried to screw him; he sensed his brother was somehow behind it all once again.

Paul did extensive contracting work for the city at a cheap rate, but it came to an abrupt end only six months later when Windels was dismissed.

Despite Paul's attempts to turn his leisure club into a year-round social mecca for the northeast, a more modestly priced club opened nearby. With bankruptcy looming, he kept thinking, *I had a moneymaker and ruined it.*

During one particularly masochistic moment, Paul got in his car and drove to the first day of construction of Orchard Beach up in the Bronx. He watched as his younger brother was chauffeured in a huge Packard to the VIP viewing stand. La Guardia introduced Robert as the man who had single-handedly conceived of and found funds for this wonderful gift to the people of New York: "This is his very first outing as a candidate, so please give a warm welcome to the next governor of the State of New York, Robert Moses!"

As Mr. Robert appeared on the rostrum, and applause died down, Paul began to feel nauseous.

"Hello, ladies and gentleman," Robert began. "As you all know, I'm running for governor of this great state with your interest at heart. As you might remember, I tirelessly worked as secretary of state under the great Al Smith . . . and before him I worked under Mayor Mitchel where I . . . I tried to devise a method of standardization to help eliminate bureaucracy . . . Well, that didn't go too well . . . but, see, that wasn't my fault. What happened was . . . well . . . it's just too difficult to explain here and now . . . but if you look at the record, you'll see that I was stonewalled time and again . . . It's too difficult to explain, but let me assure you that this will not happen again if I am governor of this fair state. No sir." Paul watched as his brother paused and stared blankly over the bewildered crowd. "All I'll add is if you vote for me, you'll greatly improve your own lot. Thank you!" Sweating profusely right through his shirt and cotton suit, Robert Moses stepped off the stage.

Paul found himself deeply moved by his brother's awkward naïvete and began clapping, leading others to join in.

After the ceremony broke up, Robert hurried to his car, but Paul remained in the parking lot. At that moment, he knew there was no way in the world that Robert was going to win this election; in fact, he would never get elected to *any* public office. His brother was simply too dismissive of the working man and too arrogant to learn how to grovel.

Ecstatic when he got home that night, Paul relayed his brother's public humiliation to his wife, who was only happy that he was happy. The next day, he called the *Moses for Governor* campaign headquarters and requested Robert's entire schedule of public appearances. As time allowed, Paul would pop in at various appearances and was always pleased to see that even though his brother had shaken off his initial stage fright, he wasn't really improving his delivery. If he wasn't bored or arrogant, the man was simply hostile.

One day when Paul felt particularly depressed, he saw that Robert was giving a speech up in Nyack. He drove all the way there, only to discover that it was a press conference.

"Mr. Moses," one reporter asked, "aren't you concerned that your public works projects will take vital funds from welfare programs for the people of this state?"

"Please don't bother me with moronic questions like that," Robert replied. "The projects will help the people get work, period."

"But Mr. Moses, Governor Lehman said—"

"He's even less informed than you are, if that's possible," Robert grumbled back.

The man wasn't merely a bad candidate, he was clearly resentful of the entire campaign process. Comments like "You won't understand" and "Leave it to the experts" punctuated his extemporaneous remarks. Over the ensuing months, the polls gradually reflected his caustic personality. It was about six months into his run that Paul caught an article about Robert's slipping numbers. He had now fallen behind the formerly unpopular incumbent. The election had been his to lose and now he was losing it.

The next time Paul saw Robert was at a synagogue in Great Neck. At the end of a wooden speech about how he would improve the economy, the candidate offered to take questions. Someone asked about his faith. Exactly how devout was he?

"I'm not really Jewish," Robert responded to the packed synagogue.

"But your name is Moses," pointed out the rabbi, allowing Robert a chance to more fully explain.

"I didn't pick it," he snapped back. "And unlike my namesake, I have no intention of leading anyone out of bondage." After some additional perfunctory remarks, he thanked the stunned crowd, told them to remember to vote, and left the temple.

The margin by which his brother lost the election made Paul feel warm all over. Yet soon after this triumph, Paul got a tax bill for ten thousand dollars and found he had no money to pay it. The end was near. The bank immediately initiated foreclosure proceedings on his pool property.

"I worked so hard and came so close," he complained over the dinner table. "I was almost there. I mean, it's a solid investment. Now I'm going to lose everything."

Teresa got on the phone and within a week her father and aunt had ponied up yet more loans.

Someone must've dug all these rocks out of the earth, Uli realized, snapping away from Paul. He left the storage depot and pushed past the chain of drone laborers, heading back down into the dim dome-shaped room. He gazed up and for the first time noticed the large uneven tower of modified wooden desks. It resembled some kind of primitive ceremonial structure. Hanging from the top was a rotting corpse. Uli examined the body in the flickering candlelight and realized it had undergone some kind of outlandish transfiguration. The feet were violently twisted backwards. Worse, though, was the missing head, replaced with a long-snouted skull.

A dull clinking of hammers drew Uli away from the corpse and over to a large hole in the wall at a corner of the chamber. Once he descended into the dark hole, he found a small tunnel shooting upward and a larger corridor that corkscrewed downward. Other smaller tunnels began spiraling off from the corridor and soon he feared that he was getting lost. He flicked on his flashlight and noticed wires above him held together along a single small wooden bridge like a violin. Tinkering sounds surrounded him. People were digging. Moving along this main artery, he realized the wires along the top led into the various side tunnels. Suddenly, a box of rocks crashed out of one. Crawling down the tunnel roughly fifty feet, Uli came upon the bottom half of a sweaty, half-naked man digging furiously into the earth. He wore something black wrapped like a turban around his face and head; Uli assumed it was an improvised air filter.

"Hello!" Uli called out.

"Fuck off!" the digger shouted. Uli withdrew to the outer corridor, where he fingered another wire leading to the next cave. This time he encountered another seminude turban-headed digger. Again, when Uli greeted the man, he was instructed to fuck off.

He continued examining the ten or so guide wires fastened to the low ceiling above him until he heard the tinkering of yet another man.

"Who's in charge?" Uli called out.

"Fuck off!" the crazed miner responded, as though following the same script. Eventually, Uli turned around and crawled back up the circular passage. Emerging in the domed room, he wiped dust off himself and followed the line of drone workers up the service tunnel toward the storage depot. After a few minutes he discovered they were now being led by someone. He sped up along the side of the tunnel. A middle-aged lady was directing the passive chain gang into the upper caves.

"Hello!"

"What?" the lady screamed, almost jumping off her feet.

"I didn't mean to startle you."

"Fuck off!" she shouted, lifting her hands defensively.

"Why is everyone so angry here?"

"We've all been trapped in this dungeon for years. What d'you expect?"

"Who's in charge?"

"Did you see the diggers in the Convolution?"

"If you mean the hole that leads to the little caves with the nasty bastards, yes," he said. Nodding behind the chain gang, he added, "I also see these poor bastards carrying rocks out of the tunnels."

"That's called occupational therapy, asshole! They're senile. I found them starving to death, and I rescued them."

Uli didn't respond. Making them into unsupervised laborers wasn't exactly a rescue or therapy.

A few moments elapsed before she said, "Sorry if I'm a bit rude, it's just the best way to deal with most of these guys. This place makes everyone very agitated. I can see by your short beard that you're new here." She resumed leading her group upward.

"The congregation back in that catch basin didn't seem particularly angry. And yes, I just got here."

"The people back there in the basin are just very sad," she said, as she continued leading the group up through the storage area and into a new labyrinth of tunnels. "They realize that if they all cling together, they can help each other survive. But they have no real hope of ever escaping."

"That must be why they pray."

"All the guys who made it up here work nonstop. To

their credit, they're still trying to get out, but none of them get along so they don't work together." She paused. "They're each intent on finding their own way out."

Uli extended his hand and introduced himself. The woman said her name was Root Ginseng.

"Hell of a name."

"I was born Persephone, a bad name for this illiterate age. When I was growing up, most people who read it pronounced it as *Percy-phone*. When I moved to San Francisco, I worked in a health food store and people jokingly called me Root and it stuck."

"Nice to meet you, Root . . . Hey, what is that central room anyway? And what the hell is that thing in the middle of it?" Uli asked, referring to the tower of stacked wooden desks.

"We thought this was the bottom of an old missile silo."

"If that's the case, wouldn't there be a launch opening directly above it?"

"That's why we built the tower and dug up into it, but it turned out to be a dud."

"How'd you manage to get all these guys to work on it?"

"Sandy and I somehow got most of them to put aside their differences and collect desks to build that tower up to the ceiling." That accounted for the absence of desks right near the Sticks. "But soon they were all fighting again."

"Fighting over what?"

"You name it. 'That's my chisel.' 'You drank my water.' 'This is my area to dig.' 'Quit breathing so loud.' Constant trouble."

"No truce lasts forever," Uli said as he walked with her.

"They got about fifteen feet into the rock before they started shoving each other for elbow and leg space." She paused again. "I'll never forget hearing that awful scream as the first man fell to his death. Then a few days went by, and another man was pushed. Soon we realized they weren't just fighting, they were actually sacrificing people up there. When there was only the original group of about eight left, they gave up and went back to lateral drilling . . . You'll excuse me for asking, but who exactly are you?"

"I own a pool club in Pennsylvania and—" He caught himself. "Actually, I just crawled out of the sewer and I'm looking for a way out of this hellhole . . ."

Moments later, Root reached her new destination and said it was time to take care of the babies.

"You have babies?!" Uli asked as he followed along.

"That's just what I call them cause they're as helpless as infants."

She headed into an abandoned cave and lit some candles. Uli saw right away that it was covered with dirt and human excrement. Root grabbed a shovel and scooped out the waste as though the place was a giant litter box. Then she laid down some new dirt and a chemical that seemed to mask the odor and spread out some pieces of cardboard— voilà, it was transformed into a giant bunk room.

Root moved into another dimly lit cave where others were standing around waiting. Following her lead, Uli grabbed a bucket and the two washed the group down, then dried them with pieces of old cloth. Next they led the men into another cave, where they handed out crackers and cups of water. After the meal, Roots escorted another group into a cave where she had them sit on a long bench with holes in the seats—a makeshift row of toilets.

21

Paul imagined that his brother would someday retire up in Albany as a minor government functionary, a body second from the left in the third row of various group photos with central politicians in the front. When the first few expressway projects were announced, Paul made a joke about Mr. Robert wearing a T-shirt while digging ditches and shoveling blacktop out in Long Island. The highways cutting across so much private property—little farms and homes—immediately reminded Paul of the bad press Robert had drawn trying to enact his controversial Standardization Plan under Mayor Mitchel nearly twenty years before.

When Paul read that his brother had declined both city and state salaries and was living off his stolen inheritance, he concluded that this was one of the great secrets to his success. Though Paul couldn't contest the will without jeopardizing his little nest egg, he figured there had to be something he could do to turn his meager trust into more cash. He decided to call the garment shop and see if he could sell them a long-term lease for a lump sum.

"Tell you what," said Mel Green, one of the proprietors, "would you take forty thousand dollars for the thirty-year lease?"

"Let me think about it," Paul said, but he immediately knew that this would be more than acceptable. He also knew that he wouldn't be able to reach Robert by phone, so he typed up the proposal and mailed it to him. A few weeks later, he got a letter back from his cousin Willy:

Dear Paul:

Robert and I have carefully considered your request and have decided that this really isn't a wise offer. We understand you've been shortchanged by these people in their monthly payments, but they still owe us all that money, and the depression should be over soon. Bowery Wardrobe promises to pay all back rent with interest as stipulated in the original agreement. Hold tight and I guarantee you'll get all the money that is owed to you. My best to Teresa and the kids.

Sincerely,
Your cousin,
Wilfred Openhym

After a terse follow-up phone conversation with his cousin, Paul hired a lawyer and brought a suit against Willy and Robert, stating that they were deliberately mismanaging his trust in order to bleed it for their own funds.

Willy, in turn, showed up with his lawyer at a subsequent arbitration meeting; he stated that Mr. Robert Moses was unable to attend due to government commitments. After reading the briefs and listening to arguments on both sides, the judge found Paul's complaint about mismanagement of the trust to be groundless. On the other hand, he ruled that it was unfair for Willy and Robert to extract income when the primary beneficiary wasn't earning his due. So he ruled that until Paul got his full back payments, they were not permitted to withdraw another cent. Although he wasn't able to accept Bowery Wardrobe's offer, Paul still felt he had won a victory by depriving Robert of his money.

Meanwhile, Robert's professional life took a turn for the better with his greatest achievement to date—connecting Manahattan, Queens, and the Bronx with just one bridge. The throne for this accomplishment was the newly created

Triborough Bridge Authority, of which Robert would be king. The endless stream of revenue from tolls would be used solely at Robert Moses's discretion.

"How can this be legal?" Paul shouted while reading the details in the *New York Times* at the counter of a coffee shop on Third Avenue and 52nd Street.

"Hey, buddy, you're scaring my customers," said the proprietor. Paul ripped the newspaper in half, slapped a dime on the counter, and stomped out.

"I met him a couple times," Root said to Uli as he helped her bring some of the tired workers into a cave.

"You met Paul Moses?" Uli hadn't said a word about the onslaught of thoughts rushing through his head.

"No, Plato, the guy who got elected leader. The one thing I fault him on was his family. I think he left them cause his boy was handicapped. I told the kid he could have access to C-rations if he ever needed any."

"As far as I can tell," Uli said, "you've done a lot more than this leader in terms of finding a way out of here."

"Yeah, if overseeing a bunch of dead-end tunnels ever helps anyone. Hell, most of them are pointed downward or run parallel to each other."

"Why do they even bother? The only way out of here is obviously up."

"Long ago, Plato told everyone that there were stair-wells at the lowest levels of this place."

"Can't the diggers come up with a plan so at least they each take a different direction?"

"A man after my own heart!" she said, smiling. "I have to confess, it's exciting to be able to talk about this with someone."

She led Uli off to a small cave that she had converted into a private office. She carefully lit several candles, re-vealing a strange model built out of little sticks and blocks that resembled a spiraling tree lying on its side with eleven branches. The largest branch of the tree was the central corridor of the Convolution.

"These tunnels move in different directions," Root explained, pointing to several branches, "but most of them are loosely parallel."

Over a dinner of canned prunes and two square tins of Spam that she had been saving for a special occasion, Root told Uli how she had first climbed out of the sewer with a group of others about five years before. All were immediately warned against going into the Mkultra. They were told it was pure savagery. Over the first couple of years, she watched as her compatriots fell victim to the memory disease that ravaged the place. One day, though, she noticed that the ropes rising from the sewer were twisting wildly. A large man climbed up. His name was Herman, and after being warned against leaving the catch basin, he declared that he would get out of this place or die trying. She asked if she could join him and he consented.

They started off by climbing three levels through the vast, abandoned installation. They cooked white rats and drank from the buckets of runoff water as they fought back roving gangs, psychopaths, and a host of other lost souls. Together, they hatched the plan to turn a group of mentally damaged men into miners.

"What happened to Herman?"

"He instructed me that when the day came that he couldn't remember his own name, he wanted me to kill him."

"Any idea why you were never affected?"

She shook her head.

"You didn't take any kind of medicine?"

Again, she shook her head.

"And you've been alone with the diggers ever since?"

"Actually, there was another woman already here when we arrived."

"Who?"

"She was suffering from partial memory loss and couldn't remember her name, so I just called her Sandy Corner, since she used to sleep in the sandy corner of the storage depot downstairs. She wasn't as far gone as the others."

"What became of her?" Uli asked.

"If you were in the silo, you probably saw her hanging there."

"I hope you're not referring to that mutilated body?"

"Yeah, but the miners actually liked her. They decided that she would be a great offering to the gods, so they strung her up there."

"They liked her so much they killed her?"

"She was pretty out of it by then. It was more like a mercy killing."

"God," Uli murmured, "human sacrifice."

"The more dire a situation, the greater the need for some divine intervention. This is probably how all religions get started."

"What did they do with her head?"

"Lopped it off and replaced it with that dog skull."

"Where did they get the dog?"

"The Mkultra was originally a big laboratory, and scientists used all sorts of animals for experimentation."

"But why did they cut off the poor woman's head?"

"One of the miners, a chubby Italian guy, came up with the idea from some weird Aztec calendar he had found on his way through the Mkultra. Sandy's body represents the death guide Xolotl: head of a dog, body of a human. And we're all in someplace called the Mictlan."

Uli was genuinely impressed by this woman. Working alone for several years now, she had somehow managed to control all these crazed human mole rats. In doing so, she had become the closest thing to a central force that this subterranean termite hill had. Inspecting the three-dimensional model of the tunnels, Uli asked, "Would the most efficient number of tunnels be—"

"Six, each going in a different direction." Pointing to her mock-up, she added, "These tunnels would maximize our chances of getting out of here."

"Why don't you tell the miners?"

"Oh, I tried—years ago. I begged them! But all they say is *Fuck off*. Most of them are pretty blind. Hell, half the time they're just trying to find their own tunnels."

"What do you mean?"

"After working for hours, they crawl out and sleep in the storage depot or Lord knows where. When they return, those wires along the top of the caves help direct them back to their own tunnels."

"Why don't we just redirect the wires so that they go into the six tunnels that you selected?"

"The real problem is scheduling them so they don't overlap," Root said. "If one finds another in his tunnel, it's over."

Uli started checking through his ratty pants. "I thought I had a watch, but . . ." But he was thinking of the pocket watch Paul had been given in Mexico.

"Why do you need a watch?"

"With it, we could track everyone's work and sleep patterns, right?"

"Not a bad idea," she affirmed.

The two headed up into the Mkultra, venturing far out to the furnished part of the Lethe. Searching through several hundred desk drawers, they found stacks of old Mkultra documents and boxes of No. 2 pencils which they could use to track the diggers. Root came upon an old windup alarm clock.

"What time shall we make it?"

Uli said he greatly missed the bright rays of early-morning sunlight, so they set it for 7:00. Since there was no indication of a.m. or p.m., it was something they'd have to monitor carefully. The next stage was simply drawing up a list of names, or at least some way to assign the tunnels to different miners. Root said that so many of them had died or vanished—only to be replaced by others—that she had never bothered trying to learn many names. She just thought of the diggers as types: There was an Italian guy, a black guy, an old guy, and so on.

Over the next few days, Uli and Root took turns waiting in the large silo, jotting down the times of their comings and goings, as well as their sleeping habits.

It quickly became a lot trickier than Uli had expected. Some of the miners would sleep erratically, while others rested at steady four- or six-hour intervals.

22

In 1940, Teresa's father and aunt began asking Paul to pay back his loans. Out of work for several years, Paul was unable to comply.

Exhaustion had deprived Uli of all strength to resist visions of Paul, and Paul in turn was overwhelmed by his brother's achievements: Along with the Queens Midtown Tunnel, the Belt System—which included the Cross Island, Gowanus, Whitestone, Laurelton, and Southern Parkways—was also designed under Robert's stewardship during the early '40s. Paul visited the various construction sites, watching the huge earth-moving machines alter the city's landscape. Rather than slowing anything down, the war seemed to be accelerating his brother's victories.

When Paul's wife said she'd finally had enough and didn't want to hear about Robert anymore, Paul tried to keep it to himself. One morning, though, she woke up to his shouts. When she asked what was up, Paul yelled that Robert had demolished the New York Aquarium in Battery Park as an act of revenge against those who had protested his Battery Bridge project.

"I want you to stop this!" she demanded.

"Stop what? *He* did it!"

"Did what?"

"He had the fish dumped into New York Harbor." Paul wept as though Robert had drowned his own children.

That was it for Teresa. She told him she was frightened. "I don't want you back in the house until you see a psychiatrist."

He reluctantly agreed. He knew there was something

wrong with him. After a dozen phone calls, Teresa located Dr. Hiram Moshbeck, a distinguished older man with a thick crop of wild gray hair.

On the doctor's soft leather sofa, Paul felt great pleasure in telling the older man how he once loved his brother. Though Robert was only a year younger, Paul had felt a strong urge to protect him against their overbearing mother. Even when his little brother would fight against him, he knew Robert was only trying to be a good kid.

"He couldn't see it, but instead of rebelling against her, he rebelled against *me*," Paul deduced. The psychiatrist let him go on, and Paul explained how the only real problem began when Robert stole his birthright.

"What exactly did he do?"

"He conned my mom into cutting me out of her will."

"Did you hate her for doing that?"

"No, I don't think she would've done it if she was in her right mind. I mean, we fought a lot, but we always made up. I never doubted Bella's love for an instant."

"And what was *his* relationship with your mother like?"

"He did everything she said." Paul then relayed the entire history of Millie, who he had loved and followed down to Mexico, and how much his mother had hated the girl.

"It sounds like your mother punished you and rewarded your younger brother because he listened to her and you didn't," the psychiatrist summarized.

"That's all behind us now."

"Your wife says you're obsessed with your younger brother."

"You must've read about Robert Moses in the news?"

"Sure."

"He's also prevented me from getting jobs. Jobs in the government."

"What about moving to another city?"

"I'm not going to be pushed from my home."

"Okay, then *you* have to push *him* out of your thoughts, don't you?"

"Just look at all he's done! He's behind all the highways, he's building bridges, parks, pools. It doesn't end!"

"So what? Why can't you just live your life and let him live his?"

"The man is a power-hungry megalomaniac and he should be stopped!"

"Then he will be," the doctor replied in a calm voice. "But how does that concern you?"

"He controls everything! You think I'm crazy? Just go look at all his accomplishments. He's behind everything."

The doctor sighed and asked Robert if he would repeat a simple statement.

"What kind of statement?"

"A declaration of independence."

"Sure," said Paul, mostly to appease the doctor.

"Robert Moses did not pay for these pools, parks, highways, and bridges . . ." the doctor began.

After a moment, Paul sighed and repeated the words.

"He did not design, nor build, nor does he own these pools, parks, highways, and bridges," the shrink said.

Paul felt idiotic as he recited the phrase.

"He is just one of a list of bureaucrats who is affiliated with the construction . . ."

As Paul echoed the doctor, he told himself, *This will make Teresa happy.*

"And if he were not alive, these highways and bridges and pools and parks would be built anyway . . ."

Paul slowly repeated the doctor's declaration.

". . . by mayors, borough presidents, governors, with people's tax money and Board of Estimates votes, and by the countless people they hire. Robert Moses is merely one of many, many names. And, most importantly, he does not control my joy or pain. Paul Moses is master of Paul Moses."

When Paul finished the ridiculous recitation, the first

session was officially over. The psychiatrist scheduled a second appointment, but Paul never showed up. When his wife asked why he hadn't gone, he said he didn't need it. The doctor had put things in perspective and he was feeling much better.

Teresa woke up one night soon after to hear her husband quietly weeping into his pillow. The next day, she found him making strange expressions at the breakfast table. She realized he was desperately trying to restrain his rage while reading the newspaper. Later in the week, while chatting with her kids, she heard a sharp yelp coming from the bathroom. Paul stepped out with a strange smile on his face. The following morning, Teresa delicately told Paul that she and the kids had become uncomfortable in his presence. She asked him to move out—she wanted a divorce.

After a week with the clock, Uli was able to keep track of both the habits of the miners and the tedious passing of his own long days. On the back of an old document recovered from the Mkultra titled "Project Artichoke," he and Root kept careful records, each taking turns sleeping so one of them was always awake. During that time, Uli told Root about his own amnesia, explaining that it predated his arrival in this place. One day he asked her about how she had ended up down here.

"I got here the same way as everyone else—trying to escape from Rescue City, Nevada."

"So you were living in the real New York City when it was attacked?"

"Oh, no. I came with the second wave a few years later, in '72, when they decided that antiwar activists were terrorists. I was one of the Diggers."

"Diggers? You mean like these guys?"

"No, the Diggers were a group in San Francisco in the late '60s who helped young hippie arrivals. They were started by a guy named Emmett Grogan who's still in Rescue City."

"Were they anarchists?"

"Most were. When I joined there were half a million U.S. troops in Vietnam—the My Lai massacre occurred a few months later. Then Bobby Kennedy and King were assassinated. A bunch of us went to the Democratic National Convention in Chicago where we all got beaten with billy clubs and arrested, so we—"

"I remember," Uli interrupted, wanting Root to continue with her story instead of giving him a history lesson.

"We eventually wound up on the attorney general's list and found ourselves detained in Rescue City. Emmett and some of us soon got tired of all the bad smells and hippie crap in Staten Island and decided to go up to Queens instead. This was just as the Piggers were taking over the Bronx and Queens and the Crappers were claiming Manhattan and Brooklyn. We refused to participate in all the partisan violence or declare allegiance to either gang, so a group of Piggers approached us and said we had to leave their borough."

"What happened?"

"We barricaded ourselves in a city park and decided we weren't going without a fight. To avoid a conflict that might've brought in the Crappers, the Pigger's told us that if we moved down to Brooklyn and vanished for six months, they'd meet us near the drain hole in Staten Island and give us the escape drug."

"Why'd you trust them?"

"Emmett had defected and joined the Queens Pigger party, but we knew we could still trust him."

As Uli and Root talked, several of the miners left their tunnels while others came and resumed work. Root noted their movements.

Uli didn't know if it was just empathy stirred by Paul's painful yearning for Teresa after she filed for divorce, but he found himself quietly attracted to Root, a tough, smart survivor alone in this world of whackos.

23

Two weeks after Teresa asked him to leave, Paul dusted off his electrical engineering degree and his honorable discharge from the army and got himself a wartime posting. He was appointed Superintendent of Construction at the U.S. Navy base in Bayonne, New Jersey. He was glad to finally have a steady job and paycheck, but it was too late to save his dying pool business, much less his marriage. Despite the impending divorce, he was still intent on paying back his loans to Teresa's family. The loss of his business and family left Paul, who had just reached fifty years of age, constantly tired and listless. He put all his possessions in a storage facility and slept on a squeaky metal cot in his Jersey office.

Over time, Paul began to enjoy his time in New Jersey. He threw himself full force at his work as though he were fighting the war all by himself. He had never felt so utilized. He mailed a portion of each paycheck to Teresa as if he were buying back his hocked self-esteem.

One morning in late 1944, Paul woke in his cramped office and discovered an envelope from his ex-wife sitting in his mailbox. Inside, he found his latest check, uncashed. A simple typewritten note said, *PAID IN FULL, good luck in life, Teresa*. His debt was finally over. He called to tell her that he wanted to help with her kids' tuition, but the maid said that Teresa no longer wished to hear from him.

After the war came to an end, while everyone else celebrated, Paul wondered what lay ahead for him. He offered to stay on as an employee at the navy base.

"Paul, we don't really need any electrical engineers,"

said his boss. "But hell, I'm sure your brother can get you more work than you know what to do with."

Paul sent out his resume to a few select places for jobs that truly interested him, but with the war over, an army of young men was coming back looking for employment. Fortunately, the Depression was over too, so Paul started once again seeing some income from his inheritance.

After he moved out of his New Jersey office, he rented a room in a cheap Times Square hotel—the Longacre—intending to live there only temporarily while looking for a new home.

As he'd return to his hotel room at night, however, the emptiness of his life began to suffocate him. Joining some other guys he had befriended in the area, he took to spending his days in the balmy spring of 1947 hanging out in Bryant Park. Most of them were veterans from the First World War and conversation was always lively. One older fellow who had also fought in the Spanish American War showed him tips for living on the cheap, like taking him to soup kitchens. Paul didn't mind joining the ranks of nameless men eating side by side in basement benches. In a way, he felt he deserved it for failing so miserably. His greatest fear was being spotted by any of his former friends, so he made a habit of pulling his fedora over his face and never making eye contact with passersby.

One morning, while walking up Fifth Avenue, he spotted Teresa heading uptown on the other side of the street. She was wearing high heels, a beautiful dress, and a tiny black hat, holding a clutch purse. She looked like a million bucks; oddly, it occurred to Paul that he didn't look half bad either. He had just gotten a haircut and happened to be wearing a nice shirt with his best suit. He experienced palpitations as he crossed the avenue and slowly approached her from behind. He was about to tap her on the shoulder when he caught a profile of her beautiful pixie face. She looked happy, an expression he had rarely seen during their final years together. Fearing that his presence could only depress her, he stopped in his tracks and let her walk away.

Paul spent his days wandering around Times Square, which suited him given the state of his life. At the main branch of the New York Public Library—the best in the world—he became well-acquainted with a small community of lost scholars and drunken intellectuals that time had forgotten. He found that he could effortlessly sneak into movies and the second halves of Broadway plays during intermission. From St. Clements Church on the West Side and St. Agnes on East 43rd Street, he would collect used clothing and free food. Every morning he'd get copies of the *New York Times*, the *Herald Tribune*, the *Wall Street Journal*, and the *New York Sun* to check for his brother's name over scalding cups of black coffee.

One afternoon while hanging out in front of the Horn & Hardart's Automat across from Grand Central Station and skimming the *Daily News*, he heard a shrill female voice shout his name.

Before he could slink away, a beautiful dark-skinned woman was standing before him: "Paul Moses! How are you?"

"Fine," he said quietly, not rising or revealing that he had no clue who she was.

"Paul! It's me—Lucretia."

He wondered if she had worked at Con Ed when he was there, or perhaps he had met her at the library.

"Maria's daughter!" she finally added.

"Oh my God!" It was the daughter of his mother's maid. He hadn't seen her in years. When she hugged him, it felt so strange being touched by another person—something he hadn't experienced in so long.

"How are you?" she asked.

She looked to be in her late twenties, but had to be in her thirties.

"Just fine. How's your mom?"

"She passed away."

"No!" Paul couldn't believe it; she was less than ten years older than him.

"She got lung cancer two years ago and died shortly after."

Paul wanted to give his condolences, but he couldn't even speak. Tears came to his eyes and for the first time, he felt distinctly old. Poor Maria was the very first girl he'd ever had a crush on. And she had always been so fond of him.

"She tried finding you but you weren't listed," Lucretia said.

"The phone was in my wife's name," he muttered without looking up.

"What are you doing here anyway?"

"Waiting for a friend," he answered, instead of telling her that the St. Clements soup kitchen didn't begin serving until 6.

"Are you still working at Con Ed?"

"No, but I consult for them from time to time. How about you?"

"I'm an accountant," she said. "I have about a dozen clients, all in the Bronx."

"Oh, that's right, your mother lived up there."

"Yeah, she left me the place. Hey, you have to come up for dinner."

"I'm not very good company these days."

"You have to! No one has ever made me laugh like you."

"Where in the Bronx is the house?"

"East Tremont. Don't you remember it?"

"Things have been a little frantic for me lately," he said. "But what's your address?"

As she scribbled it down along with her phone number, he thought he would just throw it away after she left, but then she asked, "How's Saturday at 7 p.m.?"

"I don't know, I . . ."

"Promise me you'll be there."

"The Bronx is up north, right?" he kidded, knowing when he was licked.

At the bottom of a box of rations, Root found a tiny kid's compass that looked like it had come from a Cracker Jack box. They were now able to determine north, south, east, and west. Numbering all the tunnels in Root's three-dimensional model, they figured out the most practical caves to focus on. The trick now was to fool the men into digging in the selected caves around the clock.

After having monitored the sleeping habits of the miners—some snoozing like clockwork, others entirely unpredictable—Uli and Root were ready to turn them into a coordinated digging machine. At one point while the two passed through the silo, Uli glanced at his companion and saw tears in her eyes as she watched her old friend hanging from the desk tower.

"There are corpses all over the place," Uli soothed. "Do you think they'd notice if we put another body up there instead?"

"I know where we can find a headless corpse," she replied after several moments.

"Let's try it."

The two hiked up to the funereal cave. Clamping their mouths and noses, they lit a torch and Root led him to the decapitated remains. The body was recently deceased, so it didn't smell too bad. They carried it back into the silo, then Uli scaled the tower of desks and cut down Sandy's naked body. With a rope, he hoisted up the new corpse and strapped it in below the dog's skull. Just to be on the safe side, he wrenched the feet backwards like Sandy's had been. Together they carried poor Sandy's headless body back up into one of the empty caves and interred her. Root gave Uli a grateful kiss on the cheek. For the first time since he had been consigned to hell, he actually felt good, and so did Paul . . .

24

. . . in fact, he spent a whole buck on a haircut and shave, complete with the cloud of talcum powder and a spritz of cheap cologne. He bought a new button-down Arrow shirt and picked out his least threadbare suit, which he went over with a lint brush. Then, at Grand Central, Paul gave the guy two bits for a dime spit shine. He bought a bouquet of flowers along with a box of Whitman's chocolates. Hopping on the IRT 6 train, he rode all the way up to the Bronx for dinner with his former maid's daughter. The closer he got to her house, however, the more angry he became with himself. Why the hell was he having dinner with some kid—a skinny, shy schoolgirl who would giggle and blush a lot—who he barely remembered? Maria never would've permitted this. He should've simply said no when she gave her invitation.

Forty-five minutes later, he finally deboarded the IRT at 174th Street. From what he remembered, East Tremont was the Bronx's equivalent of the Lower East Side, working-class Italians who couldn't find anything on Arthur Avenue and Jews who couldn't afford the Grand Concourse. As he schlepped along, he tried to dream up subjects to talk about with this young girl. Should he tell her about his failed marriage? Or perhaps his failed career? He could describe his rootless life of reading newspapers and living off charity. Or he could talk about what everyone else talked about—Robert's tremendous success.

After crossing through beautiful Crotona Park—another of his brother's recent renovations—he searched for her address. He was delighted when he arrived at the elegant old house with a worn wraparound porch that he had last seen twenty years earlier.

As he knocked on Lucretia's door, a small dog started barking. A moment later, when she opened the door, his heart stopped. With her hair bundled up, wearing a beautiful dress, the young woman was truly ravishing. A tiny Yorkie barked incessantly as he stepped inside her spacious house. She put the animal in the yard and quickly made Paul a gin and tonic—his favorite drink from twenty years before.

"I once came up around here with my ex-wife to attend her cousin's wedding in Pelham Park."

"Oh, the rich part of town."

"So what's this part?" he kidded.

"The further south and east you go, the worse things get," she said as she served him a Waldorf salad. "This is the middle, where the rich meet the poor. But at the rate things are going, I think in the next ten, twenty years even the South Bronx will improve."

Instead of revealing the miserable truth of his life, Paul served an appetizing lie: The pool club had been a modest success. He had sold it after ten years. He and his brother were the very best of friends. Though his marriage had failed, he was still close to Teresa and the kids.

Soon dinner was ready, a terrific grilled fish and mango platter. He had to cover his mouth as he ate, because they spent the entire time talking without a single awkward pause. She asked many questions, about his mother, about growing up wealthy, about his time in revolutionary Mexico—things he no longer mentioned to anybody.

"When I was a kid," he confessed after dinner, "I had such a crush on your mother."

"Well, that's a coincidence," she replied, staring softly into his eyes. "Because I've always been head over heels about you." He coughed as she giggled.

The first miner to exit his tunnel was the short balding

Italian from cave fourteen who was working on one of the slower eastern routes. They refixed his guidewire so that it trailed into the more efficient tunnel fifteen, just a short turn away. Root pointed out that the closer they kept the diggers to their original tunnels, the less likely the men were to doubt themselves or cause a fuss.

Something else occurred to Uli and he hastily squirmed on his belly down cave fourteen. Sure enough, the Italian had left some things behind—a small crucifix, several cutting tools, and two empty jugs, one for urine and the other with water. Rolled in a corner was the stolen vest with the Day-Glo stripe. Uli then climbed down tunnel fifteen and found that six boxes of shattered stones had been shoved in there—a detail that would've blown their scheme. Uli cleared it all out and placed the miner's possessions at the very end. Then, to disorientate him further, Uli and Root piled large stones in front of his former tunnel.

The next tunneler to break for sleep was his buddy, the black guy, another eastward tunneler. Again Uli raced in to grab his personal effects, while Root altered his wires to one of the targeted upward caves. Root was a little worried because the rock he would be cutting into was much harder than that of his former tunnel, but she agreed that it was a risk worth taking. The third tunneler already inhabited one of the selected caves, so they left him alone. Soon, all tunnelers had been rerouted to new caves except for one digger in a southwestern tunnel. Root suspected that the poor man's brain had turned to mush, as he seemed to sleep, eat, and crap around the clock in his dusty hole.

Before long, Root slipped back in her chair and nodded off. Uli let her sleep, but he noticed that a stick of gum had slipped out of her pocket. He hadn't seen any gum in the stock area, and he didn't ever remember her chewing it, so he assumed she was secretly hording it. When she awoke later, he didn't mention it.

"Want to take a nap?" she offered once she was up and about.

Though exhausted, he declined, anxious until he was sure all the miners had returned and this phase of the plan was working somewhat smoothly. The miners would reach up in the blackness and finger their particular strings, almost like harpists, to guide them into their caves. He and Root listened attentively as the rested diggers vanished inside their new tunnels. A moment later they would hear the hammering resume and hug each other excitedly. For the next few days, it became a complex juggling act of men and tunnels. Uli was elated . . .

. . . as though he had won some incredible lottery. Not only was the food that night the best he had eaten in years, but his former maid's beautiful young daughter felt like the antidote to a painful venom that had poisoned his heart and soul. It was the first time he could recall the weight of so many failures lifting from his shoulders. As he rode the IRT back down to grungy Midtown, he felt like a child again. It felt like fifty unsuccessful years were being miraculously rewritten. But as soon as he arrived back at his little room at the Longacre—his minimum-security prison cell—his life suddenly seemed all the more painful.

When Lucretia rang him a few days later, it was the first call he had received from outside the hotel.

"I really enjoyed our dinner together," she said.

"Me too."

"Well, why don't you get back up here and we'll have supper again tonight?"

Induced by his guilty conscience, he replied, "I just got a big job so I won't have any time for the next few weeks, maybe a month."

"Well, you can't be busy forever."

"I'll call when things slow down."

Three weeks later she called again. With tremendous difficulty, he said he was still busy. Hanging up the phone, he felt his heart break. He spent the week walking around in a haze. When she called once more a week later, it felt like hope and possibility were on the phone.

Instead of flatly turning her down this time, they talked

late into the night. Finally he asked, "Do you believe some people are cursed?"

"No, just dumb."

The comment stuck like an ice pick, and Paul decided it was time to come clean. He didn't want to do it on the phone since it was apparent she was not easily put off. He finally consented to a second dinner.

It had been muggy and overcast all day, and rain just started falling as Paul stepped off the train. He walked six blocks with a newspaper folded over his head. When he arrived, he was winded and soaked. This time he made no effort to disguise his true self: His wet shirt was yellowed with sweat. He was unshaven. His threadbare suit was too loose on him and filled with holes, and his shoes were worn in the soles. She handed him a towel to dry off as he sat in the living room. Toto, her Yorkie, sat in her lap.

He wasted no time: "I lied to you before and, frankly, I want to set the record straight."

"Why would you lie about anything?"

"Because I was embarrassed."

"What can you possibly be embarrassed about?"

"Everything: I don't have a job. My pool business went belly-up. My marriage fell apart. And I'm basically broke."

Lucretia rose from her couch and moved to sit next to him. She wrapped her fingers around his and said, "The you that I liked was the oldest scion of a prosperous family who treated my mother and me like queens."

"Maybe that's why I lost everything," he said with a smile.

"I didn't know you *had* everything."

"I don't have a job. I don't have a family. I don't even have a life."

"All you have, all any of us have, is ourselves," Lucretia said, "and I think you're a good person."

"You're not going to quote the Bible, are you?"

"Why, do you need religion to be good?"

"Whatever I am, I'm worthless," he lamented.

"If you're a good person, you're not worthless."

Paul chuckled in frustration. "I don't think I'm getting through."

"You're sitting here telling me you're worthless, and I do believe what you say about not having any money, but most of all I'm wondering why you're trying to get me to think poorly of you."

"Because I'm bad luck. Everyone who comes into contact with me lives to regret it."

"You could've told me all this on the phone," she said. "I think you've come all the way up here because you like me. And I know I like you. I was never after your money, so it doesn't matter if you don't have it. I still like what I liked about you all those years ago."

He found it difficult to make eye contact. Outside, the rain was still coming down. In a moment, thunder filled the darkened sky. As Lucretia moved through the house closing windows, Paul thought about her situation: With her mother's demise, she was all alone. The interest she was showing in him was nothing more than an infatuation, a search for a father she never knew. In him, she found a man her mother had once looked on trustfully and approvingly. If Maria were here now, he thought, she would want him to be fatherly toward her only daughter.

"So, are you seeing anybody?" Paul asked Lucretia paternally.

"Yeah, you," she said with a smile.

"Look, I'm divorced and old, and I know it's a difficult process, but you have to stick with it and keep looking."

"Paul, I have just one question: Do you find me attractive?"

"You're very attractive, but you're too young for me."

"Are you dating anyone else right now?"

"I'm virtually a bag man living in a Times Square hotel, so the answer is no."

"If you don't want to date me, that's fine," she said. "But if you think you're standing in the way of some Prince Charming, or that I'd be dating someone much younger than you, you're very much mistaken." She rose and headed into the kitchen with her Yorkie at her heels. Paul assumed she was preparing to serve dinner. Instead, she returned with a dozen pots and pans, all piled inside one another. Paul just sat there while she walked around the house placing the cookery under various leaks that were starting to sprinkle down.

"Why don't you hire a roofer?" Paul asked.

"I've been saving up. But my first money is going toward the plumbing and electricity."

Paul asked Lucretia to give him a quick tour of the place, during which he recalled his own inspection two decades earlier. Very little had been repaired; small problems had become big ones.

"Have you ever considered selling this house?"

"I could never sell it," she said emphatically.

"Lucretia, you live alone. Why do you need all this space?"

"Because someday I plan to have a family and this will be our home."

"How much money have you saved so far?"

"Just a little over fifty bucks." She grinned. "Not enough to do anything yet."

"Actually, fifty bucks should be enough to fix your roof."

"I had it estimated for seventy-five dollars."

"We can do it together," he said. "I'll show you how."

"I couldn't ask you to do that."

"You don't have to. I wanted to help out when I first came here with your mother, but I was too busy. Now I only got time."

"You really want to fix my roof?" she asked with a big smile.

"This is our last date together," he said as he grabbed

his jacket. "I'll be back early tomorrow to start work."

The rain began to taper. Lucretia watched as Paul walked out and up the block.

The next morning when he didn't show, she wondered if he had simply decided to vanish. At noon, though, he arrived in a Checker cab and started unloading things on her front porch. She dashed out to help him. Ten rolls of tar paper, two buckets of tar, a linoleum cutter, a five-pound bag of nails, and two hammers—he had made the purchases at Jack's, a local hardware shop on East Tremont Avenue. For the next eight hours, Paul rolled and cut the tar paper, nailing it down and then tarring the seams.

The following day he resumed his work. He was surprised by how many people passing in the street waved up at him, or called out something like, "Glad to see Lucretia's finally getting her roof fixed!" Apparently she was very connected to her community.

He left his tar-smudged clothes on the porch along with his old shoes. Not wanting to track dirt inside, he sat in the living room in his boxers and T-shirt. Lucretia made a wonderful codfish stew for dinner, which he hungrily forked down.

"I should be finished later this week," he said tiredly.

"Then you're spending the night."

"No way."

"Look, I accept that we're not going to be romantically involved, but it's ridiculous for you to go all the way downtown and then have to wake up and come all the way back up here. Especially when I have two empty bedrooms upstairs."

It took the remainder of his strength just to climb back upstairs after dinner and flop into bed. The next morning, she brought him a cup of coffee and a buttered bialy. He took a bite, slurped down the java, and went back out to the porch to put his work clothes on and climb out onto the roof. He kept at this for the next three days. In the evenings they'd listen to the radio, chat, or read the papers. She'd often sit at her desk with a manual adding machine and her accounting work, punching in numbers from a stack of ledger sheets. When he told her he knew where to find an affordable electric counter, she said she had one in the basement but it kept shorting out fuses.

After he was done with the roof, Paul checked out her electrical system. The cables were coated with a frayed fabric and connected to a haphazard array of circuit boxes with wooden backs. The place barely had enough amps to keep the lights on. Paul went to the local library to brush up on some fine points of household electricity, then proceeded to unscrew all the old fuses and pull the ancient wires from the walls. He took two days carefully upgrading her whole system with a centralized fuse box.

"You can make whatever repairs you want," she said, "but I refuse to let you pay for the parts."

He agreed to give her the receipts, but would only do so when he couldn't afford to cover them himself. Soon he finished the electrical work and plastered some of the walls. The following day, a neighbor stopped by—Ellis Dansberg, a licensed plumber. Paul asked him a dozen questions about fixing the leaky and rusted pipes.

"You wanna make sure you turn off the water to the branch you're cutting," Ellis explained in a loud, unmodulated voice. "You can use a hacksaw, but be careful not to leave burrs. I'd dry fit and solder as much of the extension on the ground as possible . . ."

He found plumbing more difficult than electrical work and was careful to only take on smaller repairs, making detailed notes as the man spoke.

Paul suddenly realized that it had been nearly two weeks since he had been back to his hotel room, and he was already in arrears. He called to learn that his scant possessions—mainly an archive of clippings about Robert—had been tossed out of the hovel.

The two of them began developing a comfortable routine: Lucretia would come home after work at 5:30 and praise Paul's latest renovations. Then she'd prepare a meal for both of them, trying to make him feel at ease. Usually around 9 o'clock, exhausted, Paul would silently head up to his room, shower, brush his teeth, and go to bed. Lucretia never tried to stop him, just wished him goodnight.

"It's my dream to someday hear the banter of children, even grandchildren, in this house," Lucretia said to Paul one morning as she held a pipe for him in the kitchen. He was soldering it to another piece.

"And someday, when you find Mr. Right, you will."

He spent the following week tapping the walls for rotten laths, ripping them out, loading the chunks of broken plaster into boxes, and piling them into dumpsters around the neighborhood at dusk. He mixed new plaster and started repairing the walls. Once through with that phase, he asked Lucretia what colors she wanted for the ceiling, walls, and baseboards.

"Let's go to Jack's together," she suggested.

They headed to the local hardware shop on East Tremont Avenue and selected four different paints, along with rollers, brushes, drop cloths, and turpentine. This time, Lucretia put on her old shirt and overalls and joined him in the ambitious paint job, a base and two top coats.

When they finished the living room, it looked so wonderfully different that she began inviting a stream of neighbors to come visit. They hadn't even begun painting upstairs. Lucretia's old friend Lori Mayer, who lived with her husband Bill in the house directly behind hers, came across the backyard and inspected the gorgeous remodeling. Another of her dear friends, May Kearne, and her huband Jimmy, both teachers at the local high school, thought the place looked positively dreamy.

26

Paul's marathon renovation job inspired Uli in his work with Root. The man's repressed feelings for Lucretia catalyzed Uli's growing attraction to his new friend.

One day, when Paul found some wilted flowers on the porch, he asked what was up. Lucretia casually answered, "Oh, it's just Leon."

"Who's Leon?"

"Leon Timmons Skacrowski." She explained that the man's mom and Maria had been the only two Jamaicans living in the area thirty years before; both had married half-Jewish men, so he and Lucretia had become childhood friends and then teenage sweethearts.

Leon's father had died about ten years before, leaving him an old scrap-metal yard on the south side of Crotona Park in Morrisania, commonly referred to by East Tremonters as the "slum."

"You should go to a game with him," Lucretia said. "He loves baseball."

"That's the one thing the Bronx has over anywhere else—the Yankees."

"When the Dodgers signed Jackie Robinson, Leon switched allegiances."

"The *Brooklyn* Dodgers?" Paul replied. "Last time I went to Ebbets Field, I fell through one of the damn seats."

"Leon will be happy to show you all the new ones."

For the next five days all went well. The laborers were moving an impressive amount of rubble. One of the diggers even commented to Root, "We'll be out soon, no thanks to you."

"That one doesn't like you much," Uli observed.

"He's really paranoid," Root explained. "He keeps telling the others I'm some kind of CIA agent."

At one point Uli noticed a fat young miner ending his shift who looked strangely familiar. Since another miner, the only black one, was due back momentarily, Uli quickly switched wires and pulled out the younger fellow's possessions, replacing them with the black man's items. Moments later, the black miner and the young, bespectacled man converged simultaneously at the mouth of the same tunnel. Uli heard a quick squabble break out, then saw the young man crawl out to the large silo and say, "Something screwy's going on here."

"What are you talking about?" Root asked.

"For starters, someone changed the path of my wire and I don't know where my things are!"

When Uli approached, the younger miner seized a rod from the ground as if he was being attacked.

"Just relax," Root intervened. Turning to the young miner, she spoke quietly: "Look, we redirected the wires, but we did it for a reason.

"What reason?"

"You seem fairly lucid, so I'm trusting you with this. I have a diagram I can show you."

"What diagram?"

"There are six tunnels going in six different directions that offer the best chance of getting out of here. Do you understand?"

Uli was now able to see the fat young miner's face up close. Suddenly identifying the man, Uli lurched over and shoved him to the ground. "You're Manny Lewis," he snapped, then turned to Root. "He killed my friend Oric outside Cooper Union in Rescue City!"

"I didn't kill anyone!"

Uli had his knees on the fat boy's arms so he couldn't budge.

"Hold it!" Root shrieked.

"He was a Pigger spy."

"I should have killed you then!" Manny started to squirm.

"You'll never have the opportunity," Uli spat.

"Root, if you let me go, I'll work with you . . ." the young miner appealed as Uli started strangling him.

"Wait a sec!" Root cried out. "We're here now and we need people on our side."

"Can't you see he's lying? He's just trying to save himself!"

"That's not true!" Manny said in a high, constricted voice. "I only went after you because of who you are."

"Who is he?" Root asked, as she tried to pull Uli off.

"Former FBI," Manny said, gasping for breath.

"You're FBI?"

"You're nuts!" Uli shot back at Manny.

"He worked for COINTELPRO in the '60s. Hoover's right-hand boy."

"I suppose the Piggers told you that," Uli said.

"No, I recognized you from your photo. So did others who were content to just let it go—but I said no. This guy did everything from planting false evidence to illegal wiretappings."

Uli slowly climbed off the kid and tried to think whether any of this made sense. Then he said what he remembered most clearly. "My name is Paul Moses."

"That's a total lie," Manny replied.

"I was born in New Haven, my siblings were Robert and Edna, my parents were Bella and Emanuel, and I attended Princeton and fought in the Mexican Revolution."

"The Mexican Revolution was something like seventy years ago!" Manny countered. "You'd have to be a century old."

"Then it was a different Mexican Revolution, cause I remember being there," Uli said.

"Look, we're all buried alive, living like rats in some massive underground crypt. We could die here," Root reasoned. "Our only chance of getting out of is by working together."

Manny said he was willing to accept a truce. Uli didn't respond—he was still wondering if what the boy had said was really true. Either way, it didn't matter; Root was right: They were all stuck down here and they needed the kid's help.

They decided to alter their plan accordingly. Manny quit digging and began helping Root to redirect the miners into the selected tunnels. Meanwhile, Uli stayed alone at the top end of the Sticks to feed and tend to the laborers. Though all seemed to be going well over the next few days, Uli felt a growing anxiety that it was just a matter of time before the other miners discovered they were all being duped.

27

Paul came downstairs around dinnertime one evening to find Lucretia sitting with her childhood friend Leon Skacrowski over a cup of coffee. The shaggy-haired half-Jamaican youth was rocking back and forth slightly as Lucretia chatted about old times. She introduced them.

"Sorry, I didn't know you had a visitor," Paul said.

"Actually, we're about to go see a movie," Lucretia replied.

"A movie?"

"Yeah, and if we don't leave now we're going to miss the beginning," Leon added. Lucretia grabbed her jacket.

"Would you mind watching Toto?" she asked Paul. He said that was fine.

This day marked the beginning of Lucretia's renewed romance with Leon. She seemed to be saying to Paul: *If you don't take me, this slow-witted man will.* One morning several days later, when Paul came downstairs and found Leon sitting at the kitchen table reading the sports pages, he realized that she had done the unthinkable—Leon had spent the night.

"I tell you," the young man said with pride, "now that the Dodgers have grabbed the pennant, there's nothing stopping them." After finishing his fourth heaping bowl of corn flakes, Leon thanked Lucretia for the wonderful night and left.

Paul exited the room in dismay. His renovation of Lucretia's house was nearly complete, so he had begun working on her overgrown garden in back and along the sides of her house. He had already cut down three dead trees and spent the day uprooting half a dozen thornbushes to lay down a flower bed. Late that afternoon, Paul stormed into the kitchen, sweaty with cuts and scabs, and shouted, "Is this is your way at getting back at me? If so, that's fine, but you're only hurting yourself!"

"What are you talking about?"

"Sleeping with that moron is what I'm talking about!"

"What business is—"

"You and I both know that you could date a thousand guys smarter and more handsome."

"I've known Leon all my life. He's a trustworthy man." Lucretia stared blankly at the far wall.

"I'll tell you what I think. I think you're dating a big dumb man just to spite me."

"And how about you?" she cried out with uncharacteristic fervor. "Why don't you admit why you're still here?"

"Twenty years ago I promised your mother I'd do some repairs and—"

"You finished weeks ago!"

Paul slumped down next to her and looked at the ground. "For me, the definition of love is . . . the supreme generosity of spirit beyond all selfish desires."

"So what are you saying?"

"I'm saying a person who feels truly worthless has no right to love someone else. I mean, the most loving thing I can do is leave here now and never look back."

Lucretia rose and gently wrapped her arms around Paul. Leaning forward, he delicately kissed her on the lips.

Uli could almost hear the quickening of Lucretia's soft breaths as he washed and fed the laborers. It took him a moment to realize that there were faint screams coming from the direction of the distant silo. Then he heard feet racing by his cave. He hoped that one of the miners had actually broken through into a new shaft and scurried toward the silo. When he reached the high-ceilinged room he discovered five miners surrounding Manny, who was bleeding profusely and backing toward a dark corner. Before Uli could intervene, the Italian miner came up from behind and cracked the kid across the skull. The others rushed in and started beating him viciously. Root was nowhere to be seen. Uli ran back up to the storage area to look for her. Almost immediately, two other miners rushed in from the Mkultra.

"They got the kid!" Uli shouted, pretending to be among them. Two other miners hurried down, joining the mob. Uli recognized one of them, who he and Root had labeled "Dave." Together they headed down into the silo.

"What happened?" Uli asked him.

"We found out that this bastard and that bitch were screwing with us."

"How?"

"From that," he replied, pointing up.

Uli glanced nervously at the corpse hanging from the wooden tower.

"I knew one of them had cut down Xolotl's body and replaced it with some other body," Dave said, motioning up to the suspended cadaver. "So I told everyone to be on the lookout and we discovered they were switching wires on us."

"Why would they do that?" Uli asked.

"The same reason she killed the other woman," said another miner who was listening in. "She's CIA! She's deliberately trying to make us waste our time here."

"Where is the bitch anyhow?" Dave asked.

"One of the guys grabbed her, but she hit him with pepper spray and ran away," the second miner replied. "He got a solid punch off. Broke her fucking nose. We raced after her, but she disappeared in the offices."

Uli looked over to Manny Lewis's bloody body, which had been unceremoniously dumped in a corner.

"There's another guy too," the Italian said, his vest also smeared with blood.

"Yeah, I remember a third guy," Uli heard someone else chime in.

Eventually the miners simmered down and began milling around. Several crawled back down into the Convolution toward their caves.

28

Four months after their encounter across from Grand Central Station, Paul Moses finally broke down and asked for Lucretia's hand in marriage. She wondered to herself how much longer it would take to get him to start producing children and money.

The first goal was easy. He initiated sex as soon as she woke up every morning and at night before bed—pregnancy was inevitable. Work, however, he rarely mentioned.

One Sunday after breakfast, as Paul flipped through the *New York Times*, Lucretia picked up a section of the paper he had tossed aside. It was the employment listings.

"You're an engineer, right?"

"An electrical engineer," he said, engrossed in an article about the new state of Israel.

"Let's see . . . where is that?" She carefully surveyed the various job headings.

"I've spent the past twenty years trying to secure something," he muttered absently. "Robert has built a blockade around me."

"Robert, your brother?"

Paul had worked hard not to repeat the same mistake he had made with Teresa. He had been trying to avoid even mentioning Robert.

"How exactly has he blockaded you?"

"He kept me from getting a state position in Water, Gas, and Electricity, and I'm pretty sure he blocked me from getting a city commissionership as well."

"Have you talked to him directly about this?"

"I tried," Paul said, then put his newspaper down.

"He stole my inheritance right out from under me."

Lucretia sat perplexed, wondering what to say or do. She knew that Paul no longer had access to the vast wealth that once made him master and her mother servant, but his chronic unemployment was going to complicate things considerably. Even Leon, who she thought of as little more than a glorified garbage collector, had a job.

Several days passed and Root was still missing. Although the miners slowly returned to their digs, Uli was reluctant to lead the zombielike laborers out of their caves. That had been Root's job, and he feared mimicking her movements too closely. With their daily routines interrupted, the laborers were growing increasingly anxious. Uli tried looking after them, but feeding, watering, and cleaning that many was difficult, not to mention dangerous. The more energetic ones started walking aimlessly, and a few actually wandered back into the Mkultra.

After a week, a couple of the sickliest workers died. Then one morning Uli entered the silo to see a fresh chubby body dangling from the heights of the desk tower. It wasn't until Uli found the large head, which had been cleanly circumcised and tossed in a corner, that he confirmed it was Manny. They had violently twisted his feet backwards—he was the latest offering to their bullshit death guide.

29

When Paul entered the kitchen, Lucretia and her friend May went silent.

"Paul," May began, "I was just telling Lucretia that you'd make a great high school teacher."

"Why in the world would you say that?" he asked, thinking she might be kidding him.

"Cause you're smart and patient. You're a natural teacher."

"What are the qualifications to teach in this city?" he asked.

"Just a bachelor's degree, and then you have to take some courses to get your license. But you can do substitute teaching until you get one."

Paul could see his beautiful fiancée watching him apprehensively. In that instant he grasped that he had walked into an ambush: Lucretia had been dropping continuous hints about him getting a job; now she had enlisted a neighbor. All he could do was smile.

"That doesn't sound half bad," he relented. "What's the pay and benefits?"

"Salary starts at thirteen thousand a year. There's health insurance and a pension plan, and they're always looking for people."

"So where do I sign up?"

Lucretia's face lit up.

"In Brooklyn Heights at 110 Livingston Street. Once you finish the certification, they put you on an availability list. But don't take any jobs—Jimmy will hire you right here in East Tremont so you can be within walking distance of your house. Plus, you get summers and holidays off."

Paul poured himself a glass of cold water and took a long sip. In a strange way, this simple plan could be the headstone for a much greater goal: Instead of recapturing a success he never really had and trying to shove it in his brother's face, he could focus on the more tangible targets of supporting his young wife and their offspring to come.

30

Memories of Paul were the only bright spot in his life now. Uli imagined he was sitting in the back row of a small, sweet wedding ceremony at the local Temple Emmanuel. Afterwards they held a buffet-style reception at El Sombrero, a Spanish restaurant on East Tremont Avenue. One by one, over the course of the evening, the entire neighborhood seemed to stop by to congratulate the lucky bride and groom. They left wrapped wedding gifts or envelopes of cash, which were greatly appreciated. No one from Paul's side of the family showed up—nor had they been notified.

In July of 1948, at the age of sixty, he finished his eight required courses at Hunter College while teaching several classes.

The day he received his teaching license from Albany was also the last day for that season's registration at the local high school. Lucretia called May Kearne because Paul was too embarrassed to contact her directly. Jimmy Kearne was head of the science department and juggled some assignments to free a schedule of classes for Paul.

Donning a crisp white shirt and a thin black tie for his first day of school, Paul stopped in the kitchen for coffee and hid his dread of babysitting a bunch of working-class brats. He loved Lucretia and didn't want to disappoint her.

Paul arrived early to the school's science department and Jimmy gave him a curriculum, the various chemistry textbooks to hand out, his homeroom assignment, and a class schedule.

"It's all about advance preparation. Make sure you have a box of chalk, an eraser, and if you need to go to the bathroom, do it on the breaks. Also, you've got to be on top of all the paperwork or it'll drown you: Grading papers, producing lesson plans, homework—all have to be done regularly. It's not like college, don't let the kids teach *you*. Other than that, don't take no guff from no one, but be fair and you'll do fine." Only one other brand-new teacher reported for work that day, a smart-alecky war veteran who was less than half Paul's age.

The task of teaching matched Paul's skills surprisingly well. The authority of his age worked greatly to his advantage. Within a matter of months, the gratitude in the community was visible. People in the street frequently greeted him with a cheerful, "Hey, Mr. Moses!"

Lucretia saw it clearly. His hollow form seemed to fill out. His bitterness diminished. Even Paul's stooped posture seemed to rectify itself as he took pride in his work.

At the end of the semester, Jimmy Kearne wrote in his teacher's evaluation: *Paul Moses is a gifted teacher, gently correcting students almost unconsciously. Fluent not just in the sciences and humanities, but in language skills as well. Relaxed, focused, firm, yet gentle, he is able to use his sense of humor as a motivational tool . . .*

At dinner one evening in January 1949, Lucretia announced that she was pregnant.

"Oh my God!" Paul exclaimed, then hugged her, gave her a long kiss, and said, "I just had the thought that in 2009 the baby you're carrying will be the age I am now."

Beatrice Moses was born on September 3, 1949. Lucretia wanted her baptized, and her old friend Lori who lived in the house behind theirs agreed to be godmother.

Paul had never thought he'd have a child, but as soon as he held the bundle that was his new daughter, he felt a swooning joy that seemed to pardon his many failures. He loved Lucretia and Bea more than he had ever loved anyone in his life.

After a close call, Uli admitted to himself that it was just a matter of time before one of the miners deduced that he was part of Root's team. They'd kill him immediately.

He had finally lost faith that any of them would find a way to some miracle staircase out of there. The key reason he remained was the faint hope that Root might return.

To protect himself, Uli started assembling supplies. He had already found a small hand truck, rope, even a box of medicine. Stashing the supplies behind the mountain of stock in the storage depot, he glanced at the narrow metal door near the sealed freight elevator. Lighting a match, Uli made out a small rectangular hole in the rear wall. Old cables dangling from the gap were attached to the large fuse box that had collapsed to the ground.

Through the rectangle, Uli could see about five feet up the black hole. Then he felt a cool, soft breeze. He quickly located one of the discarded metal rods that the diggers had used to carve their tunnels. Using a large monkey wrench as a hammer, he began chipping down the sides of the small rectangular hole so he could look further inside, but the stone was difficult to break. After three hours, he was barely able to fit his forehead through the small slot.

31

Inasmuch as the price of comfort is the quick passage of time, the next two years of Paul's life seemed to finally be moving happily along. Doing his utmost to raise little Bea well, he would get up with her early in the morning and look after her until he had to go off to work. Lucretia would take Bea during the days. Frequently she'd cut across the backyard and drop Bea off with Lori, whose daughter Charity was only two months older. The two would play nonstop. When Paul came home in the afternoons, he could hardly wait to hold and kiss his little girl. He'd watch her while Lucretia went out on afternoon business appointments. She'd usually come home around 6 or 7, then they'd have dinner together.

Though Paul realized he would have no grand impact on civilization, nor marry the most dazzling society girl, life really couldn't be any better.

Some habits were a little difficult to break. Paul couldn't stop scanning the newspapers to keep track of his fascist brother. One project in particular caught his attention, like a tiny blip on his radar: the Cross Bronx Expressway, which had broken ground at one end of the borough and was slowly moving across it. He figured it would probably pass near them, along the northern edge of Crotona Park.

Little Bea was growing fast, and by her second birthday she was walking and talking more than all the other children in the playground. She was speaking in full sentences, grasping fairly abstract concepts. Even her sense of compassion—reflected in her treatment of little Toto—was exceptional. Paul told his wife that he wanted to get her IQ tested, believing that she might very well be a genius.

"Maybe it'd be a good time for Bea to have a little brother," Lucretia replied.

Paul nodded silently, wondering how all this would end up.

In the middle of his excavation of the elevator shaft, Uli heard loud scuttling. He figured the rats had finally gotten across the great divide and into the storage depot. He pushed a large crate aside and was startled to discover the upper half of a small child, who was holding a long dagger in his right palm; his lower half, however, seemed to be absorbed into the earth.

"There's no need for that," he told the boy. "Put the knife down."

"Where's Root?"

"She was chased off," he said. Then it struck him: *This must be the missing leader's handicapped son.*

"Is your father Plato?"

"Yeah, he was the leader."

"Where is he?"

"He disappeared awhile ago."

"I heard he was very smart."

"He used to collect papers and read all the time—*read, read, read*. Used to say stuff over and over."

"What kind of stuff?"

"Used to talk about the projects."

"What projects?"

"Don't know. A bunch."

"Do you remember any?"

"All began with M-K. Artichoke, Leviticus—a lot about M-K Leviticus."

"What's M-K Leviticus?"

"Don't know. He used to say we're all in Langley. *Langley, Langley, Langley.*"

"Langley, Virginia?"

"Don't know."

"What happened to him?"

"He would go farther and farther down in the Mkultra."

"Why?"

"First he found all this paint you could see in the dark."

Uli remembered the glowing lines leading nowhere. "Then what?"

"He was looking for some kind of chemical, either flammable or inflammable, I can't remember. Then one day he just didn't come back." Changing the subject, the kid said, "The lady told me I can always get supplies here. We're low."

"Sure, help yourself, just be careful of the miners."

"Do you know anything about helping sick people? Cause my ma and brother, they're sick people." The kid set down the short sword. Using his hands, he pulled himself forward into the light, where Uli finally got a chance to look him over. In place of legs was some kind of scorpion-like tail that curled under and peaked out of his long dirty shirt.

"Exactly how sick is your family?"

"They're both really hot, and my brother won't stop pooping. He's covered with red spots." It sounded like chicken pox. All things considered, it was astounding that anyone down there could stay alive.

"They both have fevers?"

"Don't know. Can you come take a look at them?"

"I'm no doctor, but I have some medicine."

Uli led him to the utility closet, where he had a pile of boxes filled with tins of pills. Some were identified as vitamins. Others were antibiotics, but didn't state dosage.

When Uli lit a candle, the kid saw the narrow rectangle that once held the fuse box and asked what it led to.

"I don't know. I'm too big to climb in, but I've been shaving down the sides."

"Want me to try?" It hadn't even occured to Uli to ask.

"That'd be great."

"I'll do it if you come and look at my sick family."

"I wouldn't know what to do. Like I said, I'm not a doctor."

"Please. I need help."

Uli realized that the child with his congenitally malformed body might be the only ticket out of this place—he couldn't refuse the kid's request. "You have my word that if you climb in there and tell me what you see, I'll help you."

The kid stared at Uli for a moment, then said, "All right, but could I rest first? I haven't eaten in a while and I've walked a long ways."

Uli gave him some crackers and water, led him to a small square of cardboard, and let him sleep.

32

At 1:38 on the afternoon of December 4, 1951, ten minutes before fifth period ended, some kid knocked on Paul Moses's classroom door with a note saying that he should call home as soon as possible. His first panicked thought was that something had happened to Beatrice. Why else would he get this message in the middle of the school day? He asked Sal Berg in the adjacent class to keep an eye on his students and dashed off. When he reached Lucretia on the phone, she told him that she had just received some kind of legal notice stating that all the residents on their block had to move.

"Can this wait until I get home?" he asked patiently, imagining it was a mistake.

"I suppose," she replied, though she sounded frazzled.

When he arrived home two hours later, he found that a number of neighbors had collected in the street, chatting with each other. Lucretia quickly showed him the notice that had been taped to their door. It stated that they were in the path of the new Cross Bronx Expressway. The proposed roadway cut a swath between 176th Street and Fairmont Place, plowing through seven blocks of residential housing. Immediately he envisioned it: a man-made fault line opening from east to west—two hundred and twenty-five feet of concrete roadway coming right at them, tearing the earth in two.

According to the letter, all residents on the street, for blocks in both directions, had nine months to vacate their premises and find new accommodations.

"Hey, Paul!" he heard. His neighbor Robert Ward was

crossing the street, holding up a road map. "Check out this freakin' highway! It looks like the Bronx is getting circumcized."

"We're supposed to sacrifice our homes so that commuters from New Jersey and Long Island can get to work faster?" Paul responded.

"Paul!" he heard another voice shout over to him. "Your last name's Moses. You're not related to this clown, are you?"

It was Karl Stein from half a block down. He came over with another copy of the same letter. Glancing at the bottom of the notice for the first time, Paul saw that it was signed by his brother: *Robert Moses, City Construction Coordinator.*

"No relation," Paul replied swiftly.

"Too bad," Stein said.

Lucretia peered down nervously. She'd never had any reason to lie to her neighbors and friends before. Paul excused himself and went into their house, then dashed to the upstairs bathroom and locked the door.

I knew it! he thought furiously. *That cocksucker has tracked me down and now he's coming after my family! I should've killed him when I had the chance!* He muttered aloud, "Teresa and that shrink said I was nuts! Well, *he's* coming after *me!* Now who's paranoid?"

When he heard Lucretia knocking around nervously in the bedroom, he splashed cold water on his face, took a deep breath, flushed the toilet, and came out to comfort her.

Over the next hour or so, as more neighbors gathered along the sidewalk, they started pooling their resources. One fellow across the street had a cousin in the mayor's office; he worked for the Department of Transportation. Another woman's brother was a lawyer, but he lived in Des Moines.

"We should organize right away," Paul announced for all to hear. After watching so many other neighborhoods being ripped in half by his brother's highways, he realized immediately what they should do to prevent this.

"What's the point?" one of the more knowledgeable neighbors retorted. "No one's ever been able to reverse eminent-domain law."

"Politicians are motivated by public opinion. But we have to work quickly. We've got to make as loud a stink as we can."

"What are we going to say?" Ms. Rice asked. "That the city can't have a freeway cause we like our homes?"

"We have to tell people that if this can happen to us, it can happen to anyone in this city," Paul replied. "And we have to show them an alternative route for the expressway that displaces fewer families."

"What do you mean, like a tunnel?"

"No, they can just as easily run the highway north of the park," Robert Ward speculated.

Although their street was filled with single-family homes, the next block over had a number of large apartment buildings. Paul pointed out that they must've gotten notices too. "We should go over there and start organizing people," he suggested.

Ward, Stein, Rice, and some of the others agreed to head over on Saturday to garner support. Within a matter of days, three hundred people had joined an ad hoc neighborhood organization calling itself MCBE—Move the Cross Bronx Expressway. They agreed to meet on a weekly basis in the multipurpose room at the YMHA.

Two weeks later, everyone got a second letter stating that the Tenant Relocation Bureau was going to help everyone find new accommodations; indeed, they had already helped those in the "Section One" portion of the planned roadway.

Though he fervently wished to take a leading role in the committee, Paul remained in the background, fearful that he would be revealed as Robert Moses's brother.

He met up with three neighbors that Saturday to check on the progress that had been made thus far on the first part of the expressway. As they drove eastward toward Section One, they could hear jackhammers and see clouds of dust rising in the air. Just before they spotted the hills of rubble and the earth-moving machines, they came upon rows of barren tenements and empty single-family homes. They parked in front of a condemned apartment building. Broken furniture and garbage, including long shards from a shattered mirror that once lined the hallway, covered the floor of the defunct lobby. The stink of human excrement filled the large room. Several of the men stepped inside.

"Hey, get out of there!" yelled Karen Farkis, one of the older members of the committee, pinching her nose. "You're gonna get mugged."

As they exited the wrecked building, they passed a hard-worn blonde in her twenties pushing a stroller inside. Two toddlers followed slowly.

"Where are you're going, young lady?" Mrs. Farkis asked, fearful for the petite woman's safety.

"Mind yer damn business!"

"Pardon?"

"Who the hells are ya anyways?" said the young woman with a thick local accent.

"Allow me to introduce us," Mrs. Farkis replied. "We're from East Tremont. We all live in houses that are in the path of the Cross Bronx and we wanted to find out how the planners dealt with homeowners further down the line."

"Oh, you're in for a real treat, sis," the blonde said, chuckling snidely.

"Were you evicted?" Paul asked.

"More like evicted *to* here. We were kicked out about six months ago from our home further east of here, but the Relocation Bureau couldn't find us no place so they stuck us in this dump. The owners had already gotten kicked out of here."

"They're actually letting you live here?" Paul asked in dismay.

"Not for nothing. We have to pay rent. And we have to be able to leave within seventy-two hours."

"You're actually paying rent?" gasped another East Tremonter, Pauline Kennedy.

"Oh yeah, we're paying more than we were in our old apartment. In fact, there's another family living up—"

"You mean the city evicted the original residents from this building and now they're housing other evictees here?" Paul couldn't believe what he was hearing.

"Yeah, there are about a hundred families who were moved here. Hell, some of them have been moved two or three times. They just kick them like old cans up the eviction route," the young mother explained, then barked at her two children who were playing among shiny shards of broken glass.

"Have you at least asked to get into one of the new public houses the city is building?" Paul asked.

"We were told to get in line. There's a six-year waiting list."

"What kind of apartments did the Tenant Relocation Bureau offer you?" asked Bill Lawrence from the committee.

She let out a sharp breath in order to keep from crying and said, "You wouldn't put a dog in those places. I ain't fooling. And you can see my family is living in this hell hole. I mean, I've come down in the morning with my kids and found a bum taking a shit in the corner, so believe me, we'd take damn near anything."

"It's criminal!"

"Of all the families they evicted," she went on, "I don't know a single one that got housed permanently through that bullshit Re-Eviction Bureau. They just want to get you the hell out."

The group was aghast. The fact that a government

agency in a democratic country could treat it's citizens this way was unthinkable.

Paul took five dollars from his wallet. Others pitched in, and without saying a word, they offered the money to the young mother, who quickly snatched it and moved along. They walked around the vicinity and spotted at least a dozen other empty apartment buildings. Windows had been broken, doors were hanging off their hinges, piping had been vandalized, yet people were still living in some of the apartments. As the group drove back to East Tremont, terrified of what lay ahead, not one of them spoke.

Soon, another flurry of mimeographed letters arrived offering all owners and renters the generous incentive of two hundred dollars if they moved within the next six months. The letter reminded everyone that they would all be evicted anyway, so resisting it would only cost them unnecessary legal expenses.

The committee countered with fliers posted on street corners:

> We Have to Hang Together
> or We'll Hang Alone.
> Don't Move an Inch,
> MCBE's Fighting for Your Home!

Yet within a month, as word spread about how the city had treated the people of Section One, a third of all residents along the projected route had grabbed the offer and moved out.

"The wires are dead," Uli said to the scorpion-spined boy, referring to the electrical cables dangling precariously from the rectangular hole, still connected to the fallen fuse box. "You don't need to worry about getting shocked."

Uli hoisted the kid's malformed body into the chiseled rectangular space. The boy was able slip his head inside, but his shoulders were slightly too broad. After pushing painfully for a minute, the kid climbed down.

"I got an idea," Uli said. He went out to the stock area and located a small can of machine grease. "Take off your clothes and rub this on."

The kid removed his filthy button-down shirt that hung over his midsection like a dress. Uli was distressed to see the severity of his deformity as the kid slathered his shoulders and midsection with grease.

With Uli's help, the boy slowly worked himself into the stone opening. It was almost like watching a small animal trying to free itself from some trap. Then, suddenly, the kid vanished completely.

"You okay?" Uli yelled into the rectangular window of darkness.

"Yeah!" the kid called back.

"Want a candle so you can see what's up there?"

"Yeah." A little hand reached out of the hole and Uli passed him a candle and some matches.

When the kid struck a match, Uli asked, "What do you see?"

"It goes straight up, then turns right, then . . ." The kid's voice grew muffled as he moved further inside. The faint glow disappeared.

"Is it wide enough for me to climb through if I can get in there?" Uli called out.

"Don't think so," he heard back.

"Does the tunnel continue?"

"It goes over there," the kid explained; he was obviously pointing at something.

"Can you climb *up* the tunnel?"

"I need something to hold onto. There are two thingys with holes in them."

"How high up can you see before it gets dark?"

"Can't tell."

"Well, what can you see?"

"Don't know." The kid's voice was clearer now.

"Can you see past my height?"

"Oh yeah, about three or four times your height. That's when it gets black and kinda narrow." If the boy's sense of scale was at all accurate, that distance was already higher than all the tunnels in the Convolution.

"All right, come on back out here."

When Uli helped the youth out of the hole, he asked, "How narrow does it get?"

"Don't know. I saw two lines of holes running up the back of something big."

"The elevator shaft?"

"I guess, but I don't know how I can climb up and hold the candle at the same time."

"How far apart are the holes?"

"Don't know, maybe . . ." The kid stretched his hands about two feet apart.

"And you can push your back against the wall?"

"Yeah."

"How big are the holes?"

"About . . ." The kid curled his fingers to roughly an inch in radius.

Uli collected a bucket of water and a bar of brown lye soap and let him scrub off all the grease. The boy started talking about his family again—he wanted to get resupplied and take Uli to look at his brother and mom, as promised.

All Uli could think about was the possibility of escaping from this underground tomb.

33

During the following weeks, Paul watched his neighbors walking around like zombies, their eyes downcast, their postures hunched. Some complained about being unable to sleep or eat. The elderly who hadn't yet abandoned their apartments stared sadly out their windows as though on a sinking ship. Those still motivated to put up a fight converted MCBE into the East Tremont Neighborhood Association. The elected head of ETNA, Lillian Edelstein, lived in one of the nicer buildings on the street with her sister's family and their mother. During one of their early meetings at the YMHA, they came up with a plan to enlist local politicians in their cause. Within a week, State Senator Jacob Gilbert, Assemblyman Walter Gladwin, and Congressman Isidore Dollinger had all vowed to help them.

Bronx Borough President James J. Lyons was the linchpin. He had a seat on the Board of Estimates, which needed to sign off on the project before Robert Moses could get final approval for his precious highway. Unfortunately, Lyons seemed to constantly be elsewhere. His secretary suggested that they confer with the Bronx Commissioner of Public Works, Arthur V. Sheridan, who Mr. Lyons said had much more clout. Sheridan, in turn, sent them to someone else, who referred them to Edward J. Flanagan, who ushered the little group into his office.

Flanagan launched right in: "I've been following your situation very closely." Pointing to a wall map of the Bronx, he indicated the proposed route. "I don't understand why they don't just run the expressway along Crotona Park North."

"Brilliant idea!" Lillian Edelstein replied, not mentioning that they were already lobbying for this alternative.

"It looks even shorter and more direct," added Mr. Lassiter, another ETNA member.

"We need an engineer to make an assessment and demonstrate that this route would be more efficient and cost-effective that the planned one," Flanagan concluded.

Paul went home that night feeling like they actually had a chance of winning this. The next day in class, he got another message asking him to please call home during his next break. When he did so, Lucretia answered the phone in hysterics. He couldn't tell if she was laughing or crying.

"What happened?" he shouted.

"We're staying! We're NOT moving!"

"We won?"

"No," she choked out, breathing deeply to regain control, "we got . . . a letter stating . . . that we're . . . we were . . . *miscondemmed*."

"What does that mean?"

"Due to a reappraisal, several houses on our block are going to be spared!"

"Which ones?"

"Abraham Hoff's home, and Lori and Bill's."

"How about all the others?"

"I think they're still getting evicted . . . but we're spared."

"That's great," he muttered, looking nervously around, "but . . ."

"Do you think your brother—"

"No way," he cut her off. "But I think we should keep this under wraps for a while."

Lucretia agreed.

Paul felt relief at first. Then, when the next period ended, he felt a gnawing guilt as he watched some of his students leaving his class, their families still facing eviction. Throughout the rest of the day he found it difficult to focus. He resolved that no matter what, he would remain in the fight with the rest of his neighbors.

Several days later, though, at the next ETNA meeting, May Kearne approached Paul and said, "We heard that your place is being spared."

"Yeah," he replied, embarrassed, "but I'm still with you guys."

"It might be better if you weren't," she said tersely.

"Huh?"

"Paul, we all know Robert Moses is your brother. Since you were being evicted, we didn't mind, but suddenly your house is being spared. Come on, we're not stupid."

"I haven't spoken to my brother in years! He doesn't even know I'm in the Bronx."

"Lucretia's a dear friend, and we're all grateful for your help so far, but there are people here who think you're spying for him, so it really would be safer for you guys if you just stopped coming to the meetings."

Paul felt like a quisling as she walked away. It occurred to him that Robert could have found out he was living there and given him and Lucretia this reprieve only to alienate him from the community. Lucretia was a proud member of the neighborhood and would feel profound shame for the situation he was putting her in. Although he didn't think she'd leave him, as Teresa had, he feared that this would drive a wedge between them. He therefore decided to keep quiet on the fact that he was asked to leave ETNA. That night, when Lucretia inquired about the meeting, he simply said it had gone well and didn't offer another word about it.

The following week, during the time when he'd usually attend the ETNA meeting, Paul took a walk around Bronx Park. The week after that, he checked out the Jewish section of Grand Concourse and the Italian part of Arthur Avenue. Subsequently, he headed south through the Negro areas of Morrisania.

As he returned home one night, he passed by a sign

that read, *Skacrowski's Scrapyard*. A pack of dogs behind a hurricane fence barked ferociously at him until a heavyset man operating a large machine looked over.

"Hey, Paul!" he heard. It was his wife's one-night lover, Leon.

"Howdy," Paul greeted, walking quickly by.

"My mom told me that you guys were spared from the wrecking ball."

"More or less," he responded, stopping in his tracks. Abandoning discretion, he said: "Lucetia doesn't know this yet, but I was asked to quit ETNA because they think my brother was behind our exemption."

"You should tell her," Leon suggested.

"I know, I just feel awful."

"You did nothing wrong."

"I know. But this is what happens when your brother is the devil."

Leon's mother was away, so he invited Paul inside for a beer. They ended up chatting for three hours. Paul found himself ranting about how much he hated his power-hungry brother.

"What can you do?" Leon asked, opening another beer.

"Give him what we used to call a Mexican send-off," Paul said.

"What's that?"

"Five sticks of dynamite wired to the ignition of his Packard."

Leon laughed. "Sounds like a plan."

"He's more powerful than the mayor or the governor because he can't be voted out. He single-handedly makes million-dollar decisions that take money from education and social services, not to mention buses and trains. And no one can stop him!"

"Maybe you *should* kill him," Leon said somewhat earnestly.

Paul laughed. "I've been saying this for the last twenty years and finally I've found someone who agrees with me."

"Listen," Leon said, "if you want to work off your anger without risking the electric chair, you should come out to Ebbets Field with me. I got two tickets to the game this week and things are just beginning to heat up."

"Sorry, but I'm a dyed-in-the-wool Yankees fan."

"Yankees, spankies. Have you ever seen Pee Wee Reese or Jackie Robinson at bat?"

"Too bad the Giants keep kicking their asses . . ."

"Hey, with Gil Hodges in the infield, Duke Snider out in center, Roy Campanella behind the plate, and Don Newcombe on the pitcher's mound—"

"They still can't beat the Yankees."

"Give them time, they're gonna get there. They won the pennant five times since '41."

"Yeah, but they were beaten by the Yankees each time."

"Wait till next year," Leon said. "Just wait."

As Paul walked home, he felt calm. Just a few beers and a little ventilation and he was so much stronger. When Lucretia asked about the meeting, he sat her down and said he had something important to share, then relayed his conversation with May Kearne.

"Screw them," she said, causing Paul to burst out laughing.

He returned to Leon's place a few days later with a cold six-pack of beer. Once again, the two talked into the night. Paul went on about why his brother deserved to die, and Leon went on about the Brooklyn Dodgers.

After the scorpion boy had scrubbed the grease off, Uli gave him some Spam and crackers and had him draw a diagram of the fuse-box tunnel. As best as Uli could speculate, thousands of pounds of concrete had been poured down the elevator shaft, but had apparently solidified before it could ooze around the back of the tracking, thus creating this narrow passage that went straight up.

"Did you see any light coming from above?"

"No, why?"

"It might go all the way up to the surface."

The kid looked perplexed. After a while, he rolled onto his back and dozed off. When he woke again, roughly two hours later, Uli was waiting with some gear he had assembled.

"I was thinking . . ." Uli began, holding up an old construction helmet, a small lantern, and some wire. "If I can attach this lantern to this helmet and we can strap it around your chin, you can use these to climb up that tracking . . ." He indicated two large hooks with wooden handles.

"You said you were going to come and look at my sickers first."

"Well, that's true, but you just told me the entrance is narrow, didn't you?"

"Yes, but . . . you said you'd help my sickers first!"

"Fine," Uli replied, surprised by the kid's stubbornness. "Let's get going."

34

O ver the ensuing months, Paul watched in anguish as the ETNA members fought desperately to save their homes. Neighbors in the group continued saying hi to Paul and Lucretia, but they rarely mentioned any progress in their efforts.

When Paul would see them handing out fliers on East Tremont, he had the urge to remind them that the only real power was money. He knew that if just one of them sacrificed their single-family home and sold it for ten grand, a donation like that to Lyons's reelection fund might make all the difference.

"Paying Murder Inc. five grand to make your brother disappear could also make a difference," Leon suggested.

One day upon opening the New York Post, Paul found ETNA's entire proposal laid out over a couple of pages. An unnamed engineer had performed a feasibility study demonstrating that by swinging the highway two blocks south, 159 buildings housing more than 1,500 apartments could be saved. It would also save the city millions of dollars. The next day's paper quoted Bronx Borough President James Lyons as stating that the proposal seemed worthy of consideration. Robert Moses countered by telling the press that the only reason Lyons was sticking his nose into this was because it was an election year.

A six-member Board of Estimates meeting scheduled for the following month was going to cast the first of a series of votes on the highway. At that meeting, which would probably be presided over by the mayor, Lyons had a key vote.

"It's a shame we have this stooge Impellitteri in City Hall instead of La Guardia," Paul remarked to Lucretia.

"He probably steals money just like his predecessor," she said. The previous year, the O'Dwyer police corruption scandal had been smeared over the papers and had compelled the former mayor to resign in disgrace.

"At least La Guardia would have told Robert to move the frigging route. I'm just hoping Lyons has a backbone."

As the Board of Estimates meeting approached, Paul, who had excellent attendance at school, took one of his sick days. He watched as roughly two hundred people, mainly housewives, lined into four chartered buses on East Tremont Avenue and headed down to City Hall. In deference to the general distrust that many of them had toward him, he walked east and caught the Third Avenue El. At the Municipal Building at City Hall, he stayed in the back of the large hearing room while the wives filed in and sat in the front rows.

Five minutes after the board members, including James Lyons, entered the chamber, Robert Moses arrived, leading the mayor. Mr. Robert pointed to the chair next to his own as though Impellitteri were one of his flunkies. Soon the room was packed. Scattered throughout were members of the press.

Mayor Impellitteri introduced himself and, rapping a small gavel, called for order. "We will be hearing from everyone regarding Section Two of the Cross Bronx Expressway through East Tremont, and we'll discuss an alternate route proposed by the East Tremont Neighborhood Association, then we will put the matter to a preliminary vote. Everyone testifying will get one minute to talk."

The housewives of East Tremont got to speak first. One by one, in an order orchestrated by Lillian Edelstein, they rose to the mic. Each stated how long she had lived happily in their little Bronx community. They explained how the construction of the expressway would force them to move, tearing apart not just their lives, but the whole community. As they testified, Paul noticed the members of the board growing slowly disinterested. Some scribbled notes. Others whispered to their aides. One was clearly reading a newspaper. He watched as his brother chatted softly with the mayor; at one point the two men actually chuckled as if sharing a dirty joke. When a housewife went beyond her one minute, a court clerk would drop his little hammer and mumble, "Time."

After roughly forty-five minutes, Lillian Edelstein gave a summary statement: "Mr. Mayor, Borough President Lyons, Construction Consultant Moses, and members of this esteemed board, there is simply no need for any of this grief since we have an alternate route that will save the taxpayers millions of dollars." To the mayor, she politely presented a coil of large pages, the formal blueprints that had been carefully drawn by a sympathetic engineer. Without removing the rubber band, the mayor handed them off to some assistant.

"Mr. Moses," the mayor said next, "would you care to respond before this board votes?"

Robert Moses stood before the mic, smiled pleasantly to all, then spoke: "We put a great deal of thought and effort into the planning of this expressway, weighing the interests of both this neighborhood and the city as a whole. My team of engineers selected the best possible route. They didn't do this for the concerns of a few, but rather for *all* New Yorkers, present and future. Let me add that I take no pleasure in asking anyone to move and that we are all grateful for your sacrifice."

The more vocal members of ETNA started booing, followed by others. The mayor's gavel repeatedly hit the table as he called, "Order! Order!"

"We were told that we would be given a fair hearing!" Lillian Edelstein shouted.

"And so you shall. Mr. Moses's opinion is not entirely

the opinion of this board," the mayor replied. He then mumbled something to a skinny, bald man who turned out to be a city engineer. He took the ETNA blueprints to a nearby table and inspected them closely. All eyes were on the engineer five minutes later when he walked over and started whispering something to Borough President Lyons. An exchange between the two lasted a few minutes before Mr. Robert tiredly rose to his feet and walked over to Lyons's seat. He bent down and whispered something in the politician's ear that couldn't have been more than a word or two, then returned to his seat. Several more minutes passed before Lyons leaned forward and muttered into the mic, "In light of what I've just heard, I'm going to have to support Mr. Moses's route."

"You've betrayed us!" Lillian Edelstein called out. The housewives began frantically talking back and forth.

"There will be silence in the chamber!" the mayor spoke up.

"Traitor!" someone yelled.

"I said you'd get your day in court, and this is it!" Lyons shouted at Edelstein. "There are many factors that—"

"Betrayal!" she shot back.

"You owe Mr. Lyons an apology," Impellitteri stated. Moses started snickering at the women.

After more shouts of recrimination, the mayor tapped his gavel and a group of court officers entered. The room soon slipped into silence.

"We will now put this matter to a vote," Impellitteri said. "All in favor of the proposed route, please raise your hand." Three arms rose. "All opposed." The other three hands went up. It was a deadlock, the resolution would have to go to a larger vote in several weeks. But everyone knew that this had been the only real chance to stop the expressway.

Robert Moses, the mayor, Lyons, and other members of the board quickly exited through a side door as the housewives of East Tremont glared and booed at them.

"Your brother beat us! Happy, smart guy?" one of the East Tremont wives snapped at Paul, who was sitting solemnly in the back.

He looked down.

"What do you mean *brother*?" another housewife asked. "He's my boy's teacher."

"Gilda told me: Paul is Robert Moses's *older* brother."

"Mr. Moses, is this true?"

As Paul rose silently and tried to exit the packed meeting hall, he heard others shouting:

"Yer whole family should drop dead!"

"Stay outta da Bronx, you bastid!"

"Give him a break, he lives in East Tremont too!" someone called out in his defense.

"Yeah, and they spared his house," another responded. "Big surprise!"

When he finally got out of the Municipal Building and pushed through the crowd out front, Paul was filled with rage. He walked aimlessly for a while, his heart pounding in his chest. After half an hour he looked up to find himself standing in front of the house on lower Bowery, number 168, the principal of which still technically belonged to him. He started beating on the stone walls of the old building until his knuckles bled.

Uli followed the legless scorpion kid as he gracefully angled up the long corridor and out through the barren zone that led to the Mkultra. Forty-five minutes later, they reached the first groups of desks that the kid seemed to move right through while Uli stumbled around them. When they came to a spot with a small crack in the ceiling, the kid scurried up along a huge wooden pillar. Uli was unable to squeeze through, so the two had to walk another twenty minutes to a larger hole. Uli began wondering if the boy's body was defective at all, or if it had merely adapted to this perverse new landscape.

After traveling a distance on this upper level, they slipped back down to a lower floor, then after yet another stretch, the kid led him back up a level once more. Eventually, Uli lost track of where they were.

"Can't we just stay on a single story?" he finally asked, tired of climbing.

"Some floors are blocked and some sections are real dangerous."

"How are they dangerous?"

"They either do things to your middles or they're the people who don't like eating the rats or rations no more."

At some point, Uli commented on the absence of rodents.

"They don't come this far down, but you're lucky."

"Why's that?"

"Cause when things first started out, there were a bunch of other animals a lot more dangerous—monkeys and cats and other stuff—but people killed them all off."

Uli noticed occasional spaces on walls where signs had evidently been removed. Along the wooden floors, he also observed more freshly painted phosphorescent lines leading into the distance, where he could make out far-off figures that seemed to be aimlessly following them. Uli briefly considered that the futile circles the captives were traversing at least distracted them from their impending starvation. Though he spotted a few rotting corpses as they continued, the roaming zombies soon became sparse and then nonexistent. Soon, too, the desks stopped. Then even partition walls disappeared so that there was only open space and concrete pillars. Swinging forward with his hands, the boy never seemed to tire.

At a leaky hole in the ceiling next to a steel column, the scorpion kid climbed through to yet another upper floor. Five minutes later, when Uli finally flopped up onto the next level, completely winded, he immediately smelled the harsh aromas of fire and death.

He followed the kid for another twenty minutes until he began tripping over something hard and crunchy on the floor. He flicked on his dimming flashlight and saw that this area, which looked like it had once been a massive filing room, was covered with carbonized bones and burnt body parts. They were spread between rows and rows of empty filing cabinets stretching for dozens of yards at three-foot intervals. Reaching down, Uli realized that fueling this improvised crematorium were the contents of the filing cabinets. *Where does the smoke go? And for that matter, where does the oxygen down here come from?* There had to be circulation vents somewhere, but Uli hadn't seen a single one.

They climbed across the various filing cabinets until they reached a long wall marking the end of the floor. The kid seemed to know the entire place inside out. Arriving at a spot that appeared completely random to Uli, the boy slipped up the side of the wall and squeezed past a panel of wood in the ceiling. Uli pulled a burnt-out filing cabinet over and used it as a stool to climb through the ceiling and into an abandoned tunnel that might have once been an air vent.

The kid struck a match and lit a candle, revealing that his father had created a secret nook here for his sad family. A skinny middle-aged woman, deathly pale and feverishly thin, was staring past Uli, sitting in her own waste.

"Hello," Uli said, to no response. Something was moving under her filthy shirt. To his astonishment, he saw a small baby's head wiggling out—it was suckling on her flaccid breast.

"That's my brother," the scorpion boy said. "I call him Baby."

"I don't understand," Uli thought aloud. "The entire Rescue City is suffering from some kind of infertility plague—but here in this sealed dungeon babies are being born?"

Instead of responding, the scorpion kid reached into his mother's shirt and pulled his brother out. Uli was horrified to see that the body seemed to be little more than a long tail resembling a pink tadpole, but with little flapper arms. It couldn't be more than a few months old.

Over the course of the next hour, Uli helped the kid clean them both off as best they could and wash down the floor of the little nook.

The malformed baby indeed felt feverish. Uli inspected the red dots along his tubular body but was confident it was only a rash, not chicken pox.

"What should we do?" the kid asked.

"Let's get them back to the storage depot. The water and air are better. They'll recover more quickly."

Uli carried the skinny salamander baby while the kid put a rope around his mother's wrist and tied the other end to his own. Slowly they made their way back into the Sticks. Because it was no longer possible to move up and down through the various levels, they chanced it and stayed on the first floor—the Lethe level—moving cautiously around the many desks and occasional decomposed bodies.

When they reached an area with desks piled so haphazardly that it became difficult to traverse, the kid asked Uli for help moving his mother.

"Maybe I can give you a hand," they both heard.

The dark outline of a man approached and lifted the mother in the air, so that Uli was able to grab her arms and together they moved her over the desks.

"Now, maybe you can help *me*," the man suggested. He was fully dressed in clean clothes. His shaved head and handsome face were covered with light stubble—a new arrival.

"How?" Uli asked, holding his ground, ready for a fight.

"When you passed through here earlier, I thought I heard the kid say you guys know a way out."

"What we found is little more than a hunch."

184 ❦ Arthur Nersesian

"A hunch is more than I got." The man had a rigid charm. As Uli conversed with him, the boy and his family lagged slowly behind. "You have a clarity of mind that's rare down here," the guy said to Uli, attempting to make small talk. "May I ask what you were in your life?"

"I was never affiliated with either gang in Rescue City, if that's what you mean." He wanted the man to go away, but since he looked fairly strong and wasn't being violent, Uli figured he'd let him ramble on until he just grew tired and left.

"Me neither."

"You seem like a nice guy," Uli said, "but I've learned not to trust anyone down here, and I'd advise the same of you."

"Where are my manners?" the guy asked, extending his hand. "I'm Tim Mack."

"Paul," Uli responded, and shook the man's hand.

"By the look of your beard, it appears you haven't been here very long either," Tim said.

"Actually, I've been here for a while. I just cut it every few weeks," Uli replied, not wanting to reveal anything about himself.

"Are you worried about this mental degeneration that seems to have afflicted most people here?"

"It seems to miss some of us, thank God," Uli said. Glancing around, he suddenly realized he was alone with the nutcase. "Hey, kid!" he shouted, but there was no response.

Dashing back into the darkness with Tim following close behind, Uli discovered that the kid and his family were nowhere in sight. Without the scorpion boy, there was no chance of escaping.

"You!" Uli knocked the bristly man to the ground and jumped on him. "Where are they?"

"What are you talking about?"

"You distracted me while someone grabbed them!"

"I swear to God I didn't."

Leaping to his feet, Uli left the man on the ground and rushed back in the direction from which they had come. After searching through the twinkling darkness, he eventually found the mother's tattered shirt on the ground. His flashlight illuminated distinct tracks from what appeared to be at least four people. They were clearly dragging something. Unswept by wind and not muddled by other creatures, the tracks were easy to follow over the filthy wooden floor. At one point they vanished, and Uli looked up to find a hole in the ceiling. He was able to climb up to the next level where the tracks resumed. He followed them until he heard sounds in the distance. As he closed in, he saw there were five large men—a small hunting party. One oaf was half-dragging, half-leading the naked mother behind them. Over another man's shoulder was the salamander baby who was making slight barking sounds, seemingly in pain.

"I'm hungry now!" said the man holding the mother's rope.

"We got to cook them first," advised a short, obese troll-like man who appeared to head the expedition. As Uli drew closer, he could see the scorpion kid hog-tied upside down and strapped to the troll's back. He seemed to be unconscious.

Noticing a four-foot section of pipe sticking out from the ceiling, Uli pulled a desk over, leapt up, and yanked it loose. He shadowed them for another ten minutes until they came to a large rupture in the floor. Uli decided this was his best chance. The three biggest men went down first, then the mother and kids were lowered into the hole by two other hunters. Uli raced forward and walloped one across the head, cracking his skull.

"They got Slammer!" shouted the second man before Uli attacked him with the pipe.

The three large men on the lower level grabbed their fresh meat and hustled off. Jumping into the hole, Uli glimpsed a bonfire across the vast room—this was their camp. He watched as the three remaining captors, apparently believing the attack was coming from a larger group, began scurrying through the darkness. Uli sprinted after them and slammed his pipe over the lead troll's skull, but then the other two immediately realized Uli was all alone. One man knocked him down. Bigger and stronger than Uli, they started punching him. A few other tribe members lumbered over from the bonfire and joined the fight. They began kicking him from all directions. One man grabbed his arm and twisted it behind his back.

"I want his other arm!" one of them bellowed.

Suddenly, a gun shot rang out; then a second.

"Shit, I got hit!" one troll gasped.

The group immediately scattered, leaving Uli with the beleaguered family. Tim emerged from the darkness holding a pistol.

"How many more bullets do you have?" Uli asked, panting.

"Three, maybe. Why?"

"Cause they'll probably come back."

Tim wanted to grab the little family and run, so Uli untied the unconscious kid and gently smacked him until he came to.

"We're lost and they're coming after us. Which way should we go?"

The kid glanced across the large floor and mumbled the quickest route back to the Sticks. After twenty minutes of running without any sign of being followed, they began to calm down.

"I'm sorry," the kid said to Uli. "They grabbed us from behind. I should've stayed with you."

"It worked out okay," Uli said. "We now have a new member of our little group."

They eventually reached the Sticks and headed down the tunnels into the storage facility. Behind the mountain of crates, hidden from clear view, they fashioned a relatively comfortable bedding area for the ill mother and her baby. Tim, who hadn't eaten since leaving the catch basin, chewed down a box of stale crackers. Uli bathed the salamander child in a tub of cool water to bring down his fever. Then he applied some topical creams for the rash and gave him both antibiotics and vitamins. He instructed the scorpion kid to keep giving his brother and mother water—they appeared severely dehydrated.

35

As Tim slept and the kid tended to his family, Uli returned to the utility closet. Digging his chisel into the hard stone, his mind drifted back to Paul and Lucretia. They tried to regain a semblance of a normal life, but their community was being torn apart piece by piece. Neighbors weeped openly in the streets. They heard other couples fighting in their apartments about where they would go after eviction.

Miss Dombrowski and the old folks stopped sitting out front on warm nights. The few neighbors who still spoke to Lucretia mentioned having trouble sleeping. It was as if the people in East Tremont were suffering the effects of a protracted battle that was bypassing the rest of the city.

On his way to work one day, Paul saw a sign taped to the Kearnes' door. In big red letters it announced, *If you do not vacate within 5 days, legal action will be taken.* When he looked through the windows, he realized the place was vacant. All their furniture was missing. The couple who had been so helpful in getting Paul his job had moved on without a word. Paul learned from a remaining neighbor that James Kearne had transferred to another school out in Jackson Heights, Queens. Lucretia burst into tears when she learned that May, her dear friend of many years, had left without even saying goodbye. The entire block, which used to be filled with families and children playing in the streets, was soon empty.

On January 1, 1954, New York City took title of the last scattered parcels of real estate in Section Two of the expressway. Despite this, some of the poorer and older fami-

lies stubbornly hung on, living illegally. Increasingly ter-
rifying edicts from the city were taped to doors and lamp-
posts. More threats of people losing their possessions or
being thrown into the street followed. The elderly were the
last to go. Many were foreigners—widows and widowers
who had fled countries ruled by emperors and czars. They
were just trying to wait out their remaining time. But one
by one, before the city marshal arrived, they too seemed to
just vanish.

Through one of her old friends, Lucretia learned about
the plight of a family who had lived directly across the
street all her life. The Orecklins had a disabled child and
owned a nice single-family home that the father, Cecil, had
fastidiously maintained over the years. They'd had their
place appraised a few years earlier at twenty thousand dollars. Robert Moses's office offered them eleven thousand.
When Cecil argued that they were dramatically under-
valuing his property—something any outside land assessor
could verify—he was told that this was a one-time offer,
take it or leave it. Without any alternative, the Orecklins
had absorbed the loss and moved away.

While the little family recuperated, Uli tried to explain the
Sticks to Tim, cautioning him about the insane miners below who had already killed one of his compatriots. Then
he showed Tim the hole in the utility closet. Eager to get
out, the stubble-headed man made it his personal mission
to hammer through the narrow stone walls, almost never
leaving the little closet. After a few days, when the salamander baby's red dots started clearing up and the mother
seemed to be improving as well, Uli softly asked the scorpion kid if he was ready for his climb.

"I don't want to leave them alone yet."

In preparation for the kid's ascent, Uli weaved a small
body harness out of ropes, like a window washer's safety
belt that the boy could tie around his narrow waist and

broad shoulders. To protect against a fall, he'd be able to hook the sides into the eyes of the metal track running up the elevator shaft. Uli also wired the lantern he had scavenged to the top of the helmet. He calculated that if the candles weren't tipped over, they'd each last roughly an hour while wax drained safely out the back.

Hunting through the storage depot, he located a bag for holding C-rations and three water bottles that could all be strapped to the kid's back. This would give the boy enough supplies for roughly two to three days. He also found several large balls of twine that he could tie to the youth in order to mark the height of his climb.

"I know you don't want to leave yet, but I thought maybe we could do a bit of preparation."

None of it looked comfortable, but it all fit. The kid let out a deep sigh, clearly regretting ever having agreed to this. Uli knew he was going to have to convince the kid of the importance of the climb, but before Uli could start in on him, the boy said he really needed to be left alone with his family. Uli gave him the space, then resumed helping Tim in the closet.

While they worked, Tim kept steering the conversation to his life in Rescue City. "The place has turned into open warfare; I figured I'd have a better chance of survival if I tried to get out. I just want to put it all behind me."

"Put *what* behind you?"

"First the bombing of Crapper headquarters, then the retaliation killings of a bunch of Pigger officials. And finally the brutal slaying of those two beautiful P.P. workers."

Uli remained silent and looked down at his feet.

"I know that a lot of people in Rescue City have done a lot of awful things, which is why they were sent there," Tim said, "but I was never a political type."

"Someone told me about the Crapper headquarters being blown up and some woman mayor getting elected," Uli said, playing dumb in an attempt to extract some details about the latest developments. "But I haven't heard much else."

"Things have gotten a lot worse."

"Worse how?"

"Somebody apparently blew up the sandbags holding the sewage back from Manhattan. The city's now flooded with shit."

Uli shook his head in despair. All hope that the place would become a more civilized society once the Crappers took over was gone.

36

In 1955, just as Leon had repeatedly vowed, it happened again: The Brooklyn Dodgers won the National League pennant. The Subway Series kicked off in Yankee Stadium and, just as most people had predicted, the Dodgers duly lost the first two games. Then, surprising everyone, they won the next two at Ebbets Field in Brooklyn. Back in the Bronx, the Dodgers lost their third game, but they won the next—so it was an even three to three. It all came down to the tiebreaker, to be played on the Yankees' home field. Paul and Leon watched the game on a small RCA set. With each hit, Leon would jump in the air and his dogs would bark. But with each progressive inning, Paul kept thinking, *You're only setting yourself up for a big fall.* Soon, though, it was the bottom of the ninth and somehow the Dodgers were still in the lead. Despite his declared loyalty to the Yankees, Paul found himself rooting for their crosstown rival. When the game ended with a Brooklyn victory, both men jumped in the air and hugged like school boys, then they finished off all the remaining beer and passed out. Around 1 in the morning, Paul woke up, turned off the TV, and drunkenly walked the long stretch of empty blocks back home. The entire time, he kept asking himself, "Dodgers won the World Series?" It sounded so unbelievable.

"Look, I'm not forcing you to do anything you don't want to do," Uli began his talk to the scorpion kid while Tim was sleeping. "So if you don't want to do this, you and your family can leave and I'll somehow figure it out myself. But if you help us and we escape, I promise that the first thing we'll do is get your mom and brother to a doctor. And I'll do everything I can to try to find your dad."

"So what exactly should I do once I'm up there?" the kid asked testily.

"I'm going to tie some twine to your waist. I want you to climb as far as you can up that shaft so I'll know how high it goes. And I want you to use the string to measure the narrowest parts."

"And then I'm done?"

"After you come out and we review what you saw, you're all done."

"Okay."

"But first I want you to train a little cause this is going to be tough."

"Train for what?"

"Climbing and lighting candles in total darkness and other stuff."

"How and where?"

"Well, I want you to practice using these big hooks, but the only thing to climb around here is the tower of desks in the silo. We have to be very quiet cause we don't want to alert any of the crazy miners."

When they went to the silo, Uli noticed fresh blood splattered around. Boxes had been knocked down and metal rods caked with blood suggested there had been a major struggle. After a brief search, Uli locate two bodies: The guy he called Dave and an elderly miner appeared to have been strangled to death. There was no sign of any other miners in the vicinity.

Using the open area as a training zone, Uli instructed the boy on how to climb the desk tower.

"I don't need these," the kid responded. He set all the equipment aside and zipped right up the pile of desks like a chimpanzee. "How's this?"

"You've got to use that rope belt and clip into each new perforation as a safety precaution, in case you fall."

"What's a perfation?"

"The metal holes in the sides of the tracking."

"But there are no holes in these desks."

"Well, pretend there are."

"I've been thinking," the kid said after he completed his first ascent up the tower while clipping his belt into imaginary holes. "I'd like something else."

"What?"

"I want my mom and brother."

"They're already here."

"I need them up in that hole with me."

"You mean in the utility closet?"

"Yeah. They're both small and they can fit in there. It has this long flat ledge inside where they can wait."

"But they're still sick. Why would you need them in there?"

"They'd be safe and I could watch them."

"I'll keep an eye on them for you."

"If you want me to do this, then they have to stay with me. We almost got killed when I took them out of our home."

Nodding his head, Uli reluctantly agreed. He just wanted this to be over with. He spent many hours over the next few days drilling the kid on the fine points of climbing elevator shafts.

"Since you'll have a candle attached to your head, you'll need to keep your head tilted back so you don't spill hot wax on yourself."

"You sure all this needs to be done?" the kid asked, covered in sweat.

"The more prepared you are, the better your chances of surviving and escaping," Uli said for the third time that day.

After a final round of training, Uli deemed the kid modestly prepared for the challenge.

"Shouldn't I come down when I'm halfway done with the food and stuff?"

"No, cause it will be a lot easier to come down than it will be to get back up."

Uli waited until Tim took a nap before launching the kid on his great quest. The work of the newcomer had made a difference, as the kid didn't require any lubrication to enter this time. Uli lifted the mother and brother through, then passed along the various supplies.

"Listen," Uli warned up to him, "don't try anything heroic. If something looks scary, just get out. I'm not expecting you to rescue us. All you're doing is what we call reconnaissance. You're just checking out the landscape, then you'll come back here and we'll work out an escape plan together."

"Okay."

"And if need be, I can reach in and hand your mom and brother food and water. You don't have to come down for them, understand?"

"Thanks."

"Take care of yourself, pal," Uli said. Reaching into the tight space, he shook the nameless kid's hand and listened to him scamper up and away.

Over the ensuing hours, Uli watched the jerky ball of twine as if it were a clock and found himself feeling increasingly excited as it dwindled ever thinner. When the three hundred feet of twine was about to run out, Uli attached a second ball of twine to its end.

Uli wondered what he was going to do next. Even if the kid returned to say that he had climbed right up to the desert floor, Uli knew he couldn't convince any of these homicidal miners or memory-challenged inmates to collaborate on an actual escape plan.

Two loud gunshots snapped Uli from his thoughts. He raced out of the closet to find a pair of miners beating Tim, who was desperately trying to fight back. The small-caliber bullets Tim had pumped into them had slowed the men down but apparently missed their vital organs. Uli jumped up and kicked one of the guys in the neck. The other dashed down into the service corridor with blood dripping from his chest.

"I can't believe it," Tim whimpered. Blood trickled from his ears; his skull appeared to be fractured.

"I told you the miners were insane," Uli said.

"Not them . . . *you!*" he said, grimacing. "*You* killed her . . . and I went through all this . . . just to . . . to get you . . ."

"What?"

"And you . . . got *me.*"

"What do you mean?"

"Oh dear . . . I didn't mean to hit the bags . . . but they wouldn't give me the drug unless—"

"There's the fucker!" A large miner wielding a rod suddenly came barreling out of an overhead cave.

Uli dashed into the dark entrance of the Convolution. Crawling down into the ever-narrowing tunnel, he knocked into one of their steel digging rods, which he grabbed as a weapon.

He squirmed backwards into a small tunnel that would only allow one man at a time. There he was able to hold the miners at bay.

"Just wait him out," one of the men said. Two hours later, as Uli began wondering how long this would last, a massive vibration rocked the whole area.

"Earthquake!"

"You pissed Xolotl off and now we're all fucked!" a miner shouted down at him. The rest of the miners slithered back up the tunnel toward the Mkultra. Without thinking, Uli wiggled out of the cave and followed in the same direction, hurrying toward the utility closet. In the dimming candle light, he spotted something billowing out of the little doorway. It wasn't until he actually touched it that he realized it was coarse hot sand, different from the rest of the dirt he had seen underground. He screamed for the little family to hang on as he frantically started digging the room out. He found a long flat board and used it as a shovel, only to see more sand pouring down through the rectangular hole. An hour later, Uli admitted to himself that there was no chance the mother or salamander baby could still be alive.

It took a whole day of pushing the sand deeper into the storage area before it stopped cascading down into the little utility closet. When Uli was finally able to reach up into the rectangular hole, he felt around and managed to grab the mother's foot. He pulled her out first, and then her sad salamander baby. Both were dead, as he expected.

Soon, though, he located some cutting tools and continued expanding the sides of the rectangular hole. Before long Uli was able to slide into the first chamber after slathering himself in grease. Immediately he realized that the kid had lied. Once he squeezed up past the narrow entrance, the shaft was much wider than he had been led to believe. Uli smiled. At his tender age, the kid had deliberately misled Uli so that he would have exclusive control of this possible escape route. That was why he had wanted his family in there. The bad news was that inside the corridor, sand was packed as tight as a brick. Uli tied a rag over his mouth and scooped sand down into the utility closet until it was full. Then he squirmed back out and hauled the fresh mounds of sand into the storage area.

After steering and pushing the sand down and out for another day, Uli crawled up through the corridor until he found the straight vertical shaft. Here, he discovered that the kid had lied yet again. There was clearly enough space for him to climb up. But Uli couldn't figure out what he was actually seeing. Staring up hundreds of yards of shaft, he made out what appeared to be a flickering ceiling of flame. It was as though he had dug all the way to the sun. *If I try climbing up there, I'll be burnt to a crisp.* Observing the bluish fire for about twenty minutes, he considered abandoning this project and heading back to the catch basin.

At that moment he was startled by a distant voice yelling down to him. *"Help me, Uli!"* It sounded like his sister, Karen.

Peering up the narrow chute, he wasn't able to discern anything through the curling flames. "How'd you get up there?" he called to the voice.

"Help me! I'm stuck!" Uli heard, and he knew he had to get up there as quickly as possible.

37

"The circumcision"—as his neighbor Robert had called it—was a longitudinal line, a no-man's-land running several blocks wide across the middle of the Bronx. This barren stretch of the borough held the artifacts of a once thriving community. Everyone in East Tremont waited anxiously to see what kind of apocalypse would devastate the southern end of their beloved neighborhood. Weeks and months passed—nothing.

Living right on the boundary, Paul and Lucretia would hear windows being broken at night. People, probably kids, were rooting through the empty houses like vengeful ghosts. Months passed without so much as a single building being demolished. When the remaining members of ETNA who hadn't been evicted sent a letter to Robert Moses's office asking if the abandoned area could be either guarded or fenced off, they were duly ignored.

One morning in 1956, without any warning, a massive wrecking ball started slamming into the sides of one of the apartment buildings down the block. Soon a small cloud of dust covered the area. A gang of workmen besieged the place with all the annoyance of an occupying force. Jackhammers pounded constantly. For the next six months or so, the sound of demolition and the smell of brick and concrete dust filled the air. The work began at 8 a.m. sharp and sometimes continued until 7 at night. Squads of dumptrucks and bulldozers carted off the piles of stones and rubbish. With them came the battalion of surly workmen holding red flags at major intersections. It was as if a wall had partitioned the neighborhood in two. They would block the pedestrian and vehicular traffic, sometimes for hours, not allowing people to cross different sections of the sprawling construction site.

Paul and others felt a strange relief as the last homes were leveled and the rubble was trucked away. But then the dynamiting began. It turned out that the expressway was to be sunken into the earth and the bedrock had to be made consistent. For the remainder of the year, the area residents would hear periodic booms followed a few seconds later by a trembling of the earth. The mini-quakes took their toll on building foundations, resulting in an appearance of fine cracks along everyone's walls and ceilings. Gradually those cracks grew bigger.

It was in this period that Paul and his wife first heard the little coughs coming from Bea's room upstairs. When Lucretia dashed in that first time, she found the child struggling to breathe. Lucretia and others in the area began sealing their windows and ventilation ducts at night, but a fresh skin of dust was always there at the end of every day.

After thirty years, even Abe Hoff moved, leaving the Moses family as the only people still living on their side of the block. One by one, many of the little stores along East Tremont Avenue—the social hub of the neighborhood— started going out of business.

Uli climbed back down out of the rectangular hole and headed into the Mkultra where he collected six metal wastepaper baskets. He stomped them flat, then molded them around his limbs, back, and head. He gathered as many bottles of water as he could find and shoved them up into the rectangular hole with the six crushed metal baskets. After carefully angling himself back up through the tight space, he tied the metal into a tight bundle and tethered it and the bottles to his belt loops.

It was a monstrous climb. Uli heaved himself roughly a

foot at a time, resting every couple of hours. At one point, secured by ropes hooked to the metal track, he stopped altogether to take a long nap. When he awoke, he called out for Karen but got not reply.

Uli knew after some unmeasured length of time that he was getting close to the top because he began to feel the heat from the strange flames above him. In one small nook near the top of the shaft, he noticed a blackened indentation like a relief sculpted into the concrete wall. His stomach churned and bile rose to his throat. The crisp contours of a face above the jaw were all that was left of what Uli presumed to be the poor scorpion kid. In the bottom of his pocket, Uli found the two mercury dimes he had snatched awhile ago from a desk drawer. He placed them in the tiny sockets where the eyes had once been—the only honor he could pay to the deformed youth.

After another half hour of climbing toward the ceiling of flames, one mystery was solved. A large pipe carrying propane, methane, or some other flammable gas that ran above this entire chamber—buried roughly ten feet below the desert floor—had exploded. Beyond the raging torch rising from the broken pipe, Uli could make out a sliver of blue sky—freedom.

It was a sunny day on the planet earth. Uli wondered how the kid could have ruptured the thick pipe, but it only took a moment to realize that this wasn't what had happened. There must have been a gas leak. The candle affixed to the top of the kid's helmet must have touched off a dense cloud of gas, bursting an opening through the tons of sand sealing the top of the deep elevator shaft.

38

Crime rates in East Tremont exploded. People who used to leave their doors open suddenly found themselves getting burglarized. Those who would spend their summer nights sleeping out front on their porches to catch the cool air were awakened by muggers. Morrisania, near where Leon lived, went from being a modestly safe area to altogether treacherous. Though Leon was a hulking brute, his tiny mother seemed to be a lightning rod for criminals. Usually they just grabbed her purse and ran. She only kept a few bucks on her anyway. One afternoon, though, she had just withdrawn a hundred dollars from the bank and was walking along the street with her purse pressed to her chest. When some teenage punk tried to grab it, she held on with both hands. It became apparent that she wasn't letting go, so the mugger started slugging her. She finally released the purse when she fell, but the furious juvenile continued beating and kicking her. She made it to the hospital, but died two days later from internal hemorrhaging. For Leon—as Paul soon saw—his mother had been his primary companion.

Nice houses once worth a pretty penny were soon sitting empty in a buyer's market. Apartments that had attracted lines of potential tenants sat unoccupied as landlords lowered rents even further. Where Crotona Park had once been the southern border of a good neighborhood, the dividing line moved all the way up to East Tremont Avenue.

Paul felt there was a small dose of hysteria around the issue, but nonetheless took the precaution of installing stronger locks on their doors. Sure, the area had taken a hit and people had left in a panic, but he believed things were slowly stabilizing. A few of the old timers, still committed to their faith that the neighborhood would be okay, were holding the line, believing that this acute depression would eventually reverse. It was just a matter of time. A silver lining to all this was that as a wave of new immigrants moved into the communities, older neighbors who had once shunned the Moses family were now warming back up to them. People were again saying hi.

Over the dinner table that Easter, Paul pointed out how, despite everything, they were really quite lucky. They had barely escaped losing their home, but after eight years of teaching Paul was now earning a good wage at a job he enjoyed. Lucretia, too, was getting more bookkeeping work than she could handle. Financially, things were actually going quite well. As soon as summer vacation began when Bea finished kindergarten, Paul decided they had to get out of the city before things got too hot and wild. Locking up the house, he drove Lucretia and Bea up to the Adirondacks for the month of July. He had just taken out hefty theft and fire insurance policies. Glimpsing the place through his rearview mirror, he half hoped it would be burnt down when they returned.

That time in the country was just what the doctor ordered. Every moment was either relaxing or romantic. In early August Lucretia announced that she had failed the rabbit test again—she was pregnant. Their second child would be born in April.

Exhausted and covered in sweat, Uli prepared for his final surge by pouring the last remaining bottle of water over his burning scalp. Moving slowly upward, he was able to pull himself onto a narrow ledge that seemed to mark the top of the sealed elevator shaft. The heat was becoming too intense to proceed.

Uli rested for several minutes, then strapped the heat-retardant body armor fashioned from the trash cans over his clothes. The massive blue flame was blasting away just ten feet above him. He had to somehow get around it to reach the earth's surface. He removed the flattened can from his head and used it to stab into the compressed dirt, sending cascades of sand down the narrow shaft. As he progressed, he could feel his hair burning on his head. Taking occasional breaks to cover his scalp, he pressed on, shoveling a thick current of sand down past him for the next twenty minutes or so. Soon he had created a narrow upward rut along the side of the blasting spout of blue flame.

Retreating back down the shaft to where the heat abated, he rubbed his fingers over the blisters along his head, neck, and arms and caught his breath. Using the last vestiges of his strength, he scampered like a sand crab up the narrow trench he had just created along the side of the giant fiery crater. Scooping the relatively cool sand around him for relief, his hand suddenly broke through into open space. He frantically hauled himself up and collapsed onto the desert floor. Drenched in sweat, too tired and singed to even remove the body armor, he simply lay there panting under the burning sun. Smoke rose from his burnt clothes. After a few minutes, he pulled the hot metal plates off his chest and arms and passed out.

39

In late January, a week of unseasonably warm weather started melting the frozen crusts of snow. When Paul's teaching semester began, there was a sense of hope. Lucretia was in her seventh month of pregnancy and she somehow knew this one was going to be a boy. Though she didn't say anything, she wanted to name him Paul Junior.

Then one day in early February, Mr. Rafael, the new Negro head of the science department, popped his head into Paul's third-period classroom just as the kids were beginning a quiz. "Paul," he said, "I'll cover for you."

"Why? What's going on?" he asked, stepping out into the hallway.

"It's your wife, Mr. Moses," a middle-aged police officer spoke up behind Rafael. "She's passed away."

"What?" Paul asked, bewildered.

"We're not sure what happened," a second, younger cop said. "Someone found her on the ice, her skull was fractured."

"Lucretia's . . . ?" He couldn't even envision it. It was absolutely inconceivable. "Where is she? Where's Lucretia?"

"Come on," the first cop said, leading him outside. "We'll take you there."

"One of the neighbors found her on the sidewalk in front of your house. She must've been lying out there awhile. He called an ambulance," the younger of the two cops explained over the siren as they sped to the hospital. "Someone else said they saw some hooligan running away, but she still had her purse on her . . . Or else maybe she just slipped on the ice."

Paul wasn't listening anymore. Once they arrived at Cabrini Hospital, a nervous young doctor said that they would need about thirty more minutes before their examination of the body was complete.

"What the hell happened?"

"We're not sure yet, but it looks like a subdural hematoma, a head injury due to her fall on the ice."

"Did she . . . just slip or was she . . . attacked?" Paul could barely speak.

"We're trying to ascertain that right now," the doctor replied. "If she was hit we might find other marks or bruises, but she might've just fainted, which isn't uncommon for a pregnant woman."

"How about the baby?"

"I'm sorry, the fetus died with her."

Paul leaned against the clean white wall and slid to the floor. Over the course of the afternoon, Lori and several other neighbors came to visit him in the hospital, but Paul just stared off in shock.

"I'll get Bea from school," Lori offered. "She can stay with Bill and me until you're ready."

Consciousness is as tangible as any matter. It, too, must obey the laws of physics. With the velocity of decades behind it, Paul reasoned, *a life can't just come to an abrupt halt in space or time. Even if the body machine fails, the psychic energy of Lucretia's being, the components and particles of her consciousness, have to be propelled somewhere.*

Soon a detective approached him.

"Where is she? Where is she?" he called out.

A sympathetic desk nurse got on the phone and rang the pathologist in the basement who said the exam was over and the grieving husband could come down and see his wife's body. The nurse directed Paul to the basement and he was brought into a viewing room. Lucretia was wheeled out on a gurney and he was left alone with her. Only her face was visible. A sheet covered her nude, pregnant trunk. A black and red bruise the size of a walnut pushed out from the front of her skull. It seemed so unfair that this small broken part could end the rest of her. Paul pulled up a hard wooden chair and stretched forward, laying his head and arms over the top of her cold chest. The pathologist returned to the room ten minutes later to find Paul half-sitting, half-laying next to his wife.

"I'm so sorry for your loss," he said gently, "but I'm going off duty now."

"When can I see her again?"

"We'll surrender the body to whatever funeral home you want us to," the doctor explained. Paul nodded. He couldn't breathe. The pathologist asked Paul something . . . He couldn't really . . . He shook his head no . . . The man led him . . . to the elevators . . . upstairs, instead of leaving . . . he stayed in the hospital waiting room . . . one floor above the morgue . . . near . . . his wife's body . . . for as long as he could . . . passing out in the chairs . . . then waking up . . . staying until . . . the next . . . day . . . Time kept pushing forward.

The desk nurse told the hospital social worker that a friend of Paul's had left her number. She called a Lori Mayer, who called Mr. Rafael at Paul's school and left a message that due to a personal tragedy he probably wouldn't be back for a while.

Lori and her husband then visited their old friend Stuart Fell at Fell's Funeral Parlor on East Tremont Avenue. They agreed to go see Paul together at the hospital and work out the arrangements. A few hours later, when they met him in the waiting area, he nodded them off as if he were in deep thought.

Lori asked the desk nurse if Paul could get some kind of help. Soon the hospital psychiatrist, a bearded man named Dr. Hugo, diagnosed Paul as suffering from an acute case of pathological grief. He gave him a tranquilizer and held him overnight.

The next afternoon, Paul seemed to be regaining con-

nection. When he returned home, Lori brought Bea over.
The little girl gave her daddy a kiss and told him that she'd
heard that "Mommy is with God."

"I spoke to Detective Chalmers who's handling the
case," Lori told Paul. "He said they've put up notices to
see if anyone has spotted Toto."

"Oh, right," Paul replied absently. He hadn't even reg-
istered that her old Yorkie was missing.

When Lori left, Paul slumped into an armchair and
watched as his little girl moved cheerfully around the house
collecting dolls and other toys to play with. All he could
think was that every item she touched had been bought by
Lucretia. He couldn't accept that he wasn't going to see her
again. *If I ever adjust to her loss, that would reveal the limit of my love
for her. But her love for me was limitless.*

When his brother had erased him in the summer of '47,
making him a ghost around Midtown, she alone had found
him outside Horn & Hardart's and brought him back to
the land of the living. Even when he had despised himself, she had rescued and revived him. She had become a
kind of cast for his broken life, and now that she was gone
he didn't even want to try to stand. Though he loved his
little girl and knew his wife would want him to take care
of her, he simply couldn't focus. Lori, when she dropped
by around dinnertime to see how he was doing, found Bea
eating from a bag of moldy bread.

"Would you like to come over for supper?"

Paul shook his head.

"What do you want?"

"Take her."

Lori said okay and bought Bea back home with her.
The next day, Bill Mayer came by to tell him that Lucretia's
body was now at the funeral parlor. The viewing would go
on for the next two days. Solitude was all he desired, but
he knew what Lucretia would want. It took great effort to
put on a suit and comb his hair. When he arrived and saw

Lucretia in the coffin, he had to resist the urge to climb in and just lay with her, even be buried with her. He sat next to the box and stared downward as people filed along and gave their condolences. Everyone from the neighborhood stopped by, signed the book, and paid their final respects.

Lori arrived with Bea, who was dressed very nicely, and pulled up a chair for the little girl to stand on. Looking down into the coffin, Bea whispered, "I love you, Mommy. Goodbye, Mommy. Goodbye."

The heat from the bright blue flame of the blasted pipeline— even at a healthy distance—was stinging Uli's burnt face, pulling him awake. Half of him felt frozen, the other half fried. Calling out Karen's name repeatedly to no response, Uli finally admitted to himself that he must have hallucinated hearing her voice from the bottom of the elevator shaft. Despite the cold desert night, the phenomenon of freedom compelled him to simply stare at the massive flame as though it carried the very mystery of life.

Eventually, Uli crawled away into the surrounding desert. Under the vast twinkling sky, it was almost as if he had remembered infinity and all its possibilities. Uli felt born again: The sandy breeze seizing his body reminded him that the planet was alive with both cruelty and tenderness. The fact that he was no longer trapped underground with physically and mentally impaired cannibals made him giddy.

The crescent moon offered little light. Around him in the darkness, all he could see other than the distant blue flame were the outlines of hills and large rocks. He was hungry and thirsty and knew he wouldn't last long. Despite his exhaustion and pain, it would be better to walk now, at night, than under the great weight of tomorrow's unbearable sun. He rose and staggered about a thousand feet before spotting a small trench into which he collapsed.

A few hours later he began hearing sounds. Several

shapes were moving across the desert floor. He thought they were some kind of nocturnal creatures at first, but as the dark blue sky lightened, he could see they were people. Three men passed far off to his left. They appeared to be wearing striped vests, but otherwise they looked dirty and bewildered like those trapped below. The group was heading toward the large geyser of flame that roared forth from the ruptured pipe. The men seemed to be discussing something. Abruptly, two of them started pummeling the third, until the man collapsed to his knees. As the attackers moved away, Uli decided to wait several minutes before cautiously approaching the victim.

40

The motorcade made its way to Woodlawn Cemetery and Lucretia's body was interred next to her mother's grave. Afterward, Paul and Bea were driven back to the house. A couple hours later, Lori stopped by and discovered them sitting quietly in the living room, both still in their funeral clothes. She fed Paul and took Bea back home with her. Paul lingered around the house over the next few days, just sleeping and moving silently from room to room. On the afternoon of the third day, he heard a knock at the door. He answered to find Leon standing there awkwardly in torn overalls.

"Sorry I didn't make it to the funeral. After my mom's death, I just couldn't bear going through it all over again." Leon removed a fifth of whiskey from a brown paper bag.

Paul led him into the kitchen and set down two glasses.

"First my mom, now your wife," Leon said.

"None of this would've happened if . . ." Paul couldn't finish. He sucked down the burning liquor like cold water on a hot day. Leon had barely finished his first glass by the time Paul had knocked back most of the bottle. When Leon realized that Paul had passed out and pissed his pants, he shook his friend awake and told him to clean up and get dressed.

"Why?"

"I need some company."

Leon drove Paul in his old pickup a few blocks south into Morrisania and parked in his driveway. His dogs barked nonstop as he helped Paul inside. His large home was filled with foil wrappers, empty bottles, soiled clothing, and old newspapers. Over the next week, Paul ate, drank, napped, and watched ballgames on TV, all in the same tight armchair that had once belonged to Leon's mom.

Paul called Lori one afternoon and asked in a slightly drunken slur if he could speak to Bea.

"She's at school, Paul. It's 2 o'clock."

"I'm slowly getting back on my feet," he mumbled.

"No problem."

"Can you tell Bea I'll come get her tomorrow after school?"

"Sure, she'll love that." After a pause, Lori said, "Paul, I got a call from your boss at school, Mr. Rafael. He found someone to take over your classes, but he needs to know whether or not you'll be back next term."

"Great," Paul replied without really listening. Upon hanging up, he looked out the window and glimpsed the railings of that goddamned freeway several blocks north.

"He's always taken everything from me," Paul murmured to Leon. "Now it's time to take back."

"You probably want to kill more than ever now, but . . ." Leon trailed off.

"If you kill someone they don't feel pain. We have to let him feel—"

"It's over now. Maybe you should just live in peace."

"Fuck no! What that cocksucker did to this neighborhood . . . And those who stayed have been subject to years of tumult and harassment. There isn't a wall in my house that doesn't have cracks running through it. Not to mention that dust. Bea spent nights coughing herself raw. I mean, Lucretia would run tape along the doors and windows and we still couldn't keep out that goddamned dust and—"

Suddenly, shouts and screams erupted outside. Bottles were shattering, kids were fighting.

"This used to be a good street. Now we're in the middle of a fucking ghetto that's getting worse every day."

"Can you blame everything on one fucking highway?"

"THAT FUCKER TOOK EVERYTHING!!!" Paul shouted, and grabbing his overcoat he stormed out the door.

He marched angrily up to Lucretia's home, but as soon as he got to the door he felt it. Her presence was there waiting for him. He stumbled back down the stairs and wound his way along the dark, chilly streets back to Leon's place. Once inside, he gulped water right out of the faucet until he gasped for air, then he kicked off his shoes and plunked down in Leon's mother's armchair where he thought, *I'm taking it all—the whole damn city—down with me!*

He awoke very late the next day and barely made it to Bea's school in time to pick her up. After buttoning her coat, Paul took his daughter's little hand and led her down East Tremont Avenue.

"Daddy, I'm hungry," she said.

Paul bought Bea her favorite meal, a slice of pepperoni pizza and, from a nearby diner, a side of creamed corn. Back at home, he gulped down a fifth of Scotch as she ate and they both watched television. Soon he passed out on the floor. When Lori woke him up at 9, she said that Bea had run across the backyard shouting, "Daddy's dead!"

"Well, obviously I'm not."

"Paul, little girls are very fragile."

"All right," he said softly, then went to the bathroom and shut the door.

"Should I bring her back home with me tonight?"

"No," he growled through the closed door, "not tonight."

Lori helped the little girl into her pajamas, made her brush her teeth and say her prayers, then put her to bed.

"Goodnight, Mommy," Bea whispered into space. Lori gave her a kiss on the cheek and sat next to her until she fell asleep.

Early the next day, Paul dressed his daughter and gave her a Hershey's chocolate bar. After dropping her off at school, he headed south to Leon's yard in Morrisania. His friend wasn't there, but Paul let himself in and rooted through his fridge, nibbling on a half-eaten turkey hero he found inside. He searched for a drink, but the house was dry.

Paul was awoken from a long nap by noises coming from the yard. Leon and some kid were feeding scrap metal into the big chopping and grinding machines.

"What exactly are you doing anyway?" he asked when Leon was done.

Leon gave him what he called his "twenty-five-cent tour." The yard, which appeared to be just a big pile of junk, was actually an organized arrangement of various types of metal. Down the center of the yard was a small metal-processing system with assorted machinery, including a hydraulic compactor, a small crane, and great sheers for tearing up large pieces of scrap. Much of Leon's time was devoted to simply maintaining his outdated equipment.

"You okay?" Uli asked, timidly approaching the beaten man.

"My fall dey da, Play-o war me don rink and I egnor im." When the man looked up, Uli saw that his tongue was sticking out of his bleeding mouth.

"Where'd you come from?"

The man pointed at the ground and muttered something else. Uli didn't know if this poor fellow was mentally deficient or just suffering from a speech impediment. He sensed aspects of both.

"How'd you escape?"

"Play-o sho us."

"Where is he?"

"Doe know, roun ere." The man rose and started walking off.

"Where are you going?"

"Back."

"Back where?"

"E-low, Mku-tra," the guy replied, pointing downward. "You com ew, or you ge kill."

"But we're out," Uli replied. "We're free!"

"De uders righ."

"About what?"

"No un can cross da fleg-ethen. Das where de odders die."

"The what?"

"The fleg-ethen, the fleg-ethen." He pointed out across the sand.

"You mean the desert?"

The man shook his head no.

"Don dree da wada."

"What water?"

"You see." He moved off in the direction of his assailants, further out into the endless desert. Uli followed at a distance as the sun continued to rise. Soon, he spotted the other two men several hundred yards ahead on their hands and knees. But a minute later, when Uli looked again, they were gone.

Upon reaching the area where the two guys had vanished, the injured man knelt down and began fumbling around in the sand. To Uli's surprise, the guy pulled open what appeared to be a cellar door on the desert floor. Uli watched as he stepped right into the ground and vanished as well. Uli approached cautiously and found a rectangular door the same beige color as the sand. He pulled the door upward and looked inside. Metal rungs lined the edge of a dark square chute; about twenty feet down, a massive fan was anchored beneath the grating of the floor. He considered climbing down to see exactly how and where this entrance connected to the rest of the subterranean chamber, but staring into the darkness below, he feared an ambush. He slammed the door shut and looked around—dry emptiness.

His mouth felt as parched as the surrounding desert. He put a pebble on his tongue, something to form spit around, and started walking back in the direction of the blue flame, toward gracefully contoured mountains.

41

A boxy skyline ran the length of the hurricane fence along the edge of Leon's scrapyard—stacks upon stacks of large wooden crates buried under the melting snow. Each crate was about three feet wide and five feet tall.

"Why don't we just scrap these?" Paul asked.

"We can't."

"Why, what are they?" Upon closer inspection, Paul saw that each had a small black screen and a large hole toward the bottom.

"Fluoroscope machines for shoe fitting. You put on a shoe and you can see it on the screen."

"Where'd you get them?"

"Some guy dumped them here because they got some kind of radioactive crap in them. I called the government to get rid of them, but they didn't do shit. Then I wrote some letters. They keep giving me the run around, so I'm just going to take them out some night and dump them in the river."

"They're radioactive?"

"Yeah, cause your bones turn up on the screen. You can see how well your foot fits in the shoe."

"Aren't you worried about getting contaminated by the radioactivity?"

"Nah, I spend hours listening to the radio and never reacted," Leon kidded.

The next day, Paul went back outside with his bifocals and a screwdriver set. He counted 103 shoe-fitting machines in all. On the back of one, he found a diagram that indicated precisely where in the box the radioactive material was stored—in a small lead cylinder—and it showed how to safely remove it without getting exposed. He remembered some things about radioactive elements from his college studies. He knew Marie Curie had died of radioactive exposure, as had her daughter. He had read that a professor at Yale, a physicist, had died from radioactive poisoning while doing research for the government in New Mexico.

Early the next morning, after dropping Bea off at school, Paul traveled downtown to the main branch of the New York Public Library, where he turned a ten-dollar bill into a bag of nickels and proceeded to photocopy every document he could find dealing with radioactive material.

That evening, he and Leon split a six-pack and ate meatball Parmesan sandwiches while watching a college football game. Leon, however, wouldn't stop talking about the Dodgers.

"This is the Bronx," Paul said. "I mean, if you were from anywhere else in the country, I could understand your love of the Dodgers, but we can walk to Yankee Stadium from here."

"You know what? Yankee Stadium may be in the Bronx, but they should just dump it on Wall Street, cause that's where those pin-striped bastards belong. You go to a Dodgers game and you're rooting for working-class guys, and that's all I'll say about it."

The junkman went out to his truck and came back with a fresh bottle of Scotch. He twisted the top off and poured two glasses.

At halftime, Paul asked, "What would you say if I told you that the stuff in those old shoe gizmos is a distant cousin of what they dropped on Hiroshima?"

"So?"

"The radioactive material in each machine isn't powerful enough to really hurt anyone, but I know how we can make it so that no one ever drives down that fucking highway again."

"How?"

"We can dump the radioactive granules from those cylinders on it late one night, then inform the authorities anonymously. It'll be impossible to clean it up, and no one is going to drive over a radioactive highway. They'll be forced to bury the entire stretch under concrete."

Leon looked at him in silence for so long that Paul grew nervous. "What are you thinking?"

"That the next time a fucking community begs its leaders to move a highway a few blocks south, someone'll say, *Remember East Tremont.*"

"There you go."

"On the other hand," Leon added, "judging by what happened to the Rosenbergs, you'll probably fry."

They kept drinking until Leon went to bed and Paul passed out in his armchair.

The next morning, Leon headed out to work as Paul sat in the kitchen over a cup of coffee and scribbled notes, considering his new project as though it were an engineering student's assignment. Gradually, though, he found himself focusing on Lucretia's death: It was the perfect murder *they* had gotten away with. He tried returning to his plan: what to do with the cylinders. A moment later, Lucretia's face came to mind and he started weeping. He opened the bottle of Scotch, but put it down after a sip and again tried returning to the problem. Yet thinking of Lucretia—the delicate way her long fingers caressed his back and shoulders and ran through his hair, and the idea that no one would ever touch him again—led him to intense sadness, which eventually brought him to fury. He tried wiring the voltage of her cruel death to the engine of his action.

By the end of the day, repeating *They fucking killed her* under his breath obsessively, Paul attempted to walk it off, but then he passed by her old house, which he hadn't spent a night in for nearly a week. He stopped at the very spot where they had found Lucretia's body and thought, *They got away with it.*

He moved several blocks further toward the Cross Bronx Expressway, and when some portly fellow passed by staring at him, Paul shouted, "What are you looking at? You smug son of a bitch! Did you do it? Did you fucking do it? Did you?" The man sped away before Paul could knock him on his fat ass.

He stood on the overpass above that contemptible expressway cursing down at cars and waiting for pedestrians to pass. When a dark green squad car pulled up, one of the cops asked him if he was okay.

"You didn't care when they killed her and you wouldn't care if if I jumped right onto this fucking pit!" he babbled furiously.

An ambulance was called and he was carted off to the psychiatric ward at Bellevue Hospital, where he was diagnosed as suffering from acute paranoia with suicidal tendencies. Following several days of observation, the diagnosis was downgraded to clinical depression, yet still with suicidal tendencies. When the doctors finally learned that Paul's breakdown had been triggered by the recent loss of his wife, the diagnosis was further reduced to acute depression.

Two days after Paul's disappearance, Leon called the station house to file a missing-persons report. The police informed him that Paul Moses had been taken to Bellevue for a seventy-two-hour observation.

Paul, meanwhile, requested to stay at the hospital. He was given a steady dose of Thorazine and daily counseling with a rotund, pointy-bearded psychiatrist named Seth Greenwich, who quickly took a liking to him.

"I don't think I was ever happier," Paul said about his marriage. "I mean, I had really given up on life. My wife, my little girl, they brought me back from the edge. And what happens, she goes out and gets killed."

In a soft, almost dreamy voice, Greenwich asked, "Has the pain diminished at all?"

"If anything it's gotten worse," Paul said. "I keep asking myself why I'm still breathing and she's dead. I warned her that I was cursed. But I was selfish so I married her. Now she's dead and I . . . I've lost all desires, I can't sleep, eat . . . I can't do anything. I just keep thinking that some asshole killed her." He made no mention of his brother.

"Paul, I checked the police records, and after a thorough investigation they classified it as an accident."

"It doesn't really matter. All that matters is she's gone. I can't stop thinking about it. I guess I've just gone crazy."

"You're not crazy, Paul," Greenwich replied, touching his patient's arm. "I have a wife and she means the world to me. And if she were to die, I'd be sitting where you are now."

"Believe me, I want to get well. I want to clean all this out of my head and raise my daughter and enjoy what time I have left."

"Look, we've tried several different drugs and you say they're not working."

"They just blur the pain."

"There's only one thing left, but I'm not going to do it unless you really want it done."

"A lobotomy?" Paul asked.

"Of course not. Electroshock therapy. It basically neutralizes certain brain cells; supposedly it takes the edge off."

"Isn't it painful?"

"A little, but it's done over a period of time. Most patients who I've seen after electroshock are calmer."

"Will I have a different personality or anything?"

"Maybe a little memory loss, but that's it."

"Well, I'm this close to stepping in front of a subway, so let's do it," Paul said.

He was wheeled into electroshock twice a week, and

eventually, after three months, he found himself thinking about nothing. Although his memory had indeed suffered a little, on the whole he was able to function better. When the treatments ended, he was finally released and set up with outpatient counseling.

Morning seemed to last forever as Uli retraced his steps across a dry riverbed. Noticing some birds circling ahead of him, he moved forward toward them. Several larger birds appeared to be picking at some dead animal in the distance. As he drew closer, he saw that the birds were digging into the fresh corpse of a coyote. He wondered if he should try to tear off a piece of the carcass or at least drink some of its blood. Even just a few drops of moisture in his mouth would be heavenly.

Approaching the dead animal, he thought he glimpsed a clear blue pool of water off to his left. He figured it was the water that the stranger had warned him not to drink. After just a few steps toward it, he saw the bodies. Two forms, both disheveled older men, lay still on the banks of the pond. Some kind of large bird, perhaps a vulture, was digging into one of their necks. A third body floated face-down in the water. This had to be what the speech-impaired man was talking about—the mysterious Phlegethon.

Uli stared at the water and realized it was completely still; it seemed to have neither source nor drain. He dipped his finger in the liquid and tasted a single drop. At first it seemed okay, but moments later a burning sensation spread across his dry tongue, compelling him to spit out what little moisture had accumulated. The stranger with the speech impediment must have singed his tongue.

Uli sat in the shade of a huge rock several hundred feet from the toxic pond and thought, *At least I'll die under a beautiful sky.* Eventually he passed out.

He was awoken a little while later by a bird's screech and the sound of scrambling. He opened his eyes just in time to see a large, bearded black man in a loincloth lofting what appeared to be a burning trident into the pond. As soon as the spear hit the water, the fire expanded in every direction, turning it into a pool of flames.

"Holy shit!" he gasped. The large man then noticed Uli and dashed right up to him. With his last bit of energy, Uli caught his arm and flipped him to the ground.

"Just as I thought—you're trained in self-defense," the prone man observed. "Who are you with, the army or Justice Department?"

"Neither," Uli replied, struggling to keep the guy pinned to the ground. "I mean, I don't really know."

"You're probably Justice. Well, you're definitely the guy who blew up my family."

"You're Plato the leader?"

"Plato Bomber," he introduced himself. "They called me that cause everyone thought I blew up that hole from the basin into the Mkultra, but it was already there when I arrived. I just took credit to get their support."

Sensing no threat, Uli eased off him. "There was a leak in the gas pipe that exploded when your son got near it."

"He gave birth to the great blue feather then?" Plato was referring to the flame. His hippie-dippie way of talking reminded Uli of the Burnt Men in Rescue City.

"Yes, your son and I were trying to help each other escape. He had your wife and other son with him. They all died in the blast."

"They all died and you lived—good deal."

"I promise you it just turned out that way. We were working together."

"I know, I've already seen the proof." Plato glanced down in grief. "What right have I to complain? I had children, only to abandon them when I couldn't look at them anymore. My wife's brain was eaten away . . . and my two kids looked like the offspring of fish."

"You should be proud of your son," Uli said. "He was

smart as a whip, courageous, and he took great care of his mother and brother."

"I guess he took after me in some ways, but not in others." Without another word, Plato turned on his heels and began ambling away.

Too exhausted to follow, Uli lay back down and quickly fell asleep. Roughly an hour later, the man returned, this time carrying a knapsack and a canteen of water.

"I tried to work with the others," Plato began, presumably referring to the band of strangers Uli had seen earlier. "Each member of my six-man team was supposed to go in a different direction to find a way out before returning to me. Instead, they ran off and drank from the lake of fire, where half of them died and the survivors scurried back down the hole—"

"Can you help me get back there?" Uli interrupted.

"Don't you want to get out of this place?"

"I'm starving and dehydrated and . . ."

Plato opened his knapsack and dumped its contents before Uli. There were two boxes of crackers, a tin of Spam, and a container of brown water that looked like it had come from the Mkultra. When Uli reached for the water, Plato caught his wrist and said, "We have to come to an agreement first."

"What agreement?"

"You want to escape and I need information."

"What information?" Uli asked.

"Information to find a way out for everyone else stuck down there."

"You already found a way out of the Mkultra."

"Yes, but to where? Death in the desert? I need to find a way out, and for that I need you."

"I don't know any way out."

"You got out of there very quickly, so obviously you're pretty smart," the man noted. "Did you follow my lines to the stairwells?"

"What stairwells?"

"The ones behind the walls. The lady in the Sticks knows all about them," Plato said hesitantly.

"What do you know about her?"

"I know not to trust her. She's with them, but I don't think you are. Though you might be and not even know it."

"With who?"

"Maybe the CIA, maybe some other agency, maybe those Feedmore creeps, I don't know."

"What are you talking about?"

"Look," the man said, pulling a large gun from the knapsack, "I'll help you, let you eat, drink, get some strength back, but then I'm going inject you with a drug."

"Where did you find drugs?"

"Where do you think? They evacuated quickly and left everything behind. I didn't want to use it, but if experiment number 6,232 works, you'll save yourself and everyone else," he replied.

"What does it do?"

"It allegedly heightens intuition through memory hallucination."

"What were the other 6,231 experiments?"

"All I know after reading everything I could down there is that this place was one big laboratory, and we're the guinea pigs."

"What exactly is supposed to happen once I'm drugged?"

"Who knows, but it's all I got left. I've spent a month walking a two-day radius in every direction, trying to find the way out myself, and I've gotten nowhere. I can't do this alone anymore. So I'm making you an offer."

"With a gun in your hand?"

Plato passed the weapon to Uli. "That's part of the deal. I'll fix you up, inject you, then you find it and shoot the gun. It's a flare gun, so I'll be able to steer everyone else in the right direction."

"What is *it* that I'm supposed to find?"

"I'm not exactly sure, but I came across a document that described an emergency escape route somewhere in the desert. Maybe it's a phone or a dune buggy. You'll know it when you see it, and that's when you should shoot the gun."

"You think you can see a flare in this heat?"

"The flare stays in the air for around five minutes and has a twenty-mile visibility. I'll scan the sky every day just after sunset."

Seeing no other recourse, Uli agreed.

Plato removed a syringe from his bag and injected Uli's arm, then said, "Rest, eat, and drink before you start walking."

"Where are you going?" Uli asked as the guy began heading off once again.

"Back—I still have a million loose ends to tie up."

"Do you have any idea which way I should go first?"

"If I did, I wouldn't need you, would I?" The tall black man marched off in the direction of the strange cellar door. Uli promptly fell asleep.

He woke up several hours later starving and thirsty. He drank down half the container of dark water and instantly felt a surge of energy. He chomped down some crackers and opened the Spam. The oily little tin tasted like filet mignon. It was already late in the afternoon, so he loaded the remaining water and crackers into a thin sack that Plato had left with him, slipped it over his shoulders, and took to his feet. Though the pond was still burning in spots before him, there was no sign of the black man. Whatever hallucinogens had been shot into his system, he didn't feel or see anything odd. Just empty space eternally unfolding and an occasional breeze bringing little relief.

He decided to walk through the night. As the moon began to rise, he sat down on a flat stone and had a few more crackers followed by a mouthful of water. Just as he was beginning to wonder if the shot in his arm was merely some kind of placebo, he spotted something racing madly across the desert. At first he thought it was a coyote, but even in the moonlight he could see it was black, or shrouded in black. It was moving on four legs, but then it rose to two. With a hood, or long black hair, a woman was running hard. She abruptly vanished over a hilltop. He checked in his bag and verified that he still had the flare gun. He took a deep breath and followed.

42

After seeing a Board of Education psychiatrist at 110 Livingston Street, Paul successfully filed for early retirement on a psychological discharge. He got less than a quarter of what his pension would have been, but he was able to secure additional Social Security disability payments.

"What'd they do to you at Bellevue?" Leon asked when he showed up at the scrapyard.

"Fried the pain out of my head," Paul said simply. He paused before adding, "Now I can truly focus on destroying that highway."

No longer working, his days were actually more hectic than before. Bea was back with him after having lived with the Mayers during his hospital stay. Between taking her to school in the morning and picking her up in the afternoon, he would visit the Midtown library and research various models of homemade bombs and improvised land mines.

One morning, after taking his little girl to school, he sat and had a chat with Lori. "You were the person Lucretia picked as godmother for Bea," he began.

"Don't you think I know that?"

"I just want you to understand that this was a decision Lucretia made after a lot of thought. She really believed that if anyone was qualified for the job, it was you."

"It's a duty I've never forgotten," Lori replied.

"Do you know how old I am? I could drop dead at any moment."

"Any of us could."

"Well, I'm telling you this just to say that if, God forbid, something should happen to me, I want to rest assured that my little girl has a home with you."

"Paul, please, you're scaring me."

"The reason I'm telling you this is that I've made you the trustee of what little assets Lucretia and I have. That includes the house, which is paid for in full."

"I appreciate this, Paul, but I'm sure you'll live a good long life and once you get on your feet you'll be a great dad."

Paul thanked her and headed back to the scrapyard. Baseball season was kicking off the next day and Leon wanted Paul's help in selecting a new TV set.

Back in Rescue City, Uli had experienced a bizarre vision while visiting a hippie colony where he perceived bedraggled Armenian refugees being marched by soldiers from their villages to their likely deaths in the desert. He saw a young woman's husband brutally murdered and her daughter stolen from her. Eventually, the woman was taken as a slave by one of the many marauding gangs. What the hell was she doing here in *this* hallucination?

Uli continued following this sad figure through the morning, but as the day wore on he slowed down a bit. She seemed to slow down with him. By noon, he was all out of water and most of his crackers were gone. Hot and dry, Uli swung one foot in front of the other feeling like his skull was going to crack open. At one point he spotted a plane overhead and wondered if it was headed to Rescue City.

When the sun finally went down, he was hit by a wave of deep exhaustion and had to stop, but she kept going. Uli made a mental note of which direction she was moving in and dozed off by a cluster of desert shrubs. It had to be about midnight when he awoke. The moonlight was strong enough for him to continue walking. *Tomorrow morning I'll find shelter and wait out the heat*, he decided as he pressed onward through the desert. He walked for roughly eight hours, discovering along the way that even though he could discern her silhouette in the distance, the woman wasn't leaving any tracks in the sand.

When the sun started rising the next morning, he told himself, *I must be at least twenty miles from where I started out. Shouldn't I have found some means of escape by now?* A grouping of rocks offered some shade from the growing heat, so Uli curled up for a siesta.

Later in the afternoon, as the sun's rays began dissipating, Uli resumed walking toward the spot where he had last seen the refugee. After half an hour, he hadn't detected a single trace of her and began to fear that the drug he had been injected with was wearing off. He briefly considered returning to the clump of rocks where he had spied her the previous evening. Instead, he limped on a few thousand feet further before glancing up at what had to be a second hallucination. There appeared to be some kind of metal box, like a telephone booth for a midget, planted on a circular concrete foundation. Moving forward, he discovered that he was looking at a gated enclosure around a pipe sprouting from the concrete. A sign on the side affixed to the base said, *WARNING: Water Station 27, U.S. GOVERNMENT PROPERTY. Trespassing Strictly Prohibited!*↑

Although there was a latch on the enclosure, there was no lock. Inside, Uli found a small hand-operated water pump. He immediately started working the metal handle. First it was just air, but then came a rumbling, and suddenly rusty water spat out. He dropped to his knees and stuck his sweaty head under the rush of water. He laughed aloud and drank as much as he could, then he just lay there as the increasingly cool water gushed over his burning head and body.

43

Over the next few months, Lori continued to help Paul look after Bea. At the end of each night, after putting his little girl to bed, Paul quietly drank himself into a stupor. Lori sat him down one day and told him that he really needed a maid. The old house was filthy.

"Can't afford it," he replied flatly.

She shook her head in dismay.

Paul kept hoping that with time their lives would stabilize, but things only seemed to get harder. When Bea started attending grade school, he found himself thoroughly overwhelmed and Lori began taking the girl four nights a week. In an effort to avoid his neighbor's constant supervision, Paul would bring Bea down to Leon's house, park her in front of the ballgame, and proceed to get hammered with his buddy. Frequently, they'd all pass out in front of the TV. On most Monday mornings Bea would wake him up late. He'd grab the keys to Leon's pickup and hit the gas. Without even stopping at home for a new change of clothes, he'd deposit her directly in front of the school. Soon he started receiving letters from Bea's teachers about her shabby dress, her poor performance in class, and her frequent arguments with other children. When he could put it off no longer, he visited the principal, introduced himself as a retired school teacher, and explained the tragedy of his wife's death. He said he was still going through a rocky period of adjustment, but promised that things were slowly improving.

Eventually, someone filed a complaint with Child Protective Services. An attractive young woman, Honora Agnes

Burke, was assigned to Bea's case. The young social worker routinely visited the house to inspect the living situation. She'd open the fridge and find that vital foods and other requisite household items were missing, then she'd notice the garbage piled up around the house. A thick layer of dust covered everything. Paul would apologize and make some lame comment about missing a shopping day, and she'd just scribble notes into her small spiral pad.

"It's not me you should apologize to," Mrs. Burke snapped at him one day. "I have milk and eggs and bread in my fridge, and my house is spotless. It's your little girl who suffers."

One cold night that spring, he fell asleep with an electric heater running. He woke up to the smell of smoke—a stack of old *New York Times* newspapers had caught on fire. He quickly put it out and first thing the next morning went across the yard to see Lori.

"What's the matter?" she asked, seeing the misery on his face.

"It takes every bit of effort I have just to keep from killing myself."

"Please don't say that."

"Whatever I was, Lucretia made me. It's as simple as that. I didn't want marriage and certainly not children. It all came from her. You saw it. I wouldn't have even become a teacher . . . Anyway, last night I almost burned the house down." He couldn't look up. "That goddamned social worker is coming by all the time and it's just a matter of time before she starts trying to take custody of Bea. I can't put her through that."

"Paul, I have a husband and a little girl myself," Lori replied. "I can't do any more."

"Bea loves you like a mother and Charity like her own sister." He took a deep breath. "I want you to adopt her and give her a real family."

Tears came to Lori's eyes.

"By doing this," he continued, "at least I'll still be able to see her and be a presence in her life."

The next day, after Paul dropped Bea off at school, Bill and Lori came to the house and explained that much to their regret they had to decline his request.

"Bea loves you guys and I thought you felt the same way."

"Of course we do," Bill said. "Hell, we even *want* more children. We just don't have the space. Our place is really just a living room and bathroom. Charity's room is tiny."

"How about this," Paul countered. "You guys move in here. This place is over twice the size of yours, and I fixed it all up a few years back. You can check the plumbing, electricity, and paint job—I did it all myself."

"This house was Lucretia's pride and joy."

"And her daughter will still be living here."

They thought about it for two more days before they consented. Two weeks later, Paul located a lawyer who would charge a reasonable fee to do all the paperwork. Before the month was over, Paul had thrown out all of Lucretia's clothes and knickknacks that he knew they wouldn't want. He had already brought most of his own things over to Leon's home.

The Mayers moved into Lucretia's house soon after Paul had vacated. They kept possession of their own house and decided to rent it out if they could find some nice tenants.

Keeping busy to avoid the inevitable anguish of giving up his daughter, Paul carefully read and reread the diagram on one of the fluoroscope boxes. Apparently, each time the button on the box was pushed, a coiled spring flipped open the small lead cylinder holding the radioactive pitchblende and an X-ray of a foot in the shoe appeared on the screen. With much sweat and concentration, Paul was able to extract the cylinder from the bottom of one of the old machines. It looked like a small brass pipe with a panel on the side.

He was delicately removing the cylinder from a second machine when Leon walked up to him in the scrapyard and said he was worried. He had just read a frightening newspaper article: Ebbets Field was so rundown that it could no longer be filled to capacity.

"I could've told you that twenty years ago," Paul said, wiping his brow.

Brooklyn Dodgers owner Walter O'Malley was seriously looking to move them to some nice new stadium that he could finance on his own. Before Leon could say another word, he noticed Paul holding the cylinder and asked, "Is that the radioactive stuff?"

"Yep, and until I figure out how to assemble a bomb, I need some sort of lead-enforced chamber to safely store it in."

"Hey, I know where we can get a small lead-lined vault."

"That'd be a great start," Paul said.

The next day, Leon visited another scrap iron yard where he knew the owner had a collection of old broken safes. The strong box he remembered seeing was roughly three feet tall and three feet deep, with three inches of lead and steel insulating it. Leon traded his friend twice the safe's weight in copper piping for it. Then he and Paul hauled it back to his yard and dropped it to the earth right near the fluoroscope boxes.

"Let me ask you an unusual question," Leon said to Paul. "Is there any way we can detonate this stuff that might somehow further our cause *and* help the Brooklyn Dodgers?"

Uli chuckled, but then realized his pal was serious. Though he said nothing, the question compelled him for the first time to consider the idea of establishing multiple targets instead of just the highway.

"Any ideas?" Leon prodded.

"No one should have to die for baseball," Paul replied calmly.

Browsing through the listings pages of several newspapers, Paul was able to find a lead smock formerly used by a dental technician. He also picked up an old army surplus Geiger counter, but it broke after just a few days. Over the ensuing weeks, a routine formed: Paul would remove one cylinder a day. He made it a point to be done by 2 in the afternoon—in time to shave, shower, and dress so he could meet Lori outside of Bea's school and walk them home. Sometimes he'd stay at the Mayers' for dinner before heading back to Leon's place for the night.

One evening, Leon showed Paul a column about Walter O'Malley's obsession with building a new stadium. The guy wanted to plant one right on the corner of Atlantic and Flatbush over the Long Island Rail Road yards in Brooklyn. The plan was being blocked by Robert Moses, who argued that the development would create "a China wall of traffic."

"Your brother won't let the Dodgers leave New York City, will he?"

"Even Mr. Robert's not that stupid."

"Cause I got to tell you, if he did, I really would consider killing him myself, and I ain't fooling."

Soon they read that Paul's brother had offered O'Malley use of a new stadium he was building out in Queens. With that, even Paul felt some sense of relief.

Uli finished off the last of the crackers as the sun dipped out of view, then lifted the gun and pulled the trigger. The flare must have shot over a thousand feet in the air before it blasted open. This strange concrete buoy in this sea of sand had to be part of some kind of escape route. By blasting the flare into the sky, Uli had now fulfilled his bargain with the crazy black guy who had gotten him here.

That night, as he milled around trying to figure out his next move, choppy segments of Paul's memories cut through. He saw Lori repeatedly yelling at the old man for various reasons, all pertaining to Bea. The two were getting into frequent fights about parenting the girl: He didn't like the clothes she was wearing. Lori didn't want Paul feeding her crappy diner food and taking her out late at night. He accused her of monitoring Bea more closely than her own daughter. Lori said he was paranoid, and finally that she was sick of all the fights.

During the next day in the sun, as Uli imagined Lori and Paul struggling over the young girl, he simultaneously searched for the woman in black, but his hallucinations seemed to have dissipated. He closed his eyes and rested.

"What we're trying to say, Paul, is we've had it," Lori snapped. "You win. Just take her and leave us alone."

Though Paul didn't say another word, Uli knew the old guy had concluded that he needed to quietly back out of his daughter's life. Otherwise, there was no chance of her being raised by this decent family.

Suffering from severe hunger pains, Uli filled the container that Plato had given him and set out due west. A shiny half-moon and a million little stars allowed him some visibility to keep an eye out for potential food sources. The night grew steadily colder. Then he thought he saw her again, the Armenian apparition, walking across the desert floor in the opposite direction. He tiredly switched course and followed.

Rising sharply up to a small plateau of rocks, he spotted about a dozen large lizards enjoying the residual heat from the day past. They were each about three feet long from tail to snout. He found a flat rock and quietly tiptoed up and managed to slam three of them dead before the others disappeared. He slipped their hard little bodies under the rope he was using as a belt. He could still see the dark figure of the Armenian woman standing in the distance. He walked stiffly toward her until he realized it was merely the outline of a rock.

He pressed on for a couple more hours before he started shivering. Fortunately, he came upon a dried-out tree, so he snapped off some of the smaller branches, peeled strips of dried bark, and rolled them into a tight bundle. Using matches he still had with him from the underground storage depot, he lit a fire at the base of the tree. After a few minutes, the trunk was up in flames. He flopped the dead lizards on the fire and warmed himself while they cooked. Soon their skins were black and bubbling. When they cooled down, he ripped the short little limbs from one of them and chewed slowly. They were rubbery as hell, but they tasted good. He intended to save the other two cooked reptiles for later, but after months of C-rations, the roasted meat was just too tempting and he gobbled it all down. He spent the remainder of the night and most of the following day in a cool little rock hollow resting up for more hiking. Without even thinking, he drank through nearly half the container of water.

44

At the main branch of the library on 42nd Street, Paul began reviewing published dissertations and scholarly articles to try and figure out how to turn a hundred-plus cylinders of radioactive material into a bomb. All bombs required a shell, an explosive element, and a detonator, but instead of shrapnel, the most deadly part of Paul's creation would be the pitchblende. The lead safe that Leon had gotten for him could serve as a bomb shell. The real trick was finding enough dynamite to blow it open along with the lead cylinders inside. It all came down to cash. When Paul mentioned this to Leon, his friend asked how much was required.

"Maybe a thousand dollars for a box of dynamite."

Leon told him they could earn it scrapping.

That summer, the two men worked hard at cutting, grinding, and compressing ferrous and nonferrous metals from Leon's yard, then hauling them down to a blast furnace and other recycling plants.

"You know," Leon said tensely, seeing the yard clearer than he ever remembered it, "I wish to hell your brother would cut the crap and allow O'Malley to build that fucking stadium in Brooklyn."

"I wish my brother would die painfully."

"I mean, think about it, the Brooklyn Dodgers should be in Brooklyn, not Queens. Am I right?"

"Sure, but hell, O'Malley's not being particularly flexible on location."

In the hot days of August, Paul woke up one afternoon with a hangover and realized that Leon was still in bed.

His buddy had been nauseous for several days in a row.

"You should lay off the sauce for a while," Paul suggested that evening, after working the entire day on his own.

"I don't think that's it," Leon said, struggling to get out of bed. Aside from his increasingly pale complexion, Leon was suddenly losing his hair. When Paul went to the bathroom, he saw that the sink was splattered with blood. Leon said it was nothing—his gums were bleeding, big deal. It was obviously more than that, and Paul convinced him to go to Cabrini Hospital. Leon was immediately diagnosed with late-stage leukemia.

"I was healthy as an ox till a few weeks ago," Leon said, barely able to breath.

"It's very odd, getting leukemia so quickly," the doctor said. "Do you know if any other members of your family had it?"

"No," Leon said tiredly.

"You must've been exposed to something that brought it on," the doctor speculated. He prescribed Leon a full menu of painkillers and antibiotics. Because he didn't have much money and didn't want to die in the charity ward, Leon asked Paul to help him back to his yard. Paul cared for him attentively, never voicing his fear that the crap in those shoe-fitting machines was somehow responsible. The following month consisted of nonstop nosebleeds, diarrhea, bedsores, and significant weight loss since nothing stayed in or down.

"I think that this might've been my own fault," Leon finally confessed.

"What do you mean?"

"I think this is what happens when you get radioactivated. Shit!" he mumbled, coughing. "I knew I shouldn't have . . ."

"Shouldn't have what?"

"One day while you were down at the library, I took one of those things from the safe."

"One of the cylinders?"

"Yeah."

"What did you do with it?"

"Nothing, really. I mean, first I drove out to Queens . . ."

"Where?"

"Flushing."

"Why?"

"So the Dodgers would have to stay in Brooklyn," Leon said.

"Where's the cylinder? Leon, you didn't empty it, did you?"

"No. I opened it and poured a little onto some newspaper."

"It just poured out?"

"Just like dark sand. Then I poured it all back in."

"How'd you get it open?"

"The little side panel slides open easily with your finger. It's held shut by a spring."

"Where is it now?"

"I put the cylinder back in the safe—but I never even touched the stuff!"

Paul said not to worry. Leon apologized.

Later, Paul took the old Geiger counter apart and carefully checked its bottom board lined with test tubes. When he prodded one of the old wires, the needle of the counter started bouncing. He managed to get the thing working again, so he put on the lead smock and walked around the scrapyard, where everything seemed fine. Checking inside Leon's truck, however, the dial flipped all the way to the red side and stayed there. Paul then went to the lead safe and opened it up. Again the Geiger counter's dial swung into the red. He closed the heavy door.

Paul carefully hosed down the interior of the truck, then tossed his clothes into the garbage bag and took a long shower. He got dressed, made some chicken soup for Leon's lunch, and helped him to the bathroom and then back to bed.

"I have something to tell you," Leon said later that afternoon in a hoarse whisper. "I put the house and yard in your name."

"Why?" Paul asked.

"I don't have any other relatives, so I thought you'd be best."

"But I'm an old man," Paul replied.

"You still need that box of dynamite, right?"

"Oh God."

"We didn't start this battle," Leon rasped.

"I guess not."

"They can't just tear a community in two . . . and expect to get away with it."

"That's true."

Leon looked strangely content.

When they heard the news on TV that the Dodgers were indeed leaving Brooklyn at the end of the year, neither man said a word. On September 24, 1957, Paul and Leon watched as the Dodgers played their final game in Brooklyn against the Pittsburgh Pirates. They won 2-0.

A few nights later, Leon said he had something to tell Paul.

"I'm listening."

"Remember that first time . . ." Leon was having difficulty breathing and could barely keep his eyes open. "Remember that morning when you came into the kitchen at Lucretia's . . . and you saw me sitting there eating breakfast?"

"Yeah." Paul remembered feeling his heart break, assuming she had slept with him.

"I just want you to know . . . we didn't . . . we didn't do nothing."

"What do you mean?"

Leon smiled softly and said, "It was her idea, and I probably shouldn't tell you, but she . . . she was trying to . . . to make you jealous. She called and asked me . . . to come by early and tiptoe in . . ." Paul chuckled. "Hell, we waited an hour before you . . . before you entered the kitchen."

"What are you saying?"

"She loved you and you wouldn't . . ."

"But you were her boyfriend, weren't you?"

"Never really been a ladies' man," Leon said softly. "Anyway, I guess Lucretia's plan worked."

"And all this time I thought—" Paul broke out laughing, as did Leon. Paul spent the rest of the night reveling in how clever—if not conniving—Lucretia had been. She had always seemed so naïve.

Leon died six days later. When Paul found the empty bottle of sleeping pills under the bed, he wasn't wholly surprised. He called the police and had the body taken away, then arranged a funeral. Among others, Lori, Bill, Charity, and Bea came. He hadn't seen his daughter in nearly a month, so she rushed up to him as soon as she arrived. He lifted her in the air and kissed her face all over.

Seeing his daughter in a pink outfit that matched Charity's dress, he knew that Lucretia would never have bought something so gaudy. That thought brought on a flood of memories of Lucretia's death six years earlier, and sitting across from Leon's open casket, he started weeping softly for his wife.

Two days later, Paul used Leon's pickup truck to purchase a bunch of supplies, then returned to the scrapyard. With a jackhammer, he tore a small square opening through the pavement at the outer edge of the property. The next morning he dug a hole six feet into the earth.

Using two-by-fours, Paul slowly hammered together a frame. That week, he mixed and poured several bags of concrete, fashioning a small container in the earth. When it dried, Paul carefully lowered the lead safe with the 103 cylinders down into the shaft. He topped it off with an additional bag of concrete, then covered the shell with dirt.

He didn't want to ever think about building a bomb

again. His friend had died because of it—he didn't want to kill himself and Lord knows how many others just to get back at his brother. Most importantly, though, he certainly didn't want his little girl to become known as the daughter of one of the most evil men New York had ever produced. All plans to build a bomb were officially off.

Soon afterwards, he sold the pickup truck. Next, he took the title to the property to the Mark Lukachevski Real Estate Agency on East Tremont and put the scrapyard and house on the market.

"How much do you think you can get for it?" he asked Lukachevski, a man he had come to know in the neighborhood over the years.

"At this point, you'd have a difficult time even abandoning it," the man replied earnestly.

Paul packed his few things at Leon's house and moved back down to the old Times Square dive where he had lived when he first met Lucretia years ago. It was as if he had only been gone a day.

Uli felt relieved that Paul had abandoned his suicidal plan to attack the city. He had come to assume that this bombing scheme was the very reason he was having these memories, so he wondered anew what his relationship with Paul Moses signified.

Uli crawled out of his nook and scanned the horizon for any sign of his hallucination. As usual, she was being coy.

While he slovenly marched forward into the barren landscape, a symbol kept popping into his head:

↑

He had seen it on the sign of Water Station 27. He figured it must be pointing to the next station. But then he froze. *They're probably all in a direct line!* Uli had been too distracted by Paul's grief and the Armenian guide to recognize the clue. He had to go back. Only from Water Station 27 could he hope to find 28.

45

Sitting on a wheeled cart at the library, Paul noticed a bound collection of back issues of *University of Pennsylvania Alumni Quarterly*. While perusing through several recent editions, he spotted an item from three years back. Under the heading *Class of 1915*, it read, *We've established a fund to assist one of our dear colleagues who is in special need. Millicent Sanchez-Rothschild worked tirelessly on behalf of the poor in Mexico and now needs our help. Please donate to . . .*

There was a name listed that he didn't recognize, *Irena Martinez-Smith*, along with an address on the Upper East Side. At first he was going to write a letter. But since it was a nice day and the woman lived only a mile or so from the library, he headed up to her apartment on 69th Street and First Avenue. He stopped at a diner along the way to comb his hair and straighten out his ruffled suit in the bathroom. Then he located the building and rang the bell. A handsome young man answered.

"I'm looking for a Mrs. Martinez-Smith," Paul said.

"What about, may I ask?"

"I saw that she posted a notice for funds for a Millicent Rothschild—"

"Mom!" the man shouted upstairs. He quickly vanished and an older woman came to the door.

"Can I help you?"

"I used to be good friends with Millie years ago, and I saw your notice. Since I live nearby," he lied, "I thought I'd just knock on your door and ask how she was doing."

"You knew Millie in Mexico?"

"No, here. I went to Princeton though I ended up going

down to Mexico with her. That was over forty years ago."

"What's your name?"

"Paul Moses."

"Yes, Pablo, I remember her writing about you." She invited him inside, offered him a cup of tea and scones, then told him, "Millie was disinherited by her family."

"You're kidding."

"They completely turned their backs on her when she went down there to join the revolution. She was fighting against people her own father had put in power."

"I remember. Is she okay?"

"She came back from Mexico a number of years ago. She had problems there. She got arrested in the '30s and spent a few years in jail, where she lost her sight."

"She's blind?" Paul felt numb at hearing this.

"Yes. After a while she was finally getting along, but then she had to move . . ."

"Where is she?" Paul was trying to hold back tears.

"She just got a new place, but it's all the way down in the Battery. On Bond Street."

"Is there a phone number?" Paul asked eagerly. "Can I call her?"

"She doesn't have a phone yet. That's one of the reasons I'm trying to raise money for her. She was so popular and beautiful back then. There were so many boys chasing after her. I remember one of the Rockefellers was gaga over her. He was good looking too. Would've given her the world, all she had to do was take it."

"I know," he said, almost ashamed to be among them.

"Did you know she scored number one in her sophmore class?"

"I didn't know that." At least if he did, he had forgotten.

"Smart, attractive, she could've really been something," the woman said sadly.

Paul knew that she meant Millie could've been married to a powerful man, because he also knew that Millie couldn't have lived her life any other way than she had.

Millie now resided on 98 South Bond Street. He thanked
the woman for her time, then walked over to Lexington Avenue and caught the 5 train down to the last stop in Manhattan. Forty-five minutes later he was walking around the
Battery looking for her address.

When he finally found her building, which had no
downstairs doorbell, it was already 5 o'clock. It was located
behind Fraunces Tavern, one of New York's oldest pubs.
The ancient warehouse looked like it had been built back
when the English ruled. Staring up, he wondered how he
could get inside. He considered yelling out her name, but
if she was on the top floor he didn't want to make her come
all the way downstairs, particularly if she was blind. Wall
Street workers were just leaving their offices. Paul waited
as the rush hour crowds passed by, hoping someone might
enter the old building. After an hour or so, he approached
the chipped and warped door. When he pushed it, it rattled. With a sharp thrust of his shoulder, the door popped
open.

Paul slowly climbed the long, steep, splintery wooden
steps. Halfway up the exhausting ascent he began remem-
bering the last time he had seen her. He had left her in
anger in revolutionary Mexico and was returning to New
York to take his rightful place as the prodigal son of a privileged New York family. Now, other than the fact that he
was still alive, he had nothing to offer her.

When he knocked on the door, he could hear someone
rumbling around inside.

"Who is it?" a rusty female voice called out.

"Millie, it's me!"

"Who?"

"It's Paul, Paul Moses."

"*Oh my God!*" He heard her fumbling with the locks and
the door swung open. Besides her dark glasses, she hardly
looked older, just more dramatic.

"Millie, I can't believe it."

"Paul!" She reached out and grasped him. He hugged her so hard he realized he was hurting her, but she didn't utter a peep.

"I'm so glad you're still alive," he said cheerfully.

"It took me years to understand that I took you for granted!" she replied, tears streaming down her face.

"I can't believe you're back in New York."

Her hand grazed along his face to feel his expression. As he smiled, her fingers danced along his lips and cheeks and he kissed them.

"Do you know how many times I prayed that I had left with you all those years ago?" she said, hugging him. "Almost every day since you left."

She brought him inside and made some tea. In the fifteen years after he left Mexico, various revolutionary governments had abused the sacred trust of the country's people and were quickly replaced. She had attempted to keep a foothold, working with different regimes who supposedly shared common goals.

"Tens of thousands died during those years of infighting," she explained. "At some point you realize that you're no better than those you're fighting against."

Eventually, a coalition government was established. She thought the worst was over and was soon appointed to the government as one of the three Under-Ministers of Education. Everything seemed to have stabilized for a short while. In 1932, however, one of the more ruthless generals who she had briefly collaborated with was brought to trial.

"It's ironic—we all celebrated when we heard the son of a bitch was arrested."

But in an effort to gain his own freedom, the general had implicated Millie and three others. He was ultimately executed, but she was indicted as a coconspirator in a complicated debacle that had led to the slow death of thirty orphans. Millie ended up spending five years in a women's prison outside of Mexico City. It was there that she started going blind, developing something called macular degeneration, which went untreated. She was also under constant attack as a convicted child killer, and after one of the many prison riots, she was brutally beaten and raped by several guards. When she was released in 1938, she was so sick she was unable to walk.

She discovered that many of the other oligarchs who she had worked so hard to rid from the country had resumed their former places in the government. Without alternatives, she attempted to get in touch with her mother and brothers, but none of them responded. She was dead to them.

"All the pain and the thousands who died—and little had changed. All that work and sacrifice was for nothing."

She detailed how she ended up falling on the mercy of the church, an institution she had spent her entire life hating. They helped rehabilitate her, teaching her how to walk again with a cane. She learned how to read braille. They even hired her to work around the church. When she found someone who would write for her, she sent letters to old friends, members of the committee she had been a part of years earlier, to addresses she only vaguely remembered. Most of the letters came back stamped *Address Unknown*. Finally, though, a merciful letter arrived from her old girlfriend Irena Martinez. Her husband, Paul Smith, was a successful Wall Street broker. Millie requested assistance in getting back to New York, promising she'd reimburse the cost of the ticket. Irena immediately wired her money and Millie arrived back in the city just after the war, in 1946.

Irena helped her get a job through the American Foundation for the Blind giving private Spanish lessons to high school and college students. She also helped situate Millie in a comfortable rent-controlled apartment on the Upper West Side just off of Central Park.

"I looked for you as best as I could, but your family home in Midtown was gone. I tried tracking you down through Princeton, but after you quit working at Con Ed, they didn't know anything."

"Irena said you just moved here."

"Oh yeah, my old place was . . . well, unless you spent years in a dark jail you probably can't appreciate this." She smiled. "I was able to sit in the backyard most days and just be happy feeling the sun on my face." She had almost gotten her life back together when she was forced to move. The entire block of buildings was being evicted due to the new slum-clearance program. "They were turning the place into a housing project called Manhattantown."

"Awful," he said, neglecting to add that his own brother Robert was now the head of the slum-clearance program.

"Not necessarily," she replied. "They promised to give us priority housing when they're finished constructing it, so hopefully in the next few years I'll get a new apartment and other needy families will have affordable housing too."

"How'd you find this dive?" The sound of foghorns was constant.

"Irena's son is a friend of the owner."

"Any further south and you'd be in the harbor."

"For some reason, most landlords are prejudiced against blind, impoverished seniors. This guy took me in and I'm very grateful."

"Well, the place looks big," Paul said, glancing around. The apartment was one large ramshackle room with a beautiful view of New York Harbor.

"How about you?" she asked. "What became of you?"

Paul smiled. It was almost as if the two had died and were comparing lives from heaven. He related everything that had happened—his disinheritance, the failing pool club near Philadelphia, Teresa and her kids. Just when he had thought his life was over, he had found a fleeting joy

with a young wife and a beautiful daughter, with a second child coming. Suddenly—perhaps due to a slip on the
ice—it had all been taken away.

It was soon dark and Paul and Millie were both exhausted, so they moved to her single bed and fell asleep
hugging each other tightly, just as they had forty years earlier. Her place was so big and cheap that within a month
he once again gave up his room at the Longacre and moved
in with her.

Uli desperately tried to find his way back to Water Station
27, but nothing looked familiar. As he began feeling utterly
confused, he spotted a dust cloud just past a small hill—a
jeep!

He stumbled up the hill and along the nooks and contours of the rocky landscape, where he glimpsed a man's
head behind the windshield moving toward him in the distance. With the rising sun at his back, Uli figured that the
driver was probably blinded by the low rays.

"HEY!" he shouted out, and waved.

The vehicle paused almost a hundred feet in front
of him, and Uli couldn't imagine how the driver wasn't
hearing him. It didn't matter, in a moment he'd be in
that jeep. But as he neared the vehicle, it slowly turned
around.

"Wait a second!" Uli yelled as the jeep sped away.
"Fuck!"

Instead of hunkering down in the shade somewhere
as he usually did before the day heated up, Uli feverishly
continued searching for the water station. By 10 o'clock,
the burnt skin along his back and arms started throbbing.
Around noon, unable to keep moving, he collapsed.

He awoke in darkness to the sensation of something
slithering on his neck. It was some kind of small snake. He
wasn't sure if it was poisonous or not, it didn't matter. He
grabbed it tightly, stuck its head into his mouth, and bit

down with his incisors. The body whipped and convulsed around his face.

Uli chewed as much of the snake as he could, spitting out pieces, trying to extract blood or oil or any other moisture for his dried-out mouth. He closed his eyes as insects buzzed along his ears and lips, pecking at the blood splattered everywhere. He curled into a ball, so cold now that he could see his own breath in the enchanting moonlight.

46

At seventy, Paul was finally living with Millie again. Though they were poor, they were very happy together. When weather permitted it, they'd stroll over the Brooklyn Bridge or buy a cheap bottle of red wine, a wheel of brie, and apples and take the "five-cent luxury liner" to Staten Island. The worst part of their days was the vertical trek back up the long, splintery stairs to their apartment. Millie didn't have a strong heart so he'd rest with her on the climb instead of speeding ahead. Each landing was like a small base encampment. On bad days, when she was cold and feeling arthritic, it would take up to twenty minutes to ascend to the apartment. Occasionally she had to abandon the climb, moving all the way back down the stairs to visit the bathroom at the Chock Full o' Nuts on Broadway before trying a second time.

When they finally closed the door behind them, Millie would often comment that in just another year or so, when the housing project was finished, she'd be able to move back to her old neighborhood across from Central Park.

"And the place will have a balcony where we can sit down," she speculated one day.

"And don't forget the elevator!" he added.

She smiled.

In early 1961, Paul read that stage one of Manhattantown was complete. The first group of houses were accepting applications. So the two of them headed uptown, stood in a long line, and they each filled out applications to the New York City Housing Authority for a two-bedroom apartment.

"Can I ask," Millie said timidly to a short Mediterranean clerk, "how long will I have to wait for my new apartment?"

"Well, we have a lot of applications to review."

Millie mentioned that she had been evicted from one of the buildings to make room for the new project.

"She was told she'd be getting priority," Paul chimed in.

"I see that," the clerk said, pointing to a checked box on one of her forms. "Are you a married couple?"

"Not technically."

"Do you have any children?"

"No."

Peering down at the form, the woman let out a loud sigh. "May I ask why you need a two-bedroom apartment?"

"We were hoping to live together," Paul replied.

"Well, for starters, it would improve your chances if you were married, but it would also help if you applied for a studio apartment."

"My old place extended from the front of the street to the back of the building. It was the equivalent of two bed-rooms, and I had full use of the garden."

"Lady, we have thousands of applications from hard-working families."

"But she lived on the site previously and was promised priority housing," Paul insisted.

"I know, but many, many people were displaced by the slum-clearance work. We're trying to prioritize for the neediest."

"It wasn't a slum!" Millie shouted. "It was a nice house on a nice street! And the only reason I left was so that other families could have a home."

"I understand."

"Look, she lives in a fourth-floor walk-up that takes her twenty minutes to climb, and she has a bad heart!" Paul was starting to get agitated.

"There's no need to raise your voice," the clerk responded.

"Paul, let me handle it," Millie said. He sighed and stepped aside. "When I received my notice to vacate, I also received this letter." She removed a folded piece of paper from her purse and recited from memory: "*We at NYCHA promise to rehouse you once new facilities are built on this site.*"

"Look, I don't decide policy or choose the order in which people get their apartments. All I'm trying to give you is a reasonable expectation based on the information I've been given."

"Can I get the name and phone number of your supervisor?" Millie asked. The clerk handed her a mimeographed slip—apparently this was a common request. Over the ensuing weeks, Millie left phone messages and sent a steady stream of letters to various NYCHA offices requesting an apartment assignment, to no avail.

In this period, Paul would sometimes head up to East Tremont and discreetly watch Bea leaving high school. She had grown from a little girl to a tall, beautiful young woman. She looked happy, joking and kidding around with others. *Lucretia would be so happy if she could see this*, he thought. Afterwards, he'd walk by the scrapyard.

For the first six months after Leon died, he'd drop by and feed the dogs twice a week, but he felt too depressed to sleep there. When he saw that several of the dogs had been injured, he figured that kids from the neighborhood were throwing rocks at them. They were also growing increasingly high-strung at being left alone. He brought the two most injured dogs to the vet, but the bills were more than he could afford, so he had them put down. Paul taped up signs offering the other dogs up for adoption, but there were no takers. The animals were just too old and surly. Finally, he gave in and put them all on leashes and walked the entire pack to the ASPCA. When the dogs were gone, kids started climbing over the fence, vandalizing the old yard. Before Paul could sell off the larger scrapping machines, the kids had broken them. After a while, he ceased

paying taxes; gradually, more and more time elapsed between visits.

When Uli awoke a short time later he felt a bit stronger—
perhaps it was the protein from the snake. He devised a
game with himself, seeing how far he could walk with his
eyes closed before either feeling like he'd collapse or walking into something. About an hour or so later, maybe a mile
from where he had begun, he saw the outline of a large
mesa off to his right and thought it might provide protection from the sun. But then he quickly decided he could
still squeeze in another few hours of hiking before dawn;
plus, he somehow sensed the water station was nearby.

When dawn arrived, the landscape was particularly
barren. He spotted occasional cacti but none of them cast a
large enough shadow to offer relief from the sizzling heat.
As he increased his pace searching for cover, he could feel a
slight prickling around his face and neck. Tiny insects were
still tapping against him. Tiredly, he just kept dropping
one foot in front of the other. The temperature rose steadily,
and just after noon, as he staggered forward staring at the
ground, he noticed something very odd. He dropped to his
knees on the burning sand. A massive spider had spread
some kind of webbing on the scorched earth. When he
reached down to touch it, he saw that it was too big for an
insect. Someone had delicately etched a complex pattern
in the sand, a series of small wavy lines. It took him several
minutes in his dehydrated state, but he finally realized he
was looking at tire tracks.

47

On November 3, 1962, Paul opened the *New York Times* and read that a group of housewives in Central Park had effectively stopped Robert Moses from bulldozing a small playground to turn it into a parking lot for officials. Unlike in East Tremont, this group had top-notch legal representation and their plight was plastered all over the city newspapers. Cover photos showed lines of young mothers pushing their baby carriages in unity, blocking massive earth-moving machines. After so many years, Robert's tyrannical hand had finally been stopped. His brother was being revealed as the fascist he truly was.

Paul's sense of triumph was short-lived, however, as he soon read that the fucker had retaliated against the organized mothers and the rest of New York by going after Pennsylvania Station. With expansive skylights allowing natural light to bathe its vast interior, the station had been modeled on Rome's ancient Baths of Caracalla. That granite and travertine train terminal designed by McKim, Mead & White just fifty-two years earlier was in Robert's path of destruction. He was going to rip it down and replace it with a tightly compressed, hyper-efficient conglomeration of shopping center, office building, sports stadium, and railroad terminal.

Sitting together in Washington Square Park one afternoon, Paul read an editorial in the *New York Times* to Millie: *"Any city gets what it admires, will pay for, and ultimately deserves. We want and deserve the tin-can architecture in a tin-horn culture. And we will probably be judged not by the monuments we build, but by those we have destroyed . . ."*

"I used to wonder why old people were such curmud-geons," Millie said. "Now I know it's cause it takes a whole lifetime to see that it's all just getting worse."

During their walks through Greenwich Village, Paul would try to paint a verbal picture for her of the things he saw. More and more frequently, he found himself describing an epidemic of flaky kids born in the '50s with long stringy hair and bushy mustaches. Paul read about them as well: Rock and roll music was their anthem; sex and drugs were their pasttimes. Though they were lazy, he grew to admire their disdain toward authority. They were organizing against the war in Southeast Asia.

Paul read one article aloud to Millie about their new breed of civil disobedience.

"Good for them," she said.

"I don't entirely agree with them," Paul replied. "I mean, the people of Indochina deserve the same breaks the rest of us get. If American G.I.s have to teach them that—"

"Where do you think these G.I.s come from? Some warehouse in Washington? Are *you* willing to die to free French Indochina?" she snapped.

"Calm down."

"Don't tell me to calm down. I saw thousands of good men and women die in Mexico—for what?"

"The only thing I'd be willing to die for is getting us one of those goddamned project apartments you got cheated out of in Manhattantown."

One afternoon in early December, Paul went up to the Bronx to pay a visual visit to his daughter. He saw her leave school late and then eat a slice of pizza with some cute young boy. When he arrived back at home just after 6, he opened the door to the lobby, climbed the long stairs up, and found a note on the door:

Your wife Nelly had a heart attack and is in Saint Vincent's Hospital. Please call her there.

Chuck Womack (ambulance driver)

Paul dashed down the steps and caught a cab up to St. Vincent's, only to discover that Millie had passed away.

The following day, the super's son dropped by to say he was sorry about Millie's death.

"Thanks."

"We were just wondering if you'll be moving out."

"No, I'll be staying awhile."

"The rent is the same."

"Who discovered Millie?" Paul asked.

"I did, I called the cops."

"Was she unconscious?"

"No. She just called down the stairs that she couldn't catch her breath."

"So she didn't fall?" he asked, feeling some relief.

"Oh no, she was okay. I came up and found her sitting right there." He pointed just a few steps below the top landing. "She almost made it."

The kid said he had to take out the garbage and excused himself. Paul walked over to the step Millie had reached and sat down.

Not wanting to die alone, Uli searched around for her—the raven-haired hallucination, the eternally grieving Armenian widow who had abandoned him. All he could see was a single tall cactus on a distant mesa.

He stumbled forward about a hundred feet until the ground shifted and he fell to his knees. The earth was black and hard, like smooth igneous rock. Seeing the clean white lines running up the center, he realized he was on a highway. Suddenly, he was hit by a tremendous rush of wind—a car soared right by him without even slowing down.

48

As soon as he opened his eyes every morning, all he wanted to do was join her in death. Still, a survival instinct compelled him to pull on his clothes and hurry out of the old building. He knew that only when he got outside would he be safe. He was simply too self-conscious to kill himself in public.

At a nearby coffee shop, he'd get a cup and flip through the day's *New York Times*. After all these years, the mayor had finally managed to push Mr. Robert out of his sacred spot as Parks Commissioner—but not before the old prick had managed to hijack the World's Fair and turn it into a major debacle. The only real control he still exercized over the city emanated from his sacred Triborough Bridge Authority. The new mayor, John V. Lindsay, resented Robert almost as much as Paul did, yet despite his plea to the New York State Assembly, he couldn't pry the man loose. But it was just a matter of time.

Paul now believed that the only thing keeping him alive was some kind of extraordinary drive to see his younger brother banished completely from public life.

One morning, about six months after Millie's death, he spotted something on page thirty-six of his morning paper. It was a small, grainy black-and-white photo of a group of diplomats leaving a meeting at the White House. While staring at one of the figures in the photograph, just three-quarters of the man's face, he was surprised he had even noticed him. It was his old friend Vladimir Ustinov, who had taught him to build bombs over fifty years earlier in Mexico. The caption read, *Attaché to the Russian Embassy*.

"And I thought you were dead!" he muttered aloud. *I still have his pocket watch somewhere.*

When Paul returned home, he located a picture of Millie and then one of Lucretia—it was the first time he had looked at his wife's image in several years. He pondered a casual conversation he'd had over half a century ago with Vladimir that could possibly become a genuine plan.

The more he thought about how to inflict maximum harm with the 103 cylinders of pitchblende, the further away the idea got from him. What was initially intended as an extreme act of civil disobedience evolved into a question: *Do I actually have the power to make Manhattan uninhabitable, and is this the best way to achieve my goals?* The crimes his brother had inflicted upon him—a career lost, a birthright stolen, loved ones who had died or shunned him—gradually eclipsed his concerns for the people of New York.

Like a nervous tic, his hesitation kept twitching through him over the next couple of days and nights. He began regarding it with a kind of intellectual curiosity, the very notion that he could create something significant by wiring together a couple of throwaway objects—an abandoned X-ray machine and a simple triggering mechanism. He almost believed that merely thinking about the process would purge him of the desire to follow through with it. But the temptation and allure of retribution stayed with him and eventually prevailed.

Within a few days he became giddy and restless from the notion that *he alone*—a poor elderly man, a dismal failure, forgotten by others and nearing the end of his life—could rig together a device that had the potential to bring down the greatest city of the greatest country in the world. By the time Paul finally decided to go through with the project, it had morphed into an intensely personal mission: While he felt that he had perversely squandered his own talents—being born of privilege only served to accentuate the catastrophe of his adult life—this act of political violence might very well be the closest to greatness he would ever come. Paul's thirst for importance in his twilight years rekindled a sense of power that he hadn't felt since his youth, when he still had a bright future before him, a reason to live.

Paul selected his dirtiest, baggiest clothes, then gathered as much money as he could find in the apartment, grabbed a threadbare fedora, and slipped Vladimir's old watch into his pocket. He got on a 1:30 train and slept most of the way down to Washington, D.C.

As he shuffled through Union Station, somebody offered him a dime. He thanked the man and went to a nearby liquor store to buy a pack of Salems and five small bottles of cheap Scotch. Once he had located the address of the Russian embassy in the phone book, he headed over in a cab. Paul spent the morning scouting out every doorway within a one-block radius where he could keep an eye on the large gray building. In one entrance, he unscrewed the first bottle of liquor and gulped it down, then sat back and soon passed out. It was dark when somebody shook him awake and told him to move it. He stumbled a few blocks and fell asleep in another vestibule.

The next morning, he grabbed a sandwich and smoked some cigarettes, trying not to cough. Again he slept in one of the nearby doorways. Later that afternoon he opened his second bottle of liquor. In yet another spot near the embassy, he drank himself into a slow stupor. The only conscious act he maintained was vigilantly monitoring the embassy door, watching a slow stream of people young and old as they came and went. He was awoken again a little later, this time by a cop who asked for ID. When he grunted that he didn't have any, the cop cracked his long wooden club on the pavement and told Paul to get moving. He staggered away and soon met up with a small group of winos who bummed cigarettes off of him and gave him directions to the local soup kitchen. He returned the next day, this time a block and a half from the embassy; once again, he proceeded to get plastered.

This went on for the next seven long days, until a random selection of locals came to recognize him. The merciful ones offered him handouts—cash, food, clothes—but most acted disgusted or made nasty comments as they passed. Even some of the local beat cops started getting familiar with the harmless old bum who had inexplicably made the relatively nice area of Embassy Row his own. Every now and then, Paul would beg from passersby. Sometimes he'd catch cars stopped at a light and jump out to wipe down their windshields with balled-up newspapers. Most drivers honked or flipped on their windshield wipers, but some tossed him coins. Despite repeated threats from cops, it simply wasn't worth the paperwork to arrest him.

All the while, Paul kept his eye on the old embassy building, and though he couldn't keep track of every car, he soon identified the one he was looking for.

On the ninth day of living like a bag man in this posh D.C. neighborhood, he decided it was time to make his move. He had his target, a 1963 Mercedes Benz that exited the embassy most nights between 8 and 9 p.m. On a small piece of paper in tiny script, Paul wrote:

No one has seen me. 50 years ago you asked if I was ready to tip the country to revolution. I now am, and I have radioactive cylinders, but no explosives or detonators, which I need if you are still offering help. You can find me in the area.

Pablo (your old sapper buddy from the Mexican Revolution. Viva la Revolucion)

He clamped the small note in the front plate of Vladimir's old pocket watch. Then he waited until 8, 8:15, 8:30, 9, 9:30. The dark blue sedan finally exited the compound and stopped in front of him at the corner light. Paul moved forward and quickly started wiping down the windshield. When he held out his hand, the driver simply stared straight ahead. Paul stepped back and walked around the corner. When the light changed, the car turned tightly left as it had every night, whereupon Paul dove onto the hood and rolled off to the pavement.

"*Blyat!*" The driver cried out a foreign expletive, screeching to halt and jumping out of the car. "What the fuck?"

Paul leapt to his feet, pushed past the driver, and leaned into his open door. Two older men were sitting in the backseat, speaking in Russian.

"Vladimir?" Paul asked.

"*Da,*" said one aged voice in the darkness.

Just before the driver could grab him, Paul tossed Vladimir the old pocket watch with the note tucked inside. Paul was shoved out to the ground.

"What the fuck's your problem?" the driver/bodyguard shouted, then got back inside the Benz and sped off.

Paul slowly picked himself up and limped away.

The next day, instead of buying more liquor, Paul poured cups of hot tea into one of the empty Scotch bottles and sipped it patiently. The one thing he feared most was the cold weather—that alone would force him to leave.

Hope was nearly extinguished by the week's end, but since all that remained was death, Paul lingered in the area. Over the weekend, he broke down and rented a room in a boarding house. Each afternoon he'd walk back to the Russian embassy.

On a chilly afternoon during his twelfth day in Washington, D.C., while resting on a nearby park bench, Paul awoke to the sound of footsteps; a large man with sunglasses and an upturned jacket collar marched right at him in such a menacing way that Paul was sure he was going to get hit. Instead, the man dropped a tightly coiled dollar bill on the ground before Paul without even looking at him. Paul put his foot over the dollar and quickly snatched it.

It wasn't until later, while in the bright light of his little room, that he noticed the phone number. Along the margins of the bill, in a faint pencil, he read:

> *Don't mention any names, only that you want the merchandise, and negotiate for it. Don't contact me again!*

Paul walked cautiously toward Connecticut Avenue, making sure that he wasn't being followed. After ten minutes he was able to hail a taxi cab to take him to Union Station. He waited forty-five minutes for the next train, arriving back to New York around 3 in the morning. He took the subway downtown to Millie's old apartment. For the first time in a long while, he wanted to live. He knew he had to complete this last, greatest task before he could become part of the past.

Early the next day, he called the number scribbled on the edge of the crinkled dollar.

"Yeah," said a young male voice.

"I was told you had explosives and a detonator," Paul said bluntly.

The voice laughed. "Let me save us both some time, Mr. G-man. The only merchandise of that sort I have is around 150 micro-spring release switches, but we don't know what the hell to do with them."

"What are they?" Paul was bewildered.

"A thousand bucks a pop is what."

"Are they detonator caps?"

"Nothing on them is explosive. Hell, I don't even think they're illegal."

"They work on a timer?"

"Nope, they're an Italian make that are triggered by a tiny radiation detector."

"I don't understand. How can a radiation detector trigger a release spring?"

"Beats me. I think they were produced to fit into something else, but for the life of us we don't know what."

"Can I see one?"

"Sure, for a thousand bucks."

"How about two hundred?"

"Eight. And that's the bottom-barrel price."

"Look, I just want to see if I can use it. If I can, I'll buy more."

"Eight hundred for one detonator. One hundred and fifty of them for ten grand. It's a wonderful deal."

"How about eight hundred for one, and one hundred and two additional detonators for five thousand," Paul countered.

"A thousand for one and six thousand dollars for the rest."

"Okay," Paul replied with nothing else to lose. The youthful voice told him to put a thousand dollars in small bills in a white paper bag and drop it in the public garbage can on the southeast corner of Washington Square Park at 8 p.m. the following night, then continue east along 4th Street to a pay phone on Broadway, where he would be told where to find the detonator.

"How can you guarantee you won't steal my money?"

"Just do it or don't." The phone line went dead.

Paul withdrew the money from his meager savings account, turned it into ten- and twenty-dollar bills, and stuffed it in a white bag. Then he went down to Greenwich Village and passed some time perusing books at the 8th Street Bookshop. At 7:45, he walked down to the park to see if he could spot anyone around. Nobody looked conspicuous. At 8, he dropped the cash in the can and moved on to Broadway as instructed. In his excitement, he virtually ran the whole way, and when he got there the phone was ringing.

"The detonator is in a white bag in the garbage can directly to your left." *Click*. A small white bag was indeed sitting on top of the garbage. When he got home, he studied it carefully. The item was surprisingly small, about the size of a

Zippo lighter. When activated, a tiny screened tip, which he assumed was the radiation detector, flipped a small switch. The guy on the phone was right, little metal tracks on the side suggested the component was made to clip into something bigger—but what? He doubted there was any way he could utilize this gizmo. Lacking an explosive, it couldn't be used as a detonator.

What he had was a lead-lined safe buried up in the Bronx which held 103 cylinders containing a low-level radioactive powder. Now he had this small radiation-triggered switch. *How can I make this small device release the pitchblende powder in those cylinders?* He needed some kind of explosive. Could he attach a piece of flint, perhaps from a cigarette lighter, to a fuse that would in turn detonate something?

It wasn't until he was sitting at the counter of the Broadway Chock Full o' Nuts the next morning that it dawned on him: *If I were to release one cylinder of the pitchblende, it might be radioactive enough to trigger a second detonator a block or so away.*

Trudging up the long splintery flights to Millie's—now his—apartment down in the Battery, he thought, *Maybe the spring in the detonator is strong enough to pull open the little panel of the cylinder.* Leon had said he could open it with his finger. Slowly, other thoughts started coming together: Instead of a single centralized contamination bomb, one click might be able to start a chain reaction. If the pitchblende was all concentrated in one area, it would be relatively easy to quarantine that zone. But he couldn't just leave them around; kids would grab them. They should be elevated *above* the street. Perhaps they could be positioned on the first-floor windows of key buildings. But wouldn't people see the cylinders and notify the police? Also, how the hell could he get access to the windows?

He pondered these questions as he exited the Delancey Street subway stop. While looking upward for possible places to install the cylinders, something caught his eye: an old pair of sneakers dangling from a traffic light. He walked down Orchard to Broome and saw it again—someone had thrown another pair of sneakers up around the pole of a traffic light. He turned left and headed to Essex, where he found a third pair of sneakers suspended from their laces.

"Sneakers!" Paul shouted.

One small fuck-up! Uli cursed himself, thinking that a single lapse of observation and deduction would cause his inevitable death. His head throbbed in the heat and he realized he just couldn't get up again, much less walk. He started chuckling at the thought of waking and nearly drowning in a giant sewer, only to find himself here, staring up at a massive burning sun, cooking to death on some goddamn interstate in Nevada.

Sensing the hot pavement trembling under him, he realized another car was coming. Somehow mustering a burst of energy, he rolled across the center of the two-lane highway. He heard a screeching, then he clearly envisioned this older balding man named Paul Moses. But only a young teenager jumped out of the car.

"I almost hit you, dude!"

"I know him!" Uli shouted to the kid. "I met Paul Moses somewhere."

"Dude, you look burnt to a crisp!"

"I met him somewhere!"

"You need help, man. Want me to take you to the hospital?"

"I met him, but . . . I don't know where."

"Come on, try to stand up." The teenager hauled him into the front seat of his VW Bug, then gave him the remainder of his Coke, which Uli drank slowly. "Hold tight, I'll have you back in the city in forty minutes."

As the dry wind blasted Uli's face and "Take It to the Limit" by the Eagles blared on the radio, he tried to remember where and when he had seen this strange, bitter old man.

49

Paul had never climbed the steps up to the apartment so quickly. As soon as he got inside, he placed the switch in the toe of one of his large shoes. It was a snug fit—perfect housing for a small bomb. Several major questions loomed: First, could the radioactive cylinders, which were nearly a foot long, also fit in a sneaker? Could the detonator switch be rigged in the toe of a sneaker so that it would pull open the small spring-locked side panel? Was the pitchblende potent enough—and the radiation sensor delicate enough—to trigger another cylinder a block or so away?

He simply had to build and test a prototype.

Paul's next move was to purchase a tiny screwdriver designed for fixing eyeglasses. He dismantled his thousand-dollar detonator and examined it with a magnifying glass. The radiation sensor was a fine tube filled with an inert gas. He had read that a particle of radiation can make a gas temporarily conduct electricity. This would ignite a pulse that in turn would unhook the switch that would hopefully pull the spring-coiled panel back.

The next day he caught the subway up to Leon's old scrapyard in Morrisania that had been abandoned to the City of New York along with so many other buildings in the area. After being burgled by the neighborhood kids and set on fire and finally abandoned again, the yard was swarming with rats. Lugging an old winch, complete with chains, a heavy-duty shovel, a metal milk crate, and a hand truck, Paul was able to push through a jagged gap in the old hurricane fence. He slowly dug a hole at the edge of the property. When rats grew curious and came close, Paul would stomp the ground and they'd scamper off. After digging three feet, he struck something solid and knew it was the shell of concrete he had laid down years earlier. He used the end of his shovel as a pile driver to crack through to the small vault below. Soon he had chipped enough concrete away to run chains around it. Then, attaching them to the winch and the winch to one of the steel poles supporting the fence, he carefully cranked the safe out of the hole. Its broken door opened easily.

Late that night, as rats scurried around the old yard, he remembered all the good times he'd had up in the Bronx when Bea was first born and he and Lucretia were deeply in love. He also remembered all the nights spent pitching back beers with Leon while watching the Brooklyn Dodgers. Around 4:30 in the morning, he loaded all 103 sealed cylinders of pitchblende into a blanket-lined metal milk crate. He abandoned the tools and shovel in the yard and wheeled the loaded hand truck over to the elevated 5 train, where he hauled it up the station's steps, lifting with his waist, until, bathed in sweat, he had made it to the top. The train arrived forty-five minutes later. The lonely ride downtown took almost an hour. He got out at City Hall and paid some kid a buck to help him carry the hand truck up to street level. He then wheeled it over to his apartment on South Bond Street and spent the morning carrying ten cylinders at a time up the long flights of stairs.

The following day, after recovering from this extraordinary effort, he went out and purchased a soldering iron. Carefully, he welded a tiny wire to the spring panel of the cylinder, so that when it clicked open the pitchblende would be exposed to the unsuspecting world. Paul then removed the laces from a large pair of ratty old Converse sneakers he had found in a trash can and was able to slip the cylinders inside and secure the detonator switch to one of the worn soles. When he was done, he laced the sneaker back up—it looked just like any other shoe. Using tweezers and a small knife, he cut along one side of the sneaker so that all the pitchblende would be able to spill out onto the ground.

On the night of March 29, 1968, Paul finished his first prototype. Other than the detonator switch, for which he'd spent a thousand dollars, the rest of the shoe bomb had cost him less than fifteen dollars. In the future, though, he'd also have to pay for sneakers since he was unlikely to find many discarded pairs.

Since first moving in with Millie, Paul had been saving as much money as possible, buying cheap food in China-town and used clothing from thrift shops. All the while, he still received a steady trickle of income from the little his mother had left him, the disability checks from Social Security, and a tidy sum from the Board of Ed for his early discharge. Despite all this, however, he had only managed to save a little over five thousand dollars.

It had been weeks since he had called the number Vladimir had written on the side of the dollar bill. The line was busy this time. When he tried it again an hour later, it was still busy. He continued calling it frequently for the next few days. Eventually, someone picked up, but they didn't say a word.

"Hello?" Paul finally spoke.

"Harry?" said a female voice.

"No, I spoke to some guy a few weeks ago. He sold me a gizmo that could be used as a detonator."

"Oh, yeah, sorry. No refunds."

"I want to buy the other ones."

"Really?"

"Yeah."

"Twenty thousand bucks."

"We agreed on four thousand," he lied.

"That guy's not with us anymore. You want the rest, they'll cost you twenty thousand smackers."

"I only have nine grand," said Uli, pulling the figure from thin air.

"Fuck it. Nine grand then. You know how we want our bills, small and old."

"I'll make them small for you, but it's going to be too much to stuff in a paper bag this time."

"And the numbers on the bills can't be sequential. Just drop off the cash at midnight at the same place you did last time."

"Midnight when?" Paul asked.

"Tonight."

"I won't be in town for at least three days," Paul lied again.

"In exactly one week then," the young woman replied, and hung up.

Paul immediately emptied his bank account—a little over four thousand dollars, which he converted into old five- and ten-dollar bills. He spent the next two days cutting up scrap paper into strips the dimension of dollar bills, wrinkling them, straightening them out again, and bundling them together with real bills on top and bottom to make the full amount look like nine thousand dollars.

At midnight on the designated night, Paul dropped a black plastic garbage bag with four thousand fattened-up dollars into an empty garbage can at the corner of Washington Square East and 4th Street, then dashed like a mad man to the corner of Broadway. This time the phone was not ringing. He dug through the same wire-mesh trash can where he had found the original detonator, but it only held garbage.

Shit, he thought, *they're counting the cash*. After five minutes of waiting, he knew they were on to him. He had taken three steps back toward the park when he heard the phone ringing.

He picked up the receiver and heard, "They're in a garbage bag on the other corner."

Paul looked across the street and spotted a pile of four garbage bags. He hurried over and patted along the sides of them, discovering that one seemed to contain a group of hard cubic items. He tore the bag open and there they all were, nearly fifty more than he needed.

Ambling down Broadway back to his apartment, all he could think was, *Damn, I probably could've stiffed them the full amount.*

As the VW sped across the barren landscape, Uli kept one eye open, once again searching for the phantom Armenian woman. He knew she wasn't real, yet he feared she was somehow trapped, doomed to wander this desert forever. Eventually, he saw a distant clump of buildings looming ahead of them—the sinful City of Las Vegas.

50

If the people who sold Paul the detonator switches wanted revenge for being shortchanged, he never knew it. After extensive bargain hunting, Paul found that the best and cheapest sneakers to suit his needs were a crappy Hong Kong brand that would probably fall apart after walking a single mile. He purchased 101 pairs, all in size fourteen, at the bulk rate of $150. He also bought several two-pound cones of heavy-duty string. He cut them into four-foot pieces and looped them through the pairs of sneakers so that the laces were extra long for throwing. When lacing the shoes, he poked holes on the far right and left sides of the canvas so that they would hang at an angle that allowed for maximum dispersal of the pitchblende when the side panel clicked open.

He decided to keep two cylinders to use as triggers for the whle project. It took three weeks of painstaking work to match 101 pairs of sneakers with the remaining cylinders and then solder the small wires to the spring switches of the 101 detonators. He also painted a bright white stripe along each of the little spring-shut panels. With careful positioning of the cylinder in the shoe, he would be able to spot this white stripe from thirty feet feet below; since no explosives would be used, this visual aide would be the only way to detect if the sneaker-bomb had been detonated.

Finally, he had to decide where to place his little bombs. Once he tossed the sneakers up, there would be no getting them back. He guessed that the sneakers couldn't be spread more than two blocks apart, otherwise the level of radioactivity might be too low to trigger the next bomb.

Taping a street map of Manhattan to his wall, Paul used red thumbtacks to designate targets and white tacks for bombs bridging between them. He identified major business, political, and cultural institutions: City Hall, the Stock Market, New York University, Madison Square Garden, Rockefeller Center, the Museum of Modern Art, Lincoln Center, the Empire State Building, and so on. Over the ensuing weeks, he modified his tack diagrams repeatedly.

After finishing his map, at the age of eighty-one, Paul walked the route, pausing at the 101 intersections, assessing the poles he might toss sneakers over.

In the early morning hours of March 21, 1969, the first day of spring, Paul launched his little municipal odyssey. On the first day, he was only able to sling three pairs up before heading home exhausted. The next night, he took cabs instead of walking and was able to sling sneakers around five more targets. Weather permitting, that became his daily goal. Hitting different sections of nocturnal Manhattan, he'd heave with his back, sometimes tossing a single pair of sneakers as many as ten times before looping the long laces around the arching metal poles that had to be at least fifteen feet high. Only one sneaker of the pair contained the toxic cylinder—the other was simply a counterweight.

Paul wanted a pair of sneakers dangling as close as he could manage to nearly every major target. He positioned three pairs around his brother's new Madison Square Garden. Conversely, he deliberately circumvented Grand Central Station and—despite the fact that his brother had had a hand in it—the United Nations. He also wanted to hit Columbia University—that bastion of privilege—but he didn't have the bombing capability to stretch that far uptown.

At 5:30 on the morning of August 3, 1969, seven months into Richard M. Nixon's presidency, Paul Moses hurled the last of his 101 bombs.

When he got home that night, imagining that both Millie and Lucretia were forever by his side, he tiredly announced, "Well, ladies, I've avenged you."

He had two remaining cylinders at the house that he'd use to trigger all the others. It was simply a matter of opening the side panels and dumping the pitchblende out his window—then it was over. He didn't know how quickly the dust would travel, or how sensitive the sensors would turn out to be, but he felt confident that he had done everything he could to honor the lives of all those nameless citizens whose well-being had been destroyed by his brother and the city that empowered him.

Paul spent the next several days constructing a small wooden frame to hold the two cylinders outside his apartment window. He soldered little wires to their panel doors and twined them together to attach to a single lever. Somehow, creating a formal trigger mechanism to set off the devices made this unthinkable task a little easier.

He established his own private D-day as Labor Day 1969, but the day came and went. So he established a new D-day, Halloween. At that point, some of the sneakers had been hanging for as long as six months, so he used the intervening time to check around the city and make sure they were still in place. He was pleasantly surprised to find all bombs were where they should be, so he anxiously awaited the day on which he would give the city the greatest Trick or Treat in history. But hard as he tried to detonate the trigger cylinders when October 31 arrived, he just couldn't do it. Thanksgiving would be better: No children would be out on the streets; people would be away for the holidays. Again he held the switch, but he still couldn't pull it. Christmas and New Years both came and went.

It was 1970. *How much longer will I be alive?*

Despite a lifetime of pain and failure, Paul was being inadvertently forced to consider the true ramifications of what he had engineered. Although he planned to notify the authorities once the first bomb was detonated—in order to avoid human injuries—the poor would inevitably be impacted much worse than the rich.

Furthermore, newspaper reports indicated that his brother's ties to power were being slowly clipped away. Rockefeller was finally forcing Mr. Robert out of his Triborough Bridge Authority spiderweb, which was being absorbed into the MTA.

It wasn't until the second week in January 1970 that Paul figured out what he had to do: go back across the city at night and carefully cut down all the sneakers.

With a sigh of relief, he clipped the wires to each of the two trigger cylinders, but left them hanging out of his window until he could find a suitable place to dispose of them. It then took several days to design and construct a twenty-foot pole made from three segments of light aluminum piping. He bought a flag holder's belt that came with a leather pouch to fit the pole into. On the other end he installed a large pair of spring-coiled scissors with a piece of thick string that dangled down to the bottom. He would first try to hook the sneakers to remove them, and if that didn't work, he'd pull the string and shear the laces, allowing the shoes to drop harmlessly into a heavily upholstered cardboard box that he'd place directly below. If this approach worked, the entire operation would take about ten minutes—multiplied by 101 pairs of sneakers. He planned to do it between 2 and 4 in the morning to minimize human contact. He even swiped an orange cone from a construction site, which he planned to use to block street lanes as he worked. He also bought a red vest to look modestly official.

The first night, though something felt off, he headed out. He waited until 3 in the morning, carefully screwing his three aluminum pipes together, running the string from the shears to the bottom, then heaved the contraption up. No cars were in sight in either direction so he walked into the intersection directly below what he referred to as *Sneakers #1*. He struggled to hook the rod under the long lacing. It was much heavier and more unwieldy than he had anticipated. Just as he finally caught the lace, a fist from nowhere slammed into his face, knocking him and the pole to the ground.

When Paul came to moments later, a squat, middle-aged man was standing there next to him. Paul squinted and momentarily thought that he looked familiar, but he quickly turned his attention to the fact that the guy had dismantled the pole and had already snapped two of the three pipes in half. The stranger began whacking the scissored end of the top pipe against the cobblestone until it broke as well.

Run! Paul thought as he pulled himself up to his feet. He immediately felt himself thrown forward, landing hard on the broken pavement. Jumping upon Paul's back, the man shoved a small photograph in front of his face.

"Recognize her?" The man's voice was shrill and unsteady.

It was a school photo of his daughter Bea. He hadn't seen her at all over the past year or so, since he had begun his sneaker odyssey.

"We know where she lives, and if you try doing anything to a single one of those fucking sneakers, if you even *think* about calling the police, I will fuck her while strangling her with my own bare hands."

Paul didn't make a sound.

"Think I'm kidding?"

"No," Paul said.

The man lifted him to his feet and spun him around so they were face to face.

"I can stomp you to death right this moment and make it look like one of the five unsolved murders that occur every week in New York. Or," he paused, "I can let you crawl back up to your shithole on the top floor of 98 South Bond Street and you can live out the few days you have left in peace."

"Look, those sneakers have radioactive matter in them," Paul appealed. "They have to be cut down or this city—"

"*We* will take care of those sneakers from here on. You have nothing to worry about. We're not going to let anything happen to them."

"Why don't you just let me take them down?"

"We need them up there right now, you have to trust us."

"What do you plan to do with them?"

"We just have to make a point, then we'll remove them."

"Who are you?" Paul asked, squinting his eyes again at the squat man.

The guy shoved Paul back to the ground and kicked him hard in the side. "Quit looking at me. Just get up and go home."

Paul slowly rose to his feet. Without turning around, he limped painfully down the block and back up to his apartment. He cleaned his bloodied knees, put some ice on his bruised face, and wondered what to do. He had created an elegantly simple system of bombs that someone else had stumbled upon and was protecting. Who? Why? In his ninth decade, arthritis wracked his knees and bent his fingers. He was encased in pain. Worse, he was steadily losing his focus. His mind was wandering more freely each day. He pondered calling the police, notifying them of the dire situation, and then killing himself, hoping that since he was dead, *they* might leave his daughter alone. But there were no guarantees and he couldn't put Bea in jeopardy.

"Being of sound mind and body, do you consent to continue your mission and—"

"I do." ████████████████████████████████████

"You're not going to remember this, which is why we're taping it, but I just want you to know for the record that none of this was planned. New York, the Mkultra—it was all an accident. But I don't need to tell you that, do I?"

When the patches were briefly removed from his eyes, he glimpsed a woman with two black eyes. Root Ginseng?

51

One afternoon that March, while sitting at the Midtown library studying microfilm detailing some of the complex legislation his brother had written under Governor Al Smith, Paul glanced over at a young fellow reading the *Daily News*. The headline proclaimed, *Bomb Factory Blows Up!*

Paul panicked, nearly pissing his pants. He feared the headline referred to his unaborted endeavor.

But wait, nothing could have actually blown up. I didn't use any explosives. He politely asked the man if he could scan the headline story.

"Why don't you buy your own paper, bub?"

"Here's a quarter, pal, just let me read the cover story, please."

The guy thrust the paper at him angrily. Paul quickly read the article. A bomb had gone off in the basement of some rich family's brownstone in Greenwich Village. On 11th Street, a bunch of hippies had been seen running from the blast. Relieved, Paul handed the paper back and tried returning to the old legislation he was researching, but felt too jittery. He soon left the library, and while walking along 42nd he spotted a pair of sneakers just where he had tossed them. He could still see the small bright white stripe along the inside of one shoe, indicating that the little panel was closed. All was still secure. He wondered how long the laces would hold before they'd fall on their own volition.

He calmly took the RR train down to the Whitehall station. At the top of the stairs, he paused and looked over at Sneakers #1, the pair closest to his house. A steady wind was gently swaying the shoes in a slow circle. He stood staring intently for a minute but couldn't quite confirm the little white stripe was intact. He blamed his poor eyesight and ambled home, proceeding up the four flights that seemed to have gotten longer with each year. When he reached the top landing, he noticed that his door was slightly ajar. Entering, he discovered that the wooden frame was splintered.

Someone must've kicked the door in. He had a roll of ten-dollar bills in the top shelf of his cabinet. He immediately checked and found that the cash was still there. After several more minutes of searching through the apartment, he happened to glance over to the window where he had snipped the trigger wires. Someone had manually pulled the cut wires back, releasing the pitchblende! The shock of it hit him in the gut. Someone had activated the bombs!

He grabbed the phone and called the police.

"First Precinct," answered a desk sergeant.

"I'm calling to report that you had better remove all sneakers hanging from intersections throughout Manhattan or—"

The sergeant hung on him. Paul dialed again, but before anyone answered, he remembered the suffering Leon had undergone after being exposed to the granules.

"I gotta get the hell out of here!" Paul said aloud, feeling a strong wave of panic. He started tossing clothes, cash, ID, and a few other items into a shopping bag. Seven minutes later he was downstairs. Fortunately, the wind was blowing from the east that day. Paul realized it would be safest to head up Water Street. He made his way circuitously over to the Brooklyn Bridge and hurried out onto the walkway over the East River. Twenty extremely anxious minutes later, moving as fast as he possibly could, he reached Cadman Plaza in Brooklyn Heights. He stopped at the post office to catch his breath and found a pay phone in the hallway. From the operator, he got the number for the

New York Office of the FBI. He dialed, sweating profusely, trying to think of what he would say.

"FBI. Officer Sarkisian speaking," Uli heard, recognizing his own voice.

"And what did Paul Moses say?"
"I don't know. I only know what I heard."

"Okay, I do remember an older male voice rambling on nonsensically about radioactive material that had been released throughout Manhattan, via a series of sneakers."

"And then what?"

He had no idea who was speaking. He had bandages or a blindfold over his eyes.

"—on the phone as long as I could as we tried tracing the call, but it was evident that I was talking to an elderly male who may have been senile. When I asked him if he knew the date or year, he thought that Impellitteri was mayor. Then he said something about the Cross Bronx Expressway and Robert Moses. We could only determine that he was calling from Brooklyn before he hung up."

"What did you do then?" Uli didn't recognize the voice.

"This was the same day that the Weather Underground had blown up a brownstone in Greenwich Village, and we had been getting prank calls all day. Hell, we had gotten calls like this for months after the George Metesky bombings. We had no perceived threats. The Russians didn't work like that. No one did."

"So what happened next?"

"It was a solid week before a physician at Roosevelt Hospital made the first reports: Myron Cohen, a seventy-two-year-old newsstand vendor at City Hall, had suffered third-degree flesh burns. The fallout must've dropped right on his head. Over the next three weeks there were burns, bleedings gums, fevers, a sudden spiking of leukemia cases before someone at the EPA finally went out with a Geiger counter—"

"There's no reason for this to continue, we know all about—"

███████████████████████████████████

██

███████████████████████████

Uli opened his eyes, gasping for breath. He was in a bed surrounded by strangers. Every part of his body was either numb or in pain. Two IVs were dripping into his arms and he had bandages wrapped around his limbs and face.

"Where am I?" He tried but was unable to rise.

"Under arrest at a small Pigger detention infirmary in the Bronx, Nevada. I'm Erica Rudolph," said an attractive middle-aged woman who looked like the actress Donna Reed.

At that moment someone Uli recognized entered the room. It was Ernestina Erics, his old supervisor from Pure-ile Plurality, a community service organization with ties to the Pigger gang.

"But I remember seeing Vegas," he said sluggishly.

"Miss Rudolph called me at our P.P. office," Ernestina said strangely. "She heard we were friends and thought it would be nice if you woke up to a familiar face."

"How did I get here?"

Miss Rudolph filled Uli in on the details: "Someone reported that a body had been dumped on East Tremont Avenue, presumed dead. When our morgue wagon came by half an hour later, they found you stretched out unconscious on the pavement, severely dehydrated."

"Third-degree sunburns cover more than seventy percent of your skin. It's clear you got stuck in the desert,"

Ernestina added. He had been in a coma for five days and was recuperating in a small room that resembled an attic.

"Fuck! How the hell can I be back here?" he groaned. "I remember some kid in a VW Bug picking me up on the highway . . . I got out!"

"In addition to your burns, you have dysentery and you're severely malnourished," Miss Rudolph said. "It looks like you've lost over fifty pounds since you fled several months ago."

"What now?"

"You've been convicted in absentia for several murders and have been sentenced to death."

Uli knew that there was no point in disputing the charges. When he tried to sit up again, he felt a surge of excruciating pain and passed out.

He woke up several hours later when Miss Rudolph began to wash him and change his bandages. Ernestina Erics, reclining in an armchair, was the only other person in the room.

"You okay?" she asked. A man in a ski mask stepped into the room, but Ernestina waved him back outside.

"I just can't believe that after all I've been through, I'm back in Rescue City. And if I'd been found in Brooklyn, Staten Island, or Manhattan, I'd be safe."

"Your crime report says that you were last seen in handcuffs in a car with Chain and Underwood," she told him. "It says you somehow got free and killed the two of them."

"Does that sound likely?"

"Poor Patricia Itt had her right arm severed as punishment for the killing of Daniel Elsberg," Ernestina said softly. "I know she was innocent."

"What year is it?"

"Early 1981." After a pause Ernestina asked, "What was it like down there?"

"Give me a break. I know why you're here."

"Why?"

"Standard interrogation technique—good cop, bad cop. You're the only Pigger I know who I actually liked, so it's obvious they've brought you here as the good cop."

"Not everything is as it appears," she whispered. "Just sit tight."

Though bothered by her cryptic remark, Uli felt some degree of trust toward this woman.

"What happens once you're dropped down into that sewer pipe?" she asked.

"Oh God," Uli sighed. "I don't even want to think about it . . . All those sad people down there."

"What people?"

"The ones Shub gave that Mnemosyne to and plenty of others. It doesn't work, or at least it doesn't work for the vast majority of them."

"How many were down there?"

"God, it seemed like hundreds, maybe more. They're living on C-rations and recycled sewer water."

"Why don't they get out of there like you did?"

"Something destroys their memories," he explained. "It's an Alzheimer's nightmare. They just wander around lost and naked and prey on each other or starve to death."

"Why didn't it affect you?"

"It might've been that drug that Timothy Leary gave me to take into the sewer."

"You mean Leary from the Verdant League?"

"Yeah, he put two syringes in a helmet I was wearing. He claimed his crazy Indian spirit told him to do it. So I injected myself when I climbed out of the pipe. Why do you care about this?"

"My sister Angelina and her husband John bought a passage out about seven years ago. So did some others I knew," she replied sadly. "You're the only one I've met who's ever come back to talk about it."

"That might've been before they put up the netting in the sewer. Your sister might well have made it out."

"How exactly did you get out?"

When Uli thought about all he had gone through, he simply smiled. "I explored deep into this dark underworld called the Mkultra. Some poor kid died helping me. I wiggled up through the back of an elevator shaft to a ceiling of fire, and . . . and I somehow climbed around it. I landed on the desert floor in the middle of fucking nowhere and some half-crazed black guy shot me up with some kind of hallucinogenics. After experiencing crazy visions, I eventually stumbled onto some fucking highway and got picked up by a kid in a VW, only to wind up back here in Pigger custody waiting to be executed."

Seeing that he desperately needed to rest, she said she'd speak to him tomorrow. She turned off the light and left.

As tired as he was, Uli couldn't sleep. Something, someone was pushing back into his head, and he knew it could only be one person. He closed his eyes and saw Paul running down Court Street in Brooklyn. It was just minutes after the old guy had called the FBI—him—and reported what had happened. Paul was heading for the RR train to God knows where. Racing down into the subway station, his stiff legs got jumbled and he found his large brittle frame collapsing, rolling head over heels down the steep stone steps. He felt his ribs crack as he hit the bottom landing.

"You okay, mister?" some high school kid asked, staring down at Paul.

Within five minutes, a transit cop arrived. Blood was dripping out of Paul's mouth and nose, and pain was shooting through his arms and ribs. Twenty minutes later, to his horror, an ambulance was rushing him back to a hospital in Manhattan.

An intern looked him over, gave him some pills, a shot, took an X-ray, and then wheeled him into a charity ward with three other men. He had two broken ribs, a broken arm, and a slight concussion. The good news was that neither of his legs were injured, meaning he'd be able to check out of the hospital sooner. Since he was a veteran and had no money, and desperately wanted to get the hell away from Manhattan, he was told that he could get outpatient treatment at the V.A. hospital in the Bronx.

After nearly a week, shaky and alone, he checked out and took a cab up to the V.A. hospital. During the intervening days, all he could feel was an intensifying guilt: *How could I have been seduced into constructing such a thing? What the fuck was I thinking?* He sweat through the night, begging the nurses for painkillers, sleeping pills, anything to knock him out.

One morning, he opened his eyes from a black sleep and couldn't believe what he was seeing: Sitting in front of him, smiling, was his brother Robert Moses.

"Hi, Paul."

Although he was just a little younger than Paul, Robert could still have passed for late-middle-aged. He was grinning pleasantly, as though it were 1916, before Paul had ever gone to Mexico, as though fifty-four years hadn't passed and there hadn't been a million little cuts and stabs that had turned his world into living hell.

"For starters, this is for you," Robert said, holding up two wrapped parcels. He handed over both of them. "This is a tape recording of the opening ceremonies of the Robert Moses Niagara Power Plant on the St. Lawrence River. I remember decades back when you wrote that study for Con Ed. Remember, you were dying to build the generators? And this is a biography of me."

Paul was so overwhelmed he couldn't even speak.

"One of the nurses here is a cousin of one of my drivers. He told me that you took a bad spill and were laid up, so I said, *Tell Rockefeller he'll have to wait! I'm going right over to see my brother Paul—*"

"You fucking cocksucker!" Paul finally erupted. "You

awful fucking Hitler cocksucker!!!" With his good arm, he grabbed the hardcover book and hurled it right into Robert's face.

"What the hell . . . ?" yelped Robert, grabbing his nose. Blood came trickling down.

"Because of you, it's all fucking ruined!" Paul shouted as Robert rushed out of the room. "This whole city has been destroyed, all dead because of you, you dirty motherfucker!!!"

The hospital room began to fade. Uli envisioned Paul struggling for months with his arm in a filthy cast, unable to get a good night's sleep due to the broken ribs . . . Then a few months later, when the extent of the radiation clusters was fully realized, Manhattan was declared a disaster zone. All residents in the southern half of the borough were forcibly evacuated. Uli could see Paul in a slow-moving line with many other seniors, applying for temporary housing until the contamination was cleaned up. The old man was being wheeled up a ramp out at JFK Airport, onto a plane with others who had been accepted into Nevada's Rescue City project.

Uli's final image, the terminus for this singular memory, was eighty-one-year-old Paul Moses, an ancient stick of a man, sitting on a bench in Coney Island, Nevada. Uli saw himself and remembered a previous chapter in his life, when he was a tired, short-term inductee to the community service group Pure-ile Plurality. He had plunked down on the same bench, and the older man offered him some rugelach. Uli promptly fell asleep, inadvertently leaning up against the old man who had also dozed off. Resting head to head, something had happened. It was as though the nerve endings from the older man's shiny scalp had fused with Uli's uncombed hair: Memories shot into his skull, to slowly gestate and ultimately unravel during his comatose state in the sewer.

"I know where he is! I know who did it and where he is!" Uli shouted out from his bed.

The guard wearing a ski mask came to the door and called back, "*You* did it, and you're going to die for it, pal."

Uli smiled. Strangely, he felt more at peace than he had in a long while. At least the memories of Paul Moses were finally out of his head and, he knew, gone for good. *Soon, I'll be gone too*, he thought, and closed his eyes for a deep, relaxing sleep.

Also available from Akashic Books

THE SWING VOTER OF STATEN ISLAND
by Arthur Nersesian
*The first installment in the FIVE BOOKS OF MOSES series
272 pages, trade paperback, $15.95

"Nersesian's extravagantly imagined dystopia relies—as did those in Philip Roth's *Plot Against America* and Michael Chabon's *Yiddish Policemen's Union*—on an alternate, counterfactual history."
—*New York Times Book Review*

"A sharp, strange read: Imagine William Burroughs and Philip K. Dick sharing a needle." —*Kirkus Reviews*

SUICIDE CASANOVA
by Arthur Nersesian
368 pages, trade paperback, $15.95

"Sick, depraved, and heartbreaking—in other words, a great read, a great book. *Suicide Casanova* is erotic noir and Nersesian's hard-boiled prose comes at you like a jailhouse confession."
—Jonathan Ames, author of *The Extra Man*

"Nersesian has written a scathingly original page-turner, hilarious, tragic, and shocking—this may be his most brilliant novel yet."
—Kate Christensen, author of *In the Drink*

"A tight, gripping, erotic thriller."
—*Philadelphia City Paper*

MANHATTAN LOVERBOY
by Arthur Nersesian
203 pages, a trade paperback original, $13.95

"Best Book for the Beach, Summer 2000."
—*Jane*

"Best Indie Novel of 2000."
—*Montreal Mirror*

"Part Lewis Carroll, part Franz Kafka, Nersesian leads us down a maze of false leads and dead ends . . . told with wit and compassion, drawing the reader into a world of paranoia and coincidence while illuminating questions of free will and destiny. Highly recommended."
—*Library Journal*

THE FUCK-UP
by Arthur Nersesian
*Original Akashic Books edition with chapter illustrations, available only through direct mail order or www.akashicbooks.com
274 pages, a trade paperback original, $20

"The charm and grit of Nersesian's voice is immediately enveloping, as the down-and-out but oddly up narrator of his terrific novel slinks through Alphabet City and guttural utterances of love."
—*Village Voice*

EAST VILLAGE TETRALOGY
four plays by Arthur Nersesian
240 pages, a trade paperback original, $14.95

"Award-winning playwright Arthur Nersesian has woven an effective dramatic form through four plays, each quite funny in its own way."
—Evangelina Borges, *Trying Time Press*

"Take four observational pieces, add a healthy dose of tongue-in-cheek humor, and tailor them into the play format and you have a collection which earns remarkable distinction."
—*California Bookwatch*

BROOKLYN NOIR
edited by Tim McLoughlin
*Winner of the Shamus, Anthony, and Robert L. Fish Memorial Awards
350 pages, a trade paperback original, $15.95

Brand-new stories by: Pete Hamill, Arthur Nersesian, Maggie Estep, Nelson George, Sidney Offit, Ken Bruen, and others.

"*Brooklyn Noir* is such a stunningly perfect combination that you can't believe you haven't read an anthology like this before. But trust me—you haven't. Story after story is a revelation, filled with the requisite sense of place, but also the perfect twists that crime stories demand. The writing is flat-out superb."
—Laura Lippman, winner of Edgar, Agatha, and Shamus awards